THE LABYRINTH OF SOULS

THE LABYRINTH OF SOULS

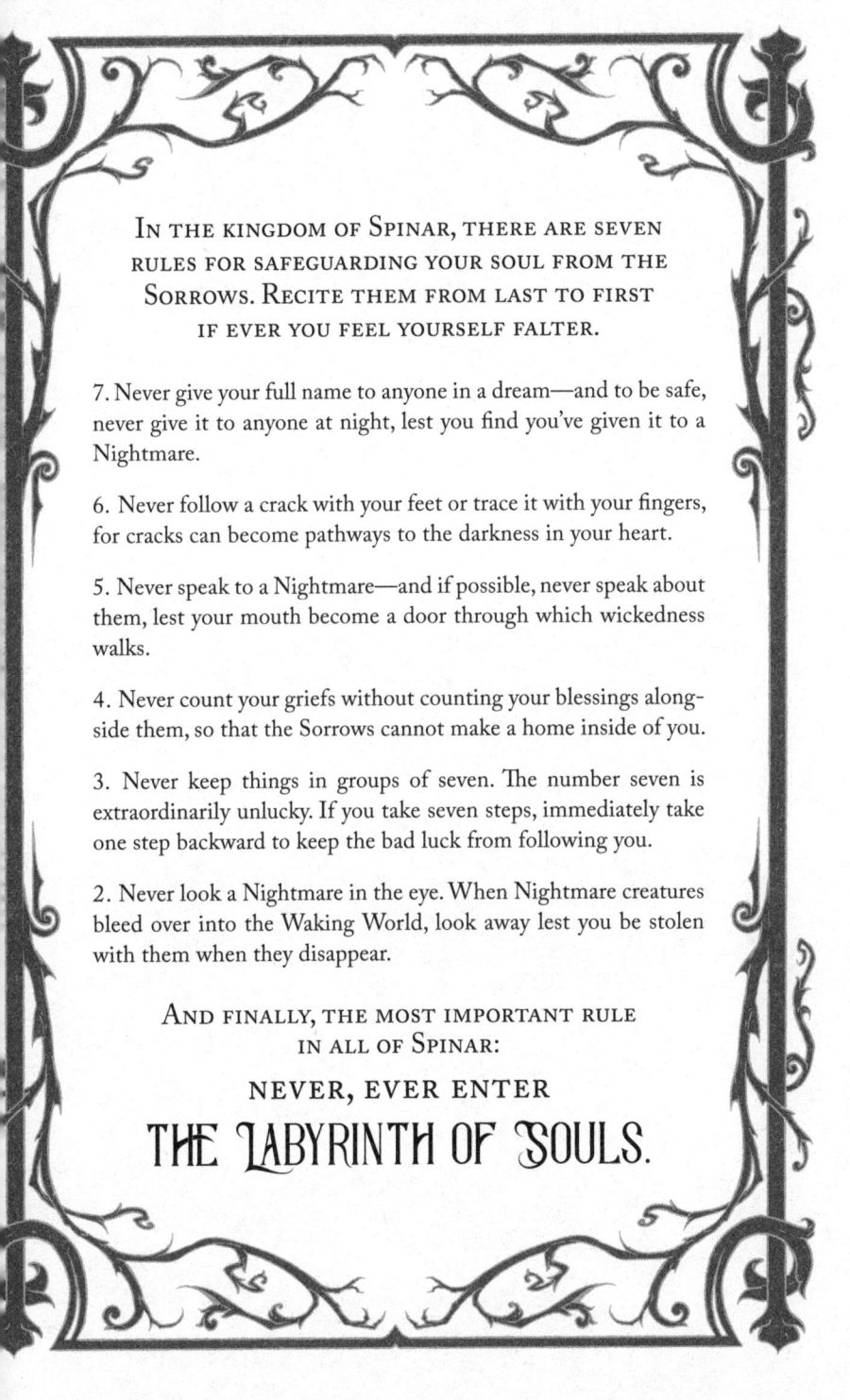

In the kingdom of Spinar, there are seven rules for safeguarding your soul from the Sorrows. Recite them from last to first if ever you feel yourself falter.

7. Never give your full name to anyone in a dream—and to be safe, never give it to anyone at night, lest you find you've given it to a Nightmare.

6. Never follow a crack with your feet or trace it with your fingers, for cracks can become pathways to the darkness in your heart.

5. Never speak to a Nightmare—and if possible, never speak about them, lest your mouth become a door through which wickedness walks.

4. Never count your griefs without counting your blessings alongside them, so that the Sorrows cannot make a home inside of you.

3. Never keep things in groups of seven. The number seven is extraordinarily unlucky. If you take seven steps, immediately take one step backward to keep the bad luck from following you.

2. Never look a Nightmare in the eye. When Nightmare creatures bleed over into the Waking World, look away lest you be stolen with them when they disappear.

And finally, the most important rule in all of Spinar:

NEVER, EVER ENTER

THE LABYRINTH OF SOULS.

THE LABYRINTH OF SOULS

LESLIE VEDDER

WITH ILLUSTRATIONS BY

ABIGAIL LARSON

putnam

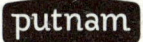

G. P. PUTNAM'S SONS

G. P. PUTNAM'S SONS

An imprint of Penguin Random House LLC

1745 Broadway, New York, New York 10019

First published in the United States of America by G. P. Putnam's Sons,
an imprint of Penguin Random House LLC, 2025

Visit us online at PenguinRandomHouse.com.

Library of Congress Cataloging-in-Publication Data is available.

ISBN 9780593699119

1 3 5 7 9 10 8 6 4 2

Printed in the United States of America

BVG

Design by Alex Campbell

Text set in Adobe Caslon Pro

To the midnight cat wrangler:
all would be lost without you
—L. V.

1

THE GIRL WHO SEES NIGHTMARES

They were whispering about her again.

Ix hunched into her long black coat, trying to disappear as she slipped out of the little brick schoolhouse. But there was nowhere to hide. She knew everyone in Brittlewick, and everyone knew her.

Ix Tatterfall. The girl who sees Nightmares.

"Ugh. It's Ick," a pretty blond girl warned her friend, sneering the nickname Ix had been stuck with since first grade. "Hurry, or the ick will rub off on you."

The two girls pushed each other out of the schoolhouse, giggling. Ix tried to pretend she couldn't hear them. Or at least that she didn't care. There were worse things than getting called names.

The first rustling yellow leaves swirled around Ix as she headed for her aunt's cottage on the edge of town. It would have been faster to take the big dirt road in the center of Brittlewick, but instead she ducked into the grackleberry bushes, then slipped through a rotted hole in the fence surrounding the overgrown garden of Whitlock Manor. When she came out, she was in an alley behind the cobbler's shop, which sagged like a rough old boot.

Ix shook old leaves and dust off her purple-striped shirt and black overalls. A stick poked her hand as she ran her palm across her dark hair, plaited into two twiggy braids that everyone said made her look like a raggedy scarecrow.

She knew every secret path and shortcut in Brittlewick. It helped that she wasn't afraid of most things that other people were. The spider-infested shed behind the school was the perfect place to read, though you had to brush away the cobwebs now and then. Ix didn't mind the brambly ditches near the Scally Woods where the rats scampered around, either. The smell wasn't great, but the whiskery rats were actually quite friendly. Most of all, Ix liked the dark: old abandoned buildings, and crawl spaces under the stairs, and especially the dead of night.

Because Ix Tatterfall had a secret.

Ix knelt beside a squashed pumpkin that had rolled off a cart into the alley. She could see something moving inside the broken shell, among all the gooey seeds: a tiny squiggle of black huddled into the hollow. A Nightmare creature.

Ix stretched her hand out toward an Inkling. Inklings were Nightmares, what people called all manner of creatures and maladies that escaped from the Labyrinth of Souls. But these were the harmless kind that mostly just hid in cracks and corners or under beds. They were hard to see because they blended into the dark, but if you caught one, they looked like splotches of ink with long, wiggly arms and legs. They reminded Ix of little stick bugs.

Some Nightmares weren't so harmless. If you had a sudden dark feeling out of nowhere, or a chill ran up your spine, or you found yourself wide awake in the middle of the night, or experiencing a run of terrible luck, maybe you were just having a bad day. Or maybe you'd run afoul of a Nightmare without even knowing it.

Most people couldn't see them, just feel their effects. But Ix was different.

The Inkling waved its arms and grabbed on to Ix's hand, wrapping around her thumb.

For as long as Ix could remember, she had drawn Nightmare creatures to her. It was kind of like moths to a flame. Except the opposite, she guessed. Maybe Ix gave off some kind of darkness that the Nightmares liked.

A sudden voice made her jump.

"Gathering ingredients for your witch's brew?"

"Arthur," Ix yelped in surprise, spinning to face her nemesis. The tall, fair-skinned boy couldn't see the Inkling, but Ix tucked the creature into her pocket anyway. "I thought you'd be across town by now."

"My gran sent us to the market," Arthur said, jerking his thumb at the boy moving down the alley behind him. Arthur's equally mean cousin, Samuel. "Then we saw you crawling under the fence from Widow Whitlock's garden. Not satisfied with witchery anymore, now you're stealing, too?"

"I didn't steal anything," Ix insisted.

Arthur looked smug. "Trespassing, then."

Ix wanted to argue that Widow Whitlock didn't care about people cutting through her overgrown garden, but she already knew Arthur wouldn't listen to her. No one ever did.

It all started when Margaret MacElroy, the schoolmaster's daughter, caught Ix talking to Nightmare creatures that no one else could see. Ix especially liked the Mistcats, with their shimmering bodies and cold curls of wispy white fur, and the Dire Frogs, whose bulging red eyes shone like lamps in the dark.

That was when Ix realized that seeing Nightmares was not considered a blessing, but a curse. It was right there in the Seven Rules: *Never speak to a Nightmare, or about one.*

Ix felt her mouth stretching into a big, creepy grin, like it did whenever she got nervous or scared. "Leave me alone, Arthur. I haven't done anything," she said, backing away.

That was a mistake. Arthur's face split in a vicious sneer. "Really? Because I can think of a few things. Like that time you put a spider in Becky Appelman's hair."

Ix bit her lip. She hadn't done that. She'd just told Becky she *liked* the spider in her hair. Ix liked spiders; why wouldn't Becky?

Samuel chimed in. "Or that day when all the lanterns blew out in the schoolhouse, and while everyone was screaming, you climbed up on the desk and laughed at us."

"That's not true!" Ix hadn't been laughing at *them*. She'd been laughing at the Fright Bat that got loose in the schoolhouse. Laughter made them go into hibernation.

Arthur moved toward her, menacing. "Or the time you pushed me into the river."

"I only did that because you were going to step on . . . something," Ix finished weakly. It was a family of Inklings crossing the bridge, getting right near Arthur's stompy feet.

"Go on, lie, like you always do," Arthur taunted her.

"Like when you burned down the bell tower," Samuel hissed.

Ix froze, her stomach squirming.

That was the thing that had turned the whole town against her. Everyone thought Ix had set fire to Brittlewick's beloved bell tower—

but she hadn't. It was a Nightmare creature, an Infurious Flame, but no one believed her. No one was even willing to listen.

"I've got an idea," Arthur said. Ix backed away nervously, bumping into the wall. "You like small, dark places, right, *Ick*? Maybe you'd like to spend some time in the crawl space under the ruins of the bell tower you destroyed."

Ix thought about fighting back. She thought about calling them bullies or pushing Arthur and his cousin into the cobbler's pile of old shoes. And then she thought about her aunt's worried face, and she didn't do any of those things.

Aunt Tara had taken Ix in when no one else would. She wasn't the warmest person, but she didn't ask Ix for much.

Just don't make trouble, Tara whispered every morning. And in that whisper, Ix heard all the things she didn't say. Trouble meant attention. Attention meant more rumors about her. More questions about her family. And Ix had already brought so much trouble to Aunt Tara's doorstep.

There was only one thing to do.

Ix made a run for it. There was no way she'd be able to squeeze under Widow Whitlock's fence fast enough. So instead she scooped up the slimy pumpkin shell and threw it at Arthur.

"Argh! Witch!" he shouted, grabbing for her with his face full of orange goop.

Ix ducked under his outstretched arm and raced for the market street.

"Catch her, Samuel."

Arthur's older cousin leapt into Ix's way. She dodged past him, flattening herself against the wall. She was steps from the end of the alley when—

Snatch!

Ix felt herself suddenly yanked backward as Samuel seized her coat.

Bumblefuzz! she cursed in her head.

A sudden commotion erupted in the street ahead. Samuel's grip went slack. Ix seized her chance, breaking free and stumbling out into the busy main way.

The street was a mess of people. Everyone in Brittlewick seemed to be there, staring at something she couldn't see. Arthur and his cousin followed her out, but they seemed to have forgotten her in the commotion. Ix pushed forward to get a better look.

"What's going on?" she asked.

It was the old cobbler who answered, his face pinched like one of his shoes. "It's Candle Corps," he said, frowning down at Ix. "They've come hunting something in Brittlewick."

Ix's stomach was suddenly as squirmy as the Inkling hidden in her pocket.

Candle Corps. The elite guard that protected the people of Spinar from the Labyrinth. The mysterious figures known as Flames banished Nightmares and punished willful rule-breakers, like criminals who consorted with Nightmares, or tried to conjure them to cast curses, or purposefully entered the Labyrinth of Souls.

Criminals like Ix, who carried Nightmare creatures in their pockets.

Ix gulped, smooshing down the Inkling that had been oozing up her elbow.

She was in so much trouble.

THE FLAMES OF CANDLE CORPS

Ix stared wide-eyed at the figures moving through the street. There were six of them, all dressed in the uniform of Candle Corps: a long, flowing black coat fastened with sashes and glinting with big silver buckles. The glossy black fabric shimmered like deep water in the sunlight. Their faces were hidden beneath their hoods.

Like all the kids in Brittlewick, Ix had grown up on the legends of Candle Corps. As guardians of Spinar, they traveled through the kingdom, banishing fearsome monsters and curing people of little maladies caused by Nightmares.

It was said the Flames of Candle Corps wielded magical weapons called Shadow Renders that could dispel Nightmares, and when they walked in the Labyrinth, they channeled their Dreamlight power into brilliant candles that drew lost souls to them.

Arthur leaned into Ix, whispering, "I bet they're here for you, Ick. They're going to lock you up in a moldy old dungeon until the rats nibble away your toes."

Ix shoved an elbow into Arthur's chest.

Once upon a time, Ix thought because of the things she could see, she might belong at Candle Corps, too. But people with Dreamlight powers repelled Nightmares—the exact opposite of Ix. Arthur was right. She was probably headed for the dungeon.

Four of the hooded figures spread out, opening shining black bags and handing out tea candles with gold wicks to the crowd. "Sprite Lights," a young man called. Ix could just make out his sharp features and curly hair beneath the hood. "Sprite Lights to protect your homes."

Ix knew she should go, but her curiosity got the best of her. Brittlewick was on the very edge of Spinar, so far out it practically disappeared in the Scally Woods. When Flames passed through at all, it was only ever one or two. This was different.

Ix was swept along with the crowd to the town square. Candle Corps might be the good guys, but they didn't show up unless you had Nightmare troubles, and everyone wanted as little to do with Nightmares as possible.

A short woman pushed to the front to meet the hooded figures. She had a round, worried face and gray hair that stuck up around her head; she reminded Ix of a twiggy broom turned upside down.

"Everyone, calm down!" Mayor Bramblebab called, raising her voice over the din. "Candle Corps is here at my request to address our recent rash of troubles."

"The turnips!" a man in a straw hat yelled.

The crowd muttered in agreement. Rows and rows of turnips had come up with strange lumps and bumps that looked like horrifying faces, and everyone who'd eaten them had terrible dreams for weeks.

"And the ghosts," the baker added, waving a breadstick from her basket. Whispery flutters of ghosts had been spotted over the wall in the Scally Woods and even at the crossroads in town. And it was nowhere near All Hallows' Eve—far too early for ghosts.

"And the bell tower," someone else called out. Ix cringed.

"Candle Corps will get to the bottom of everything," the mayor assured them.

"Let's not make any promises until we know what we're up against," a gruff voice said.

Two of the figures pulled down their hoods. The man who'd spoken was tall, with tawny skin and a shock of glossy dark hair. A jagged scar ran across his jawline up to his ear. Beside him, a blond woman with a fair, heart-shaped face turned to the crowd.

"I'm Allison Mella, one of the corps' healers. And this is Captain Tarryn Kel." Mella's face was kind. "As long as you've followed the rules, there's no need to be alarmed. We're only here to help. May the flames forever burn," she finished with the Candle Corps blessing.

"May the flames forever burn," the crowd echoed.

"I'm taking Candle Corps to the town hall," Mayor Bramble-bab said, waving to shoo them off. "Everyone, go back to your homes. Keep the Sprite Lights burning in your windows tonight and stay inside. No. Matter. What."

Ix didn't need any Sprite Lights. But she did need to get home and warn Aunt Tara to hide what was in the upstairs bedroom.

Ix hurried through the town square, head down. She passed close enough to hear the two Candle Corps members speaking low, as if they didn't want to be overheard.

"Have you uncovered any more about the disturbance?" Healer Mella asked.

Captain Kel shook his head. "No. But this is undoubtedly the source of it. Once we finish the Nightmare sweep, we'll . . ."

Ix lost the rest in all the mumbling voices. *A disturbance.* She had to get away before someone noticed her and started pointing fingers—

Splat!

Ix stopped. The Inkling that had been dangling from her pocket had fallen to the ground. It cowered from the tromping feet all around it, skittering away to hide under a fallen handkerchief.

"Come back," Ix whispered after it, following the purple polka-dot handkerchief through people's legs. "It's dangerous here!"

Ix made a grab for it. The little arms wriggled as it ran away, right toward one of the hooded figures.

Ix's heart thumped. It was going to get dispelled!

"Sorry—excuse me—pardon me," Ix gasped, not even looking at the people she elbowed past. The hanky was getting away. Ix dove forward, sliding across the cobbles on her stomach.

"Gotcha!" Ix said triumphantly, grabbing the Inkling. Right as the hooded figure tripped over her.

The Candle Corps member let out an *oof.* Their arms wheeled comically before they toppled backward onto the stones.

"Ouch!"

The voice was much younger than Ix expected. She sat up, coming face-to-face with a girl about her age. Her hood had fallen back to reveal wild red hair and a thick layer of freckles on her peach skin. The girl scowled at Ix.

"Nothing to say for yourself?" she demanded.

Ix felt that nervous grin creeping across her face. "Me? I'm nobody. And I'm not up to anything. I just dropped my hanky." Ix waved the polka-dot cloth, praying the girl hadn't seen the wiggling black shape she'd stuffed into her pocket.

The girl gave her a withering look as she stood up, shaking out the dark sweater and black skirt under her coat. "I meant an apology. I thought even country bumpkins knew how to say sorry when they tripped someone."

"Right. That. I mean, sorry," Ix fumbled, shoving the Inkling deeper and trying not to look suspicious. She scrambled up, ready to flee.

"Wait."

Ix flinched. But the girl just shoved a handful of Sprite Lights at her. "Be sure to put these in your window tonight. There are so many Lesser Nightmares in these border towns. Ugh."

"Morrigan," Captain Kel called, making the girl turn away.

Ix grabbed the candles and fled.

"What, no 'thank you' either?" Morrigan called after her as she ducked into a narrow alley. And not a moment too soon. The Inkling was practically rioting in her pocket.

"I'm sorry," Ix said, pulling the little creature out. "But you'd better stay out of sight. I don't know what they'll do to you if they find you."

The space between the buildings was so narrow it would be tough for a full-grown person to fit down. Ix tried to set the little Inkling next to a nice dark crack in the rocky wall. Only it wouldn't come off. No matter how she plucked at it, the inky body oozed all the way around her wrist, holding on tight.

She couldn't very well walk around with a Nightmare for a bracelet, not with Candle Corps in town. "What could you possibly want?" Ix asked. To her surprise, its little head bobbed in her direction, its long, thin limbs straining toward the far end of the alley.

"You want me to go that way?"

The Inkling tugged again.

Ix glanced over her shoulder. She could hear the tromping feet of Candle Corps in the square, just around the corner.

"Okay," she said. "But we better make it quick."

Following the Nightmare's directions, Ix ducked and weaved through back streets until she found herself in a crooked alley behind town hall. It was full of empty crates and smelled of musty old vegetables. The Inkling dangled off her arm in excitement, its tentacle arms waving toward something by the dead-end wall.

At first Ix couldn't tell what she was seeing. But once she got closer, she realized it was a whole group of little Nightmares huddled in the shadows. There was a puddle of Inklings oozing in the corner, along with a pair of Money-Grubber Mice, whiskery green rodents that chewed holes into people's pockets to steal their last coin. She even spotted a little Teasel Weasel cowering in a dusty old top hat. Ix would have to check herself carefully for loose threads teased out that threatened to unravel her clothes after this.

It was an odd assortment of creatures. Ix had never seen a group of them bunched up like this. All the Nightmares were quivering, their eyes wide. Suddenly Ix understood.

"You're all scared of Candle Corps," Ix whispered. The Teasel Weasel hissed, but she could hear its stubby tail thumping against the hat as it shook with fear.

Ix took a deep breath.

"Okay—let's get you home."

Ix had already seen Nightmares, talked to them, followed them, and consorted with them. She might as well break the biggest rule of them all.

Because that was Ix Tatterfall's biggest secret.

She knew how to slip into the forbidden Labyrinth of Souls.

The little Inkling swung wildly on her wrist, as if telling her to hurry. Ix closed her eyes, feeling a shiver of excitement roll down her spine. She'd only stay in the Labyrinth for a moment. Just long enough to help the Nightmares escape.

Darkness surrounded her. Ix could feel cold tendrils of mist on her tan skin. The Labyrinth was all around her, almost in reach—

Suddenly there was a great CRACK! as the splintery door at the end of the alley banged open. All traces of the Labyrinth disappeared, and Ix's eyes sprang open.

"There! Do you feel that? A Nightmare—and a big one." Morrigan's voice rang out into the alley.

Ix pulled up her hood, squeezing desperately behind the empty crates. She could see a figure silhouetted against the door. The stern captain from the square—Captain Kel.

"Do you think it could be the disturbance we're looking for?" Morrigan whispered.

"Shh," Captain Kel warned. He raised his hands like he was drawing an invisible sword. A glowing broadsword sprang to life in his fist.

A Shadow Render.

Ix had never seen one before. It wasn't metal at all but made of pure light—Dreamlight. No wonder it worked on Nightmares.

The creatures around Ix squirmed. The mice scurried up Ix's boots and the tickly Inklings slipped into her sleeves, while the Teasel Weasel clung stubbornly to her overalls. Now she was harboring fugitive Nightmares, too.

"Who's there?" the captain called harshly. "Show yourself!"

Ix absolutely could not be caught like this. She closed her eyes, desperately searching for the dark and the cool and the mist that would bring her away.

Come on, come on, come on, she begged.

Heavy footsteps crunched down the alley. Just in time, Ix felt herself tumbling to the other side, into the Labyrinth.

3

THE LABYRINTH OF SOULS

Crossing into the Labyrinth was like plunging into a deep pool of water. Only, when Ix sucked in a breath, she was no longer in the alley in Brittlewick. She was in the Labyrinth of Souls.

Swirls of mist coiled around her. Ix sagged to the ground in relief. She'd made it.

All the little Nightmares in her coat were suddenly wriggling. Inklings oozed out of her sleeves, and the Teasel Weasel landed with a thump on her foot, lumbering off into the mist.

"Watch the claws," Ix yelped as the mice hopped from her pocket.

Wait—*her pocket*?! Ix stuck her hand in only to find that the little Money-Grubbers had indeed chewed a hole and made off with her last coin. The pitter-patter of their feet almost sounded like snickering.

"Ungrateful," Ix muttered. But really, what had she expected from Nightmares?

As she stood up, she realized they weren't all gone. The first Inkling, the one that had hidden under the polka-dot hanky, was still clinging to her elbow. She tried to lift it off, but it only scrambled higher, until it sat in her collar.

"You want to stay with me?" Ix asked. "Well, okay. But I have to get back to the Waking World."

Ix looked around. She'd been in such a panic when she'd come through, she hadn't landed in any of her usual spots. The ground was mossy beneath her feet. The mist roiled around her like a stormy sea. A soft glow seemed to come from everywhere and nowhere at once.

This was the raggedy edges of the Labyrinth, where people's dreams bled into the world of Nightmares. In the distance, through the fog, Ix could see a towering arch set into the high stone wall—a pathway deeper into the Labyrinth. It looked like a great dark mouth, waiting to gobble her up.

The Labyrinth of Souls was the Between World, a place that existed between the realms of the living and the dead. At its heart was the door to the next world, protected by Death itself. Ix shivered and hurried into the gloom.

There were three ways to end up in the Labyrinth of Souls.

The first was to die. According to the stories, people who died peacefully appeared at the very center of the Labyrinth, at Death's Door, while those who were tormented by unfinished business or clung to their regrets wound up in the Labyrinth. Of course, since nobody living had ever been to the center of the Labyrinth, no one knew for sure. Ix tried to stay away from ghosts in the Labyrinth, since they could be scary and unpredictable.

The second way was to slip through in a dream, when your soul could drift away and wander in by mistake, or a Nightmare might lure you in. If you didn't get out quick, you could become trapped, a lost soul wandering the maze. Ix had tried calling to them sometimes, but they never seemed to hear her, as if they were sleepwalking. Only the Dreamlight of Candle Corps could guide them.

Finally, there were those who crossed over on purpose—

members of Candle Corps or rule-breakers like Ix. Then not just your soul but your whole body entered the Labyrinth, and that was dangerous for all sorts of reasons. Like the slithery chokeweed vines at Ix's feet, curled up like sleeping snakes. She tiptoed over them, careful not to rustle a single leaf.

There was one particular soul Ix always looked for when she came to the Labyrinth. Though, after all this time, she supposed she should really just give up.

The little Inkling rubbed its head against her cheek, distracting her.

"Thanks," she said, tickling under its chin.

A strange wind began to blow. First it was a gust, then it started to whirl around them. Ix tried to steady herself, but her shoes scraped across the stones—dragging her in toward the hungry doorway.

All at once the sucking stopped. A second later, air was blowing out instead. Ix lost her footing, tumbling end over end in the moss. Gobs of icy mist blew in all directions around her.

No, not mist. Souls!

It was as if the Labyrinth had sucked in a big breath and then blown out dozens of glowing souls. Ix gaped at a man in a dapper suit, an old woman in a nightgown, a pair of young girls holding hands—and others that were hazy, the formless shapes of souls that had been in the Labyrinth so long they'd started losing themselves.

Ix scrambled to her feet, tucking the Inkling into her collar for safety.

She'd never seen this many souls at once. And she'd certainly never seen the Labyrinth do that. It was supposed to lead souls deeper, not spit them out. She remembered what she had over-heard Candle Corps saying. A *disturbance*. Something big and ter-rible that definitely wasn't Ix.

A soul moaned behind her, its translucent arm reaching out. Ix leapt away. Her gaze darted to its feet.

Feet were how you could tell the difference between a lost soul and a soul that had already died. Lost souls had wavery feet that floated off the ground. They weren't really here, after all—their souls were still tethered to a sleeping body. But those who were dead had their feet planted firmly in the Labyrinth, until they found their way to the center and passed through Death's Door.

Ix sucked in a sharp breath. It had feet. *All* the souls seemed to have feet. And they were all turning toward her.

She was surrounded by ghosts.

Her heart hammered in her chest. The ghost grabbed for her again, and Ix dove under its hazy arms, its gnarled fingers nearly catching her coat. She darted through the knot of ghosts, looking desperately for any mist that hadn't blown away.

The mist was Ix's only way in or out of the Labyrinth. She spot-ted one small patch, already starting to disappear.

Ix ran toward it, the Inkling clinging to her neck as she hurtled over the moss. The ghosts were right behind her.

Three steps from the mist. Two—

Something slithery grabbed Ix by the ankle. She screamed out in surprise as she fell, right into the nest of chokeweed. All the vines came alive at once, surging up to swallow her. Ix gasped as a translucent hand brushed her arm, cold as a crypt in the dead of winter.

Ix froze, shocked. She knew this ghost—it was the late husband of Widow Whitlock. Only the little Inkling tugging on her earlobe saved her from being swallowed by the souls.

The chokeweed squeezed tighter and tighter. But the patch of mist was so close. Ix lunged forward with all her might, squeezing her eyes shut.

Anywhere but here, she begged as she felt the tendrils of mist closing around her.

One moment Ix was falling through the mist. Then she was falling for real, splashing into deep, chilly water. Ix came up spluttering and totally drenched.

She'd landed in the little pond behind the pumpkin patch, not far from Aunt Tara's cottage at the edge of town. The poor Inkling floated on the surface, looking miserable. It had soaked up water like a sponge and ballooned to twice its normal size. Ix fished it out and waded to shore, wringing the little Nightmare out as best she could.

"I don't know what that was," Ix whispered. "But we'd better get home." She set off at a run.

That had definitely been the ghost of the late Mr. Whitlock. But he had died years before, and peacefully. His soul should have passed on long ago. If it hadn't—if his ghost had been spat out of the Labyrinth—maybe others had, too. Like that one special soul she'd been searching for all this time.

The sun was setting as she reached the brambly little cottage and burst through the door. Aunt Tara was so surprised she nearly dropped her teacup.

"Ix, by the Sorrows, where have you been—"

Ix didn't stop to answer. She raced up the creaky stairs to the room at the end of the hall.

A figure lay on the bed, concealed in the gloom. Panting, Ix pulled the shutters to let the evening sun in.

Her father lay perfectly still, frozen. His skin was pebbled with hard, glittering crystal. He wasn't dead, but he could no longer wake. It was the fate of anyone whose soul was lost in the Labyrinth. Only, Nathan Tatterfall's fate was a little more uncertain than most.

Usually, when someone's soul was lost in the Labyrinth, their body would slowly crystallize for one year. And if they hadn't been rescued by then, the crystal cracked, and they died. As far as Ix knew, no one's soul had ever been trapped for as long as her father's. Ten years—almost as long as she'd been alive. Ix only knew him through her aunt's stories, most of them cautionary tales.

Your father was a willful rule-breaker, too, Aunt Tara told Ix one day, after she'd been chased home by a pack of Nightmares. *Nathan used to disappear into the Labyrinth for weeks at a time and consort with all manner of Nightmares. When he met your mother, it stopped for a while, and I thought perhaps he'd mended his ways. But . . .*

Aunt Tara had dabbed at her eyes.

After your first birthday, your mother went missing. Nathan was never the same. He became obsessed with reaching the center of the Labyrinth. And one day I came over to find him completely crystallized, and you just a little thing, left alone for Sorrows know how long.

Ix had no memories of any of it. But sometimes she wondered if that was when she had started to slip into the Labyrinth.

"You're still here," Ix whispered, slumping next to the bed. Disappointment stabbed at her. With all the souls out in the Labyrinth, she'd dared to hope her father might have finally found his way home.

Ix had spent many afternoons up here, tucked next to her father, plucking off the little Nightmare creatures that gathered around him. She missed him deeply sometimes, but in the way you miss a very good dream: something forever out of reach that you can never remember quite right after waking up.

Aunt Tara appeared in the doorway. She looked a lot like her brother—the same dark eyes and tan skin. But unlike Nathan's, Tara's face was creased with stress lines. "Ix, I've been worried sick. Where have you been?"

"Candle Corps," Ix said breathlessly. "They're here—in Brittlewick. They're looking for a disturbance, something causing trouble in the Labyrinth."

Aunt Tara's face paled. "It won't be long before they wind up at our door. And then . . ."

"Then?" Ix asked, swallowing hard.

Tara's eyes were soft and sad. "They'll take your father away."

They couldn't. Ix rushed to the wardrobe and wrestled out her aunt's old traveling trunk, the drippy Inkling swinging from her elbow. "Then we have to run away with him. Tonight, before they find us—"

"It's too late for that." Tara caught Ix's shoulders. "The best we can hope for is to at least stop Candle Corps from finding out about you, too."

Ix's stomach wrenched. She hadn't eaten in hours, but still she thought she might be sick. "Will they take me away?"

"I'm not going to let that happen," Tara promised. "I can't do anything for Nathan. But I swore I wouldn't let anything happen to you."

Aunt Tara straightened. She still looked scared, but she looked something else, too. Determined.

"It's late. Candle Corps will have started their Nightmare sweep.

First thing tomorrow, as soon as you're out of the house, I'm summoning Candle Corps and giving them your father. Hopefully they'll blame the disturbances on him and not look any further into our family."

"You can't!" Ix cried, horrified.

"It's all I can do," Tara insisted. "Your father's been gone for ten years. If he was going to find his way back, he would have done it by now. He would want you to be safe."

Ix's throat felt thick. She didn't really know what her father wanted. But she didn't think it was to be carted away by Candle Corps and shoved in a musty vault somewhere.

Tears welled up in her eyes. Through them, she watched a wavery-looking Aunt Tara pause at the top of the stairs.

"Promise me, Ix. Promise you won't get in Candle Corps' way or do anything to draw attention to yourself."

Ix couldn't answer. Half in a daze, she sank down by her father's bed, pressing her hand over his.

Even in the Crystal Sleep, he was the only connection Ix had to her past. To her strange abilities. And to the biggest question mark of Ix's life: her mother.

Only Nathan had known who she was. Ix had so many questions—a lifetime of questions. She couldn't lose him and her only chance at answers.

But Candle Corps would be here. *Tomorrow*. Aunt Tara wasn't going to change her mind. And Ix couldn't hide the heavy crystallized body by herself.

There was only one thing she could do: find her father's soul in the Labyrinth, tonight. Ix had been looking for years—every time she'd crossed over. But there was one thing she hadn't tried. Something so dangerous she was sure even her rule-breaker father wouldn't approve. Ix swallowed, clutching the Inkling tight to her overalls.

Tonight, she'd go looking for the Sorrows.

4

THE FIRST SORROW

The bells tolled eleven o'clock as Ix closed her eyes and sank into the darkness, drifting down, down, down into the Labyrinth of Souls.

Cold mist frothed around her ankles on the other side. Sometimes, when Ix came here by accident, she arrived barefoot and still in her nightshirt. Tonight, she'd tucked her new Inkling friend into her nightstand for safekeeping and then slipped into bed fully clothed, holding the blankets all the way up to her chin so Aunt Tara wouldn't notice when she said good night.

She'd appeared on the raggedy edges again. There were paving stones set into the mossy ground, but they didn't lead anywhere, and the Bupkis Birds sitting in the sharp Snickersnee Trees called nonsense to each other, like suggestions for dessert toppings, silly names, and bad directions.

"Left—better hang a left!" a Bupkis Bird called in its parrot-like voice.

Ix picked a direction at random that was *not* left and started walking. Bupkis Bird directions were always wrong.

There was no north here, no stars. Everything was designed to be misleading. The raggedy edges were the domain of the most fickle of the Seven Sorrows, and the only one Ix had ever met.

Chaos. The Grinning Cat.

Just who she'd come to see.

"Smiles!" Ix called into the mist.

Smiles was the nickname she'd given the Grinning Cat when she was little. He had taught Ix the secrets to surviving the Labyrinth and to always grin in the face of her fears. She was sure their friendship was just a whim on his part. But maybe he would help her, if he was in the right mood.

Ix cupped her hands around her mouth. "Smiles!" Her voice was nearly swallowed by a wall of icy mist, and she rubbed her arms against a shiver. Something cold pressed against her calf. A small Mistcat twined through her legs and ran a few paces into the dark. It turned back expectantly, its fluffy bluish-white tail curled like a question mark.

The Mistcats were Chaos's minions. He must have heard her.

"Thank you," Ix called to the cat.

The Mistcat trotted left and right, even backtracking once, but Ix followed dutifully wherever it went. Chaos didn't always make sense, after all.

The ground turned from rock to spongy moss speckled with mushrooms and eerie glowing dandelion puffs. Ix saw the big, wide grin gleaming out of the dark even before she saw the outline of the giant cat. Chaos surged out of the mist. The Grinning Cat was easily the size of a carriage. His fur was long and ragged, with thick patches that seemed to be made of darkness and mist, giving him a striped look. Giant amethyst eyes blinked at Ix like purple lanterns. The little Mistcat that had been guiding her swirled around his great paw.

Smiles crouched on his belly so that his head was at Ix's level. If possible, his smile stretched even wider. "Still wandering the Labyrinth, I see, little human."

"And you're still leaping out at people in the dark," Ix teased back. Smiles may have been one of the Seven Sorrows, the most powerful and dangerous beings in the Labyrinth, but he was also the closest thing Ix had to a friend.

The cat twitched his whiskers, tsking. "Yes, but you take all the fun out of it by not being surprised. Were you looking for me? Come to hear more tales of the Labyrinth?"

Smiles was an excellent storyteller, though he never told a story the same way twice. But tonight, Ix was after something else.

"I saw all those souls in the mist earlier," she began.

"Such an inconvenience!" Smiles moaned dramatically.

"Is the Labyrinth releasing souls?" Ix asked hopefully.

Smiles gave his paw an absent lick. "Hmm. More like spitting them up, and it is certainly not supposed to. Somebody in there isn't doing their job."

Ix wasn't sure what that meant. "What did you do with them— the souls, I mean?"

"I sent them all back into the Labyrinth, of course," Smiles said with a dismissive snuff. "Better in than out, you know."

"Oh." Ix took a breath, screwing up her courage. "If I was look- ing for a soul trapped in the Labyrinth—one particular soul— could you help me find it?"

She knew it was a risk. Asking a favor of a Sorrow was like

gambling with your soul. One careless promise, and Smiles could trap her here forever. But her father was out of time.

Smiles's eyes glowed with interest. "I don't keep human souls, you know. I just send them into the Labyrinth. I much prefer simply poking around in people's dreams."

"And luring them here," Ix pointed out.

The giant cat licked his teeth. "Well, they make it very easy. You humans are so predictable, always wanting things you can't have."

Ix pressed on. "Do you think one of the other Sorrows would know how to find a soul—or help me?"

"What a deliciously chaotic thought. A Sorrow helping a human!" The Grinning Cat laughed again, flopping down on his back and raising a heavy paw. He unsheathed his gleaming claws one by one as he counted.

"Despair is too far gone to even hear a plea. Wrath would just as soon smash your head in as help you."

Ix had heard of the Bloody Ripper's vicious temper. She avoided Wrath's domain at all costs.

The cat flicked up another claw. "Terror might listen if it amused them, but you'd have to find them without dying of fright first."

Ix's shoulders hunched thinking of the Eyeless Child and the prickle of dread on the back of her neck whenever she entered their part of the Labyrinth.

"Greed is an awful sort, who will promise you anything your heart desires in exchange for your soul."

Ix grimaced. "I'd rather keep my soul in my body, thanks."

"I figured. But Misery is generally unpleasant and unhappy to see anyone, so you're quickly running out of Sorrows."

Misery was called the Shadow Lady, a gray figure who carried an umbrella that never stopped raining from the inside. Ix had never seen her, even from afar, but she'd nearly drowned in a sink-hole of tears once. That was more than enough.

That only left the final Sorrow.

"What about Death?" Ix whispered.

Smiles rolled back up to his feet. "No one has seen the Soul Reaper in years. Then again, they always were the secretive sort . . ."

He hummed thoughtfully while the little Mistcat twined around his feet.

"Death has always had a soft spot for children," he said, and Ix's heart swelled with hope. "But . . ." His claws came out all at once, trapping the Mistcat underneath his massive paw. "For any chance to meet them, you'd have to get to the center of the Labyrinth."

Ix swallowed. *Get to the center of the Labyrinth*—the same thing her father was trying to do when he went missing. "Other souls make it, so it must be possible."

"Most of those souls wind up passing through Death's Door." Smiles retracted his claws, freeing the Mistcat. "But you're not like most humans, are you, Ix . . . ? You never did tell me your full name." His amethyst eyes glowed enticingly.

Ix bit her tongue. *Never give your full name in a dream, and especially not to a Nightmare.* Even one she'd known as long as the Grinning Cat.

Giving a Nightmare your name gave them power over you. Weak Nightmares might only be able to learn your deepest hidden desires or follow you back from the Labyrinth to whisper in your ear. But the strongest Nightmares, like any of the Sorrows, could use your name to bend you to their will.

"Not a chance," Ix said.

"You'll fall for it one day," the cat promised. "For now, your plea amuses me. Get as far as you can into the Labyrinth. I'll even offer you a shortcut."

The cat reached up and tore a jagged hole into the mist. On the other side, a stone passage stretched into the dark.

Ix paused on the threshold. "Which domain?"

"Terror," the cat hissed, with a wink. "We're friends, after all."

Ix couldn't help the shiver that crawled down her spine. Still, it was better than the alternatives.

"Thanks, Smiles," Ix said before slipping into the tear. It closed behind her with a sound like the Grinning Cat was zipping her in.

5

RAGGEDY JACK

The stone walls of Terror's domain towered overhead as Ix crept down the dark passageways. Eyes seemed to watch her from every crack. She took a steadying breath and picked a direction, dragging her fingertips along the stones as she followed the wall.

The main part of the Labyrinth was split into four equal quadrants that belonged to Wrath, Terror, Misery, and Greed. The entire misty outer ring of the Labyrinth was Chaos's domain, and the very heart belonged to Death.

The only Sorrow without a domain of their own was Despair. It was a mindless presence that traveled the Labyrinth aimlessly, devouring anything in its wake.

Ix was already deeper in the Labyrinth than she'd ever been. Usually she stuck to the outer edges. It was a mistake to think of this place as a normal maze, with passageways you could memorize. The Labyrinth was more like a living thing. Here and there, the stone walls broke away into patches of wilderness and seething bogs that made whole corridors impassable.

Each quadrant had its own look and feel. Terror's domain was bordered by dark, looming stone walls. Colonies of Fright Bats suddenly took flight from the bony limbs of gnarled trees, and pools of dark water rippled with things lurking under the surface. Terror loved a good jump scare.

Wrath's domain was the most dangerous. The rough-cut walls were covered in rusty bolts and chains, and through tiny slits you caught glimpses of the hungry eyes of rageful beasts.

Misery's quadrant was unpleasantly swampy. Water trickled down the walls like endless tears, and the whole area was prone to fungus-choked bogs and sucking sinkholes that popped up without warning.

Greed's area was the trickiest. The whole quadrant was full of sinuous twists and mirrors, with deceptively beautiful gardens and crystal lakes that concealed piles of bones just under the surface.

Ix had never ventured deep enough into the Labyrinth to know what Death's domain was like.

The pathway she was following turned sharply, and her boot splashed into a dark puddle, scattering a group of Inklings that had been clinging to the wall. Ix's heart leapt in surprise. A few of the Inklings oozed back into the cracks.

All manner of creatures called the Labyrinth home—ghosts, and apparitions, and strange Nightmare animals. But tonight, the whole maze seemed deserted.

Her footsteps echoed down the empty passageway. Suddenly she heard something up ahead—a great rushing sound, like a whisper of scurrying feet. Hairs prickled on the back of Ix's neck.

Something was moving in the dark passage: dozens of giant rats with gleaming red eyes, headed right for her. A shriek rose up in Ix's throat, but she forced it down.

Smile, she reminded herself.

Ix flattened herself against the wall. But the rats had no interest in her, scrabbling right over her boots as they fled. Three wispy Wraiths floated after them, their almost-human shapes hidden beneath hooded robes. Other creatures were fleeing, too—Bone Lizards and Dire Frogs and even a screech of Fright Bats.

"Jack. It's Jack," Ix heard the Wraiths whispering. "Raggedy Jack is looking for more friends."

A bloodcurdling scream pierced the Labyrinth. Ix wrenched her head up. A bright light burst to life high above the walls. A Dreamlight flame.

Candle Corps was in the Labyrinth.

There was no climbing the walls of the Labyrinth, no cheating your way through. But the members of Candle Corps could create Dreamlights, flickering flames that blazed like bright candles high over their heads. The lights were guides for lost souls and a way for Candle Corps to keep track of each other.

And to call for help.

Ix hesitated, staring at two forking paths. One led deeper into the Labyrinth. The other, straight for the Dreamlight flame.

This was her chance. She could slip through Terror's domain while the Sorrow's attention was elsewhere. But . . .

Another shout. Ix bit her lip. Somebody might be in trouble. She took off running toward the flickering candle, her heart pounding.

There were a lot of things that screamed in Terror's domain. Wraiths. Shrill gusts of wind. There was even a bird called the Shrieking Crow that had scared Ix out of her skin a time or two. But that scream hadn't sounded like a Labyrinth creature. It sounded like a girl.

The Dreamlight flame was almost overhead. Ix darted under

a curtain of hanging moss and found herself in one of the wild patches. Mist slithered through crumbling pillars, and an inky-black bog seeped up from the floor like she was suddenly in the middle of a frightful marsh.

On the far side of the bog, Ix saw a couple of hooded figures in Candle Corps coats leading a group of glowing souls away. Each had their hand thrust high in the air, a bright Dreamlight floating over their palms.

That wasn't where the scream had come from, though.

Two other Candle Corps members were trapped against the stone wall. She recognized the tall man, Captain Kel, brandishing his glowing Shadow Render sword. Crouched behind him was the red-haired girl, Morrigan. In the dark of the Labyrinth, the glossy black material of their uniforms had turned bright, glowing with an inner light.

Morrigan clutched her shoulder. The sleeve was stained with blood. Ix's guts lurched.

"Stay back, Morrigan," Captain Kel warned.

Morrigan nodded. But as Ix watched, the girl's Dreamlight power erupted like wild flames around her. Knifelike claws burst from her bare knuckles, and a reddish flicker at her back gave the impression of wolfish ears and a tail.

Looming over them was a human-shaped figure in a brown coat overstuffed with straw. It looked almost like a lumpy scare-crow, but far more menacing. A black-brimmed hat sat low on its head, and its face was covered by a sackcloth mask with ripped holes for eyes and a slash for a mouth. It looked like it'd been stitched together from old leftover bits. With horror, Ix realized he was devouring one of the other Nightmares. Stringy bits of Wraith hung from its jagged mouth.

This must be Jack.

Ix cringed, remembering what the fleeing Wraiths had said. *Raggedy Jack is looking for more friends.*

In all her time in the Labyrinth, Ix had never heard of Jack before. As far as she knew, most Nightmare creatures didn't have names. Just the Sorrows.

Jack wiped his mouth with a sleeve, turning toward the Candle Corps pair with interest.

"What are you?" Captain Kel demanded. "Are you a new minion of Terror?"

"Terror," the scarecrow repeated thoughtfully, tipping his head. "Terror . . . I don't think we're friends yet."

Ix couldn't tear her eyes away from the scarecrow. Water seeped into her boots from the rising bog. Suddenly a rock under her foot crumbled, and she stumbled out into the open. The scarecrow wrenched its head around, the dark eyeholes locking on her.

"How about you?" Jack moved so fast, Ix barely saw it. In a blink, he danced around the Candle Corps captain and appeared right in front of her. "Do you want to be my friend?"

Hard sticklike hands made from bits of bone and other refuse clenched on to Ix's arms. The pinkie was a discarded bent nail. Her throat closed around a scream as Jack bent down. This close, she could see the little pieces of thread strung between the mouth, stretched to their limit as he opened wide.

This was going to be her end. Devoured in the Labyrinth, her soul lost forever.

6

THE SCREAM OF TERROR

Ix felt the rough material of the sackcloth mask on her cheek as the scarecrow bent to eat her. Then there was a *yank!* as Captain Kel jerked the scarecrow back by his ratty coat. Jack's bony fingers tried to cling to her, but Captain Kel whipped his sword in between them, forcing the Nightmare away.

Someone caught Ix under the arms, wrestling her back to the wall.

"I've got you," Morrigan said. Then her green eyes widened in shock. "Wait—you're the girl from Brittlewick . . . and you're not a sleeping soul at all! You're solid! How did you get here?"

They were interrupted by Jack's scratchy laughter, the scarecrow bent over double in mirth.

"Never mind," Morrigan decided grimly, pushing Ix behind her. "Just don't leave my side. Candle Corps will get you out of here."

Ix nodded, but her insides were in knots. It didn't even look like Candle Corps could get themselves out of here. The rest of the figures with their Dreamlights had disappeared. It was only the three of them now. And Jack.

Captain Kel lunged forward, sweeping his glowing broadsword at the scarecrow. Jack leapt back, bony bits of foot clacking against the floor as he ran.

"Leave the children alone," Captain Kel warned. "You want them, you'll have to go through me."

"That sounds like a dare," Jack said. His voice was positively giddy. "And I do so love a good game." He reached down to his belt and drew a rusted half-moon sickle. "If you're wagering the children, then I guess I'll wager . . . my hat. No, one of my arms! Maybe my favorite toe, made from a fossilized snail. Which do you want?"

Ix felt a little sick.

Captain Kel's jaw clenched. "I don't want anything from you. And I'm not *wagering* the children."

"Boo," Jack hissed, eyes smoldering. "If you're not going to play fair, then neither am I."

He lifted a hand to his mouth and then reached inside, his whole arm disappearing into the black maw. When he withdrew it, it looked like he was holding two lumps of coal.

He tossed them carelessly to the ground. A sickly looking Wraith rose from one, while a Creak-o-dile emerged from the other, growing and growing until it was twice Ix's size. Its scales were dark with rust, and there was a horrible screeching sound like old metal as it opened its mouth. Both creatures had electric-green eyes Ix had never seen on anything in the Labyrinth.

"My friends," Jack explained. "Once they've spent enough time inside"—he patted his stomach—"they do as they're told. Play with the children, dears."

"Morrigan, take her and run," Captain Kel said, his voice tight.

"I can't leave you—" Morrigan protested.

"That's an order!" the man shouted, and then Jack was on him.

Morrigan gritted her teeth. "Yes, sir!" She dragged Ix away, only to find their path blocked by the wispy Wraith.

"You're one of Terror's creatures," Ix said. "You don't have to listen to Jack."

The Wraith's electric-green eyes narrowed. "I really, really do," it cackled.

The Creak-o-dile was slowly gaining on them from behind. Its great rusty tail lashed against the stones.

Glowing power blazed around Morrigan, and her knuckles sprouted those razor claws. "Do you have any kind of Dreamlight powers? A weapon?" she demanded. When Ix shook her head, Morrigan scoffed. "Unarmed and useless."

"I'm not useless," Ix shot back. She couldn't fight Nightmares, but she'd learned to use the Labyrinth against itself. Ix's eyes darted around the bog.

The Wraith flew at them. Morrigan snarled and lunged forward to meet it. Ix gasped as the girl slashed through its silvery translucent body with her glowing claws. It flew backward and tangled in the branches of a tree, hanging like a rag on the laundry line. Morrigan landed in a crouch, flipping her hair off her shoulder.

Then Ix spotted what she was looking for. Just under the surface of the water was a scatter of Sinking Stones. No bigger than a pebble, but if you accidentally swallowed one, it sank like a stone in your gut. It would double and triple in weight, leaving such a pit of dread you couldn't even move.

Ix raced down the bank. The Creak-o-dile was right behind her. She plunged her hand into the water, grabbed a handful of stones, and flung them into the Nightmare's mouth. The Creak-o-dile snorted and then swallowed. It swung its squeaky jaw back and forth, teeth gnashing as it crashed to the ground, too heavy to move.

"I guess you're not completely useless," Morrigan grumbled.

"Thanks," Ix panted.

Over her shoulder, she saw Captain Kel and Jack still battling. She looked down the dark corridors, searching for a patch of mist so they could escape. It was everywhere in the Grinning Cat's domain, but it got sparser the deeper into the Labyrinth you went.

A small figure with a scraggly white nightgown and long dark hair was coming down the passageway. One arm was thrown over their eyes, and the other dragged a shabby stuffed animal. She could even hear soft sobbing.

It looked like the soul of a lost child. And they were heading right for Jack.

Captain Kel shouted in surprise. A slimy tentacle shot out of the bog and caught his foot. Jack darted past him, right for Ix and Morrigan.

"Run!" Morrigan yelled, yanking at Ix. "What is wrong with you?"

"There's a child!" Ix yelled back. The figure was ghostly pale and crying even louder now. She couldn't see their feet, but whether it was a sleepwalking soul or a ghost, she couldn't abandon them to be eaten by Jack.

Ix shook off Morrigan's hand. She heard Morrigan shouting and Jack's uneven footsteps behind her as she threw herself to her knees in front of the soul.

"Wake up! Please—you have to get out of here," Ix begged. But the child gave no signs of hearing her.

"Got you," Jack crooned.

The scarecrow was right behind her. He lifted his rusted sickle. Then Morrigan skidded down the corridor and threw herself in front of Ix.

"Look out!"

"Stop interrupting my fun," Jack snapped. His bony hand smashed into Morrigan's chest, tossing her into the wall.

"Morrigan!" Kel shouted. The girl slumped down, unmoving. The captain had cut himself free, two writhing tentacles flopping at his feet, but another was already rising from the dark water.

Jack loomed over Ix and the child, cackling as he raised the sickle again.

Ix threw her arms protectively around the small body and was surprised to find it was solid.

The sobbing stopped abruptly. The child slowly lowered their arm to reveal a pale face. Instead of eyes, two wide, dark pits as big as saucers sank into their cheeks.

Ix's heart seized. She wanted to let go—more than anything—but she was frozen in place. By Terror.

This wasn't a soul. This was a Sorrow: the Eyeless Child.

"Jaaaaaack," the child whispered, dragging out the name. "It's not nice to play with other people's things."

Jack paused. Ix felt the sharp tip of the blade a hairsbreadth from her neck before Jack pulled it away. "Ooh, scary," he chuckled.

The Eyeless Child opened their mouth and screamed. The sound was like creaking footsteps on a dark staircase. The screech of a rusty gate. The last nail being driven into a coffin.

Ix threw her hands over her ears. Jack stumbled backward on his patchwork legs. The stitching ripped on his sackcloth mask, and for just a second, Ix saw the face underneath.

It wasn't what she expected. It was a young man's face, translucent like a sleepwalking soul, with blue eyes and pale cheeks. His gaze snapped to Ix, but she squeezed her eyes shut.

Never look a Nightmare in the eye.

Terror's scream seemed to go on and on. She heard Jack's staccato footsteps racing away into the Labyrinth. Terror slipped away from her, the stuffed animal scraping across the stones.

Smile, Ix reminded herself, grinning as hard as she could. *And count your blessings*. She was in the presence of a Sorrow.

With her ears ringing, Ix couldn't tell when the screaming finally stopped, until a warm hand settled on her shoulder. It was Captain Kel.

"They're gone," Kel said. "Terror chased after Jack. Are you all right?"

"I think so," Ix said. Her legs wobbled like noodles when she tried to stand. "What about Morrigan? Is she . . . ?"

Morrigan groaned, picking herself up. "I feel like I've been hit by a Raging Rhinuffalo. But I'm fine."

Ix's whole body sagged in relief. Then the reality of her situation came crashing down. She'd been caught, by Candle Corps, in the Labyrinth of Souls. Ix gulped as she locked eyes with the stern-looking captain. It felt like he could tally up all the rules she'd broken just by looking at her.

Kel crossed his arms. "You have some explaining to do, Ix Tatterfall."

Ix's heart plummeted into her shoes.

Her name. He knew her name. He knew who she was and where she came from, which meant . . .

Aunt Tara! Ix thought desperately.

"There's no point in running," Captain Kel warned. "It'll be better for you if you turn yourself in—hey!" he shouted as Ix dove under his arm and bolted.

There was a tiny puff of mist up ahead. It was barely the size of a wagon wheel, nowhere near large enough for an adult to get through, but maybe just big enough for a twelve-year-old girl with a lot of practice scrambling under Widow Whitlock's fence. Ix dropped to the stone, scuttling toward the mist on her elbows.

"Gotcha!" Morrigan shouted triumphantly.

She'd grabbed Ix's foot. But Ix was already sliding into the mist. For a second she was stuck, suspended between the worlds. Then her shoe popped off, and Ix hurtled through to the other side, hoping she was in time.

7

CAPTIVES OF CANDLE CORPS

Ix tumbled out of the Labyrinth into Aunt Tara's garden box, right on top of the tomatoes. Dirt sprayed in all directions. At least her aunt preferred vegetables to prickly rosebushes, or the night might have ended very badly.

Ix's socked foot smooshed into the mud as she scrambled up, racing around the house.

"Aunt Tara!" she hollered. "We have to go! Candle Corps is—"

Ix gulped down the last word as she skidded to a stop. Four figures in Candle Corps coats stood outside the cottage, one of them restraining Aunt Tara—and in the middle of them all lay a shining crystal figure, bright against the night.

Nathan Tatterfall.

"Ix! Run!" Aunt Tara cried. Her hands were bound—not with a rope or a chain, but with a thin glowing thread looped around her wrists. A very spindly, snappable-looking thread.

There was no way Ix could leave her aunt. Not when this was all her fault. Ix darted through the figures in shiny coats and grabbed for the thread, yanking with all her might.

"Ouch!" she yelped. The thread hadn't snapped—it had bit into her palm, leaving an angry red mark.

"Be careful, dear. That's sharper than it looks."

Ix spun around. It was Healer Mella, the woman who had spoken in the square. Ix realized she was the one holding the other end of Aunt Tara's thread cuffs.

Aunt Tara gasped at the sight of Ix. "Are you all right?"

Ix looked down to see a dark splatter across her chest that looked eerily like blood. There were more all over her sleeves, and even one on her sock. She probably looked like Wrath, the Bloody Ripper.

"It's tomato," Ix said, plucking a slimy red skin off her overalls. "Aunt Tara, I'm so sorry—"

"So this is the Tatterfall girl."

Ix turned. The woman stalking toward her looked about as friendly as a Dispiteous Viper. Her blue eyes burned like coals in her chalky face.

Ix shivered in fear. But only one thing mattered now.

"Let Aunt Tara go," Ix pleaded. "She isn't the one who broke the rules—it was all me."

"Funny," the woman said, tapping a polished boot, "because she said the same thing. And of course we found this *blatant violation* in plain sight." The woman jerked a thumb at the crystallized figure of her father. "Crystal Sleepers are dangerous and meant to be reported to Candle Corps immediately. Concealing one for ten years is unthinkable."

"He's not dangerous," Ix protested. "And he's not hurting us."

"It's not just a matter of your safety," Healer Mella cut in. "This concerns the entire kingdom." Mella twisted the glowing thread nervously between her fingers. "The fate of your father and the other Crystal Sleepers may hold the key to certain . . . problems that have begun cropping up in the Labyrinth."

Others? Ix's eyes widened. She'd thought Nathan Tatterfall was the only one under the Crystal Sleep who didn't die. But if there were more . . . "Can you wake him up?" she blurted out, hope flickering in her chest.

"We don't owe criminal rule-breakers any answers," the viper woman hissed.

Mella lifted a hand. "*Suspected* criminal rule-breakers, Vice-Captain Wystorm. And I don't see the harm." She turned to Ix. "We've found five others who've been in the Crystal Sleep for years without passing on, though none as long as your father. Unfortunately, we haven't been able to wake them."

"If you can't even help him, then please don't take my father," Ix begged, grabbing on to Vice-Captain Wystorm's coat.

"Such insolence." The vice-captain yanked her sleeve away. "You're in no position to plead for mercy. And we're not just taking your father. Candle Corps is taking *all* of you into custody."

Ix's heart gave a horrible wrench.

Aunt Tara's voice quivered. "She's just a child—"

"Mella, a pair of cuffs for the girl," Wystorm ordered.

This was the moment Aunt Tara had been afraid of Ix's whole life. The reason she begged Ix not to draw attention to herself every morning. And now, Ix had gotten them all taken prisoner by Candle Corps.

Ix held out her hands for Mella to slip the glowing thread around her wrist. As the loop began to tighten, there was a flash of light, and a second later, a figure was striding into the starlit grass, curls of mist vanishing around him. It was Captain Kel, looking just as stern as he had in the Labyrinth. Morrigan was nowhere to be seen.

"Stand down, Vice-Captain Wystorm," he ordered.

"I'll remind you I'm not in your squad. You don't give me orders," Wystorm bit out.

"And I'll remind you I still outrank you. They're not being detained. Let them go," Kel said.

Mella snapped her fingers. With a quick pop, the entire glowing thread disappeared, freeing them both. Aunt Tara pulled Ix into a tight hug.

Wystorm ground her teeth. "You can't ignore such flagrant rule-breaking."

"You're right, I can't. But there is another option." Captain Kel turned to Ix, fixing her with a serious gaze. "You could join Candle Corps Academy."

Aunt Tara gasped. Vice-Captain Wystorm went so red she almost turned purple.

Ix stared at him open-mouthed. "I can't join Candle Corps!" Candle Corps was for people with Dreamlights who saved souls and repelled Nightmares. Not strange, dark-loving Nightmare magnets like Ix.

Wystorm seemed to have the same opinion. "You can't honestly be considering recruiting her—" she began, lip curled in disgust.

Captain Kel held up a hand. "I'll take full responsibility. You're dismissed, Vice-Captain Wystorm. Why don't you and Mella see to the transport of the Crystal Sleeper? I need a moment alone to talk to Ix."

Vice-Captain Wystorm seethed. But there didn't seem to be anything she could do. "The Elder Flames will hear about this," she muttered as she turned on her heel.

Kel gave a grim smile. "I don't doubt they will."

Aunt Tara looked between Ix and the Candle Corps captain.

Then she squeezed Ix's shoulder. "I'll look after your father," she said.

Ix's eyes prickled. She stole one glance back at Nathan Tatterfall, hoping it wouldn't be her last one.

Captain Kel led Ix to the hill overlooking Brittlewick. The whole town looked like a firefly pond. Fog drifted in the streets like water, and all the windows shone with Sprite Lights. Ix wished she could erase all the terrible things that had happened. She'd been attacked by a Nightmare. She'd been saved by a Sorrow. She'd had her arms around Terror. And now she was losing her father—maybe forever.

"You were the one in that alley, weren't you?" Captain Kel said, giving Ix a knowing look. "I saw how you handled yourself with that Creak-o-dile. You seem very familiar with the Labyrinth."

Ix couldn't deny it. "I went in to find my father's soul. Or at least, that's how it started."

"The fact that you *can* go there at will makes you very special." Kel's voice was gruff but not unkind. "I know this is a lot to take in, but I didn't only suggest you join Candle Corps to stop you from being detained. I think you could belong there."

Ix found that hard to believe. She was one-shoed, tomato-splattered, and now that they had been standing still long enough, a Dreary Longlegs spider had started crawling up her overalls.

Captain Kel smiled. "Most students are invited to Candle Corps because they've shown exceptional Dreamlight powers. But there are others. Some people who have a strong connection to the Labyrinth also have powers they don't understand. You might be one of them."

"What if I refuse?" Ix asked, just to check.

"I don't know what rumors you've heard, but everyone brought in for breaking the rules gets a fair hearing before the members of Candle Corps' ruling council, the Elder Flames. Those found to be willful rule-breakers are either exiled or, if they're too dangerous, locked up." Kel sighed. "For you . . . exile, probably. You and your aunt both."

Ix's stomach squirmed. *Exile.*

They had nowhere to go. The Tatterfall family had always lived in Brittlewick. She couldn't ruin Aunt Tara's life like that.

"I'll do it. I'll join Candle Corps," Ix said, hoping she sounded braver than she felt.

"A wise choice." Captain Kel glanced at the waning moon. "It's almost the witching hour. I'm afraid I must get back. But here—take this." When he turned, something shone in his outstretched hand.

It was a small padlock made of glistening silver. Now that Ix looked, she realized an identical lock hung from the strap that crossed over the captain's heart.

"This is an official invitation to enter Candle Corps Academy," Kel explained. "Technically, this year's new students have already been selected and classes are about to start. But I think we can squeak you in." His expression grew serious. "Lock it, and make sure you have it on you by midnight tomorrow, and someone will come to get you. If you don't—if you choose to run—you'll be declared fugitives, and nothing I say will protect you."

Ix gulped, closing her fingers around the lock. "Thank you."

Kel shook his head. "Don't thank me. Candle Corps is dangerous, especially for those with secrets that concern the Labyrinth. But you might find some answers there, too. I'll help you any way I can. Just . . . don't let anyone look too closely at that lock."

Ix had so many questions. She couldn't hold them all back.

"Why are you helping me?" she blurted out. "I'm a rule-breaker."

Captain Kel chuckled. His whole face suddenly seemed kinder. "Let's just say I have a soft spot for rule-breakers." He turned for the house, then paused. "Oh . . . Morrigan wanted me to give this back to you."

He reached into his coat, fishing out Ix's lost shoe. Ix clutched it to her chest.

"Best of luck, Ix Tatterfall."

8

THE MIDNIGHT MIST

That night Ix couldn't sleep a wink. She got out of her bed and curled in the window, looking up at the fading stars. Something nudged her elbow. It was the little Inkling, all dried out and silky again.

"There you are," Ix said. "I thought maybe Candle Corps scared you away. Or worse." She lifted the Inkling and pressed it to her cheek, glad for the comfort.

Ix Tatterfall was about to leave home. Maybe forever.

No one in Brittlewick would miss her. The whole town would probably throw a party to celebrate getting rid of her. And maybe they'd even be kinder to Aunt Tara without Ix around.

But that didn't mean there was nothing Ix would miss.

As soon as the sun rose, Ix got up, determined to make the most of her last day. She and Aunt Tara ate waffles for breakfast, lunch, and dinner, so they could have all the best kinds: chocolate chip, maple butter, and strawberry cream. She visited all her regular spots, like the abandoned shack, the dried-up well, and the dark cubby under the stairs. And she said goodbye to all her favorite Nightmares—the Fright Bats that slept under the splintery old bridge, and the Teasel Weasel that lived in the back of her drawer, forever unraveling her ugly sweaters down to piles of loose yarn.

She tried very hard to say goodbye to the Inkling, too, but it kept crawling back into the pocket of her overalls.

"Candle Corps will be dangerous for you," Ix said, peeling the little Nightmare off her handkerchief for the third time.

The squiggly body seemed to form a question mark, as if to say, *And not for you?*

Ix laughed. "Good point. And I wouldn't mind having a friend. But if you're coming along, you need a name." She tapped her fingers, thinking. "Splotch? Or Socks?" The Inkling had spent most of the day curled up in her sock drawer.

Its inky-black arm tugged at the handkerchief.

"Hanky?" Ix asked. The Inkling straightened up quick, like an exclamation point. Ix grinned. "Hanky it is."

At ten minutes to midnight, Ix stood in the living room, watching the clock tick down. She fidgeted in her long black coat and wiggled her toes in her best pair of striped purple socks. Hanky had slipped into the front pocket of her overstuffed bag, its tiny head just poking out.

Ix's stomach churned like she'd swallowed a whole screech of Fright Bats, watching the minute hand move: 11:55 . . . 56 . . . 57.

"I guess it's time," she said.

Aunt Tara had been very quiet. Suddenly she pulled Ix into a tight hug.

"There's something I need to tell you about your mother," she whispered. "I don't know much, but the way your father talked about her, she was not someone Candle Corps would have approved of."

Ix was surprised. Aunt Tara never, ever talked about Ix's mother. No one did. "What do you mean?"

"I really don't know. Nathan was very secretive about her. And then she disappeared while you were still a baby." Tara pressed her lips together. "The last time he and I spoke, he was barely himself, sleepless and desperate. I'd come to beg him not to go into the Labyrinth anymore. He told me, *They can't find out about her.* But I don't know if he meant your mother . . . or you."

Captain Kel's words rang in Ix's head. *Candle Corps is dangerous, especially for those with secrets that concern the Labyrinth.*

Ix's heart thumped. Whatever her father's secret had been, she was about to walk right into the heart of Candle Corps.

"I can't protect you anymore," Aunt Tara said, brushing back Ix's dark hair. "I know you have to go. Just be careful. Of Candle Corps—and of the Labyrinth. It's very easy for those obsessed with the Labyrinth to lose themselves to it."

"I'll be careful," Ix promised.

Tara's face softened. "And come back to visit sometimes?"

Ix smiled. She gave her aunt one last hug and then lifted the little padlock. With a deep breath, she snapped it closed around the strap of her overalls.

Nothing happened at first. Both she and Tara looked around, waiting. Then the clock started to chime.

A single curl of mist rose in front of Ix. Suddenly mist was everywhere, spilling out of the dark cracks and swirling around like a living thing.

The twelfth bell chimed. With a great *rrrrrip!* a jagged hole split the haze.

A figure in a Candle Corps uniform appeared on the threshold. She had tan skin and a messy brunette bun, with four feather quills sticking out of it at odd angles. It made her look like a frazzled cockatiel. In one hand she held a clipboard.

"Ix Tatterfall?"

Ix nodded.

"Welcome. I'm Instructor Cadence," she said, making a sharp check mark on the clipboard. "Come on, then, we haven't got all night. You're my last one."

Ix shouldered her bag, making sure Hanky was tucked out of sight. Then with one last goodbye to Aunt Tara she stepped into the portal, the mist swirling closed behind her.

She came through into the outskirts of the Labyrinth, far from the high walls and the Sorrows. There were four other kids waiting with Instructor Cadence, two boys and two girls, all looking bored or nervous or both.

"Now that we're all here, let me give you Novices your first lesson," Cadence said, stuffing her clipboard into a bulging pocket. "Those of us who can open doorways in the mist can use the Labyrinth to get around quickly."

Ix knew that where you went into the Labyrinth was very rarely where you came out. She'd even counted on it a number of times to get out of locked broom closets and sheds after Arthur Vance shoved her in. But she hadn't known you could travel long distances—or that you could control exactly where you landed.

"The mist is the veil that separates our world from the Labyrinth. The strongest Flames of Candle Corps can slice doorways open simply using their Shadow Renders. But even those of us without that kind of power can do the same if we use a key cutter."

Instructor Cadence dug into another overstuffed pocket and pulled out a dagger with deep notches cut into the blade. It looked like an oversize key.

Ix studied it closely. Captain Kel had said the way Ix entered the Labyrinth was special. She never felt like she was cutting through anything—just slipping inside. Like there was always a doorway to the Labyrinth right behind her eyelids. She filed that away to ask the captain about.

"Stay close, and be vigilant," Instructor Cadence told them, setting off into the mist.

A tall boy with sharp features and chestnut-brown hair shouldered Ix out of his way. She would have gone headfirst into a patch of Mildew Mushroom if another boy hadn't caught her arm. He was shorter than Ix, with brown skin, floppy curls, and big round glasses.

"Thanks," she said. "I'm Ix, by the way."

"Ollie. Are you a first-timer?" the boy asked.

Ix rubbed the back of her neck. "Um, I think so."

"It just means you don't have family in Candle Corps."

"Definitely, then."

Ix heard a derisive snort from the pale boy who'd pushed past her. "I swear they'll let anybody in these days," he said.

"That's Darien Winters," Ollie whispered behind his hand. "His father's head captain and also on the Elder Council, and he never lets anyone forget it."

"Careful, everyone, we've got company," Instructor Cadence warned, holding up a hand.

Mist swirled across the stones at the head of a pack of Mistcats. When they all ran together, they looked like a crashing wave.

Someone shrieked—a short girl with peach skin and bouncy pigtails. One of the Mistcats had run through her legs.

"It barely touched you, Beatrix," the tall girl next to her groused.

"Stay calm and wait for them to pass," Instructor Cadence said, snagging Darien Winters by the coat before he followed the cats in a daze. "And for goodness' sake, if you start feeling dizzy or confused, look away."

Ollie seemed to be studying the Mistcats hard, his nose crinkled up under his glasses.

"What are you doing?" Ix asked, curious.

"Counting tails," Ollie explained. "Sometimes real cats slip into the Labyrinth. But even hiding in a pack of Mistcats, you can tell them apart by their furry tails."

Ix tried to count the swirling tails, but quickly got dizzy. "I didn't know any animals could enter the Labyrinth at all," she admitted, rubbing at her eyes.

"Cats are the only ones," Ollie said. "There are some dogs who can sense Nightmares. You know, barking at things that aren't there, twitching while they chase invisible creatures in their sleep—seventeen!" Ollie interrupted himself as the last cat ran by. "Seventeen Mistcats, and no real ones hiding among them."

"How do you know all this?" Ix asked, amazed.

"My family trains Dreamchasers." At her blank look, he added, "They're special Nightmare-sensitive dogs that work with Candle Corps outside the Labyrinth. Sometimes regular people adopt them, too, if they're troubled by Nightmares."

Maybe she could get a Dreamchaser for Aunt Tara, who was always sweeping the Inklings and sneezing when the tickly little things ran away through the dust.

"Just dogs, though?" she asked. "No cats become Dreamchasers?"

Ollie grinned. "Cats are super Nightmare sensitive, but they're totally untrainable. We have a big orange house cat, and no matter what kind of Nightmare crosses his path, he just sits there licking his paws like he couldn't care less."

Ix shared a laugh with Ollie, suddenly feeling a little lighter. She had been so caught up in Candle Corps as her only choice, *school or exile*, that she hadn't thought about being around people who could see what she saw. Maybe here, she finally wouldn't be an outcast anymore.

Ollie started to tell Ix about the different breeds of Dream-chaser dogs and what each one was especially good at, when they were interrupted by a loud fake yawn.

"I thought the boring lectures didn't start until next week," Darien Winters sneered.

Ollie blushed. "I'm sorry if I was going on too much," he told Ix, twisting his fingers. "I'm really better with books and dogs than people."

"You weren't," Ix replied, shooting a glare at Darien. "And if he wasn't interested, he could mind his own business."

Ollie gasped, and the two girls behind them snickered. Darien's cheeks colored. He shot Ix an angry glare.

"That's enough, all of you," Cadence warned. "Hurry along—we're nearly there."

She led them to a patch of mist so thick Ix could barely see her own feet. Then Cadence lifted the dagger and started sawing. Ix watched in amazement as the key-like teeth cut a jagged hole, big enough for them to pass through single file.

Darien elbowed his way to the front. "This isn't over between us, *Snot*," he hissed at Ix. Ix tried not to let it get to her. *Snot* wasn't that much worse than *Ick*.

"This is always my favorite part," Instructor Cadence said, her eyes twinkling. Then she swept her arm out, ushering them onto a wide lawn glittering with dew. "Your home away from home. Welcome, Novices, to Covenant Keep."

9

ʮOVENANT ʮEEP

Ix stared up in wonder at a giant castle surrounded by dark haw-thorn forests. It had craggy towers and glittering windows and jagged merlons along the walls that looked like grinning jack-o'-lantern teeth, all wreathed in fog.

Ollie took off his glasses and wiped them on his blue necker-chief. "Being in the Labyrinth always gives me goose bumps, even when I'm locked in tight."

"Locked in?" Ix repeated.

"Your Soul Lock." Ollie pointed to the padlock clipped on Ix's overalls strap. "Without them, we wouldn't be able to enter the Labyrinth in our physical bodies without risking our souls unte-thering and getting lost. Didn't someone explain it to you when you got your invitation?"

"Uh, maybe." All Captain Kel had told Ix was that she shouldn't let anyone look too closely at her lock. She certainly hoped she'd see him again soon, because her questions were mounting. Ix had been going to the Labyrinth, body and all, since she was little, and she'd never lost her soul.

She didn't have time to dwell on it. Instructor Cadence was already leading them up the slope and through the giant double doors into Covenant Keep.

Inside, Ix turned in a circle trying to see everything at once. There were statues and suits of armor and woven tapestries and midnight-blue rugs embroidered with silver moons. Bright lights floated inside glass baubles on the walls, flickering with white fire.

"Dreamlight," Ollie whispered, when he saw her staring.

"The auditorium is at the end of this corridor," Instructor Cadence explained. "But we won't be walking straight there. Can any Novice tell me why?"

Ollie's hand shot excitedly into the air, but Darien Winters didn't even give him a chance. "It's because of the Dreamlight seal, right?" he said, sounding bored.

"Remember to raise your hand. But yes. All of Covenant Keep is a giant Dreamlight seal used to hold back Nightmare power. Go ahead and set your bags down—we'll get them after the tour."

Everyone did as she said. Ix bent all the way down so Hanky could scurry up and hide in her pocket.

As they walked the halls, Cadence told them how the very first Flames of Candle Corps had built the tower at the center of the keep to trap Nightmare creatures and cursed objects that were too powerful to be sent back to the Labyrinth. The Dreamlight seal of the castle put them to sleep and then, over time, leached the Night-mare power away until they could be safely released. At least half the paintings on the walls were actually vessels with Nightmares sealed inside. The heavy gilt frames were wound with silver chains.

"Isn't that dangerous, having them out in the open?" Beatrix asked.

"Not at all," Instructor Cadence said. "In fact, it's necessary. The energy that maintains the Dreamlight seal comes from each and every member of Candle Corps. That's why we're walking around the outer ring of the building. Every time a Flame or even a student like you walks the ring of the building, the seal is strengthened."

Cadence stopped in front of a giant portrait of a woman in a billowing gray cloak. The longer Ix looked, the less she saw the woman and the more she saw a ghoulish face staring out at her with a wide, hungry smile. Ix tried to imagine what Nightmare was trapped in there.

She leaned in for a closer look. The painting rattled suddenly, banging against the wall. Ix jerked back in surprise.

"Strange. This one's usually very mild-mannered." Cadence frowned at the canvas, then shrugged. "Must be all the excitement."

Ix thought about the way Nightmare creatures always seemed drawn to her. She couldn't possibly have the same effect on Nightmares that were sealed away. Still, Ix resolved not to touch anything. She shoved her hands firmly in her pockets, almost squishing Hanky, who gave an indignant little wriggle.

Cadence had gone on. "Whenever you stop in front of a painting or statue in the keep, count to eight. Tap your foot eight times, or your fingers. Hum a song with eight bars. Anything. That is the rule of Covenant Keep."

"Because of the Rule of Sevens?" Ollie asked.

"Exactly. And by the same token, be especially careful of groups of seven within the keep. Your classes will be structured carefully, but never gather in groups of seven."

Cadence lifted a finger, following her own instructions and drawing eight quick circles in the air before leading them onward.

Down the next hallway, she stopped in front of a heavy door with jagged gouges torn right above the handle. It looked like something had tried to claw its way in.

"These are the Doors to Nowhere. They're how we access the Between World, where the Labyrinth is."

She swung the door open. There was nothing behind it but a gray stone wall. Cadence chuckled at their disappointed faces.

"We use the key cutter. Here, watch . . ."

She shut the door firmly and stuck her key in the dark gouge, tracing its lightning-bolt shape. This time, when she threw the door open, the Labyrinth was on the other side—swirling mist and glowing dandelions waving in the wind. A handful of fluffy seeds whipped through the door and brushed Ix's face. Cadence caught one in her palm.

"Because people are always coming and going through the doors, a lot of small Nightmares sneak into Covenant Keep. But don't worry, they're mostly harmless."

"Ooh, look," Ollie said, pointing at an Inkling dangling over their heads. Beatrix shrieked.

"We don't bother dispelling little ones like that," Cadence said. "But do be cautious. There are some larger Nightmares that can be . . . difficult. I'm sure your upper classmates will fill you in."

Ix wasn't sure about *difficult Nightmares*. But she was glad she wouldn't have to worry about keeping Hanky under wraps forever.

Cadence closed the door. There was still a little mist hissing out under the crack.

"Sometimes the door disappears at once, but some parts of the Labyrinth try to linger. Which is why Novices are strictly forbidden from opening the Doors to Nowhere. Understood?"

She waited for every single one of them to nod before leading them on.

By the end of the tour, Ix was more lost than when they'd come in. She was surprised when they turned a corner and found themselves back in the entrance hall.

The doors to the auditorium had been thrown open. The statues carved around it grinned eerily in the Dreamlight.

"Looks like they're ready for us," Cadence said.

Ix sucked in a tight breath. "Wish me luck, Hanky," she whispered.

Hanky wrapped around her fingers, giving her an encouraging squeeze. Ix squeezed back, hoping both of them were ready for whatever came next.

10

THE DREAMLIGHT INITIATION

The auditorium was enormous, bigger than Brittlewick's whole town square. Huge iron chandeliers hung from the ceiling, each one glowing with hundreds of Dreamlight flames. Stone gargoyles watched them from hollowed-out nooks high in the walls.

There had to be over a hundred students and instructors assembled, all in their dark Candle Corps coats. Some students whispered, watching them excitedly, while others just yawned, looking half asleep.

Tiny pinpricks of light glittered in the dark corners of the ceiling, almost like a night sky.

"Are those stars?" Ix whispered to Ollie.

Ollie adjusted his glasses, squinting. "Looks like a Glow Snail infestation."

"Oh," Ix said, deflating. Now that she looked closer, he was right—a few were even moving, leaving glowing slime trails behind. But it was still sort of pretty, if she didn't think about it too hard.

Instructor Cadence led them to where a small handful of students not in uniform stood near the edge of the stage. "Please join the rest of this year's novitiate class."

There were only nine of them altogether. Ix stayed close to

Ollie, peering around at the rest of the Novices. A shock of bright red curls caught her eye. Right at the center of the group stood Morrigan.

Ix was relieved to see she looked okay. If there were any bandages on her arm, they were hidden under her fuzzy sweater. Ix lifted a hand to wave, but the second she caught Morrigan's eye, the redhead scowled and turned away.

A severe-looking woman with tan skin and gray hair pulled into a tight knot glided onto the stage. She banged harshly on her lectern, and Ix jumped—then she realized the woman was just loosing a cloud of Dust-Puff Beetles. They took off in a whirl, leaving a film of dust motes in the air. The woman coughed, waving it away.

"Welcome, new Candle Corps members. And *wake up*, older students! If anyone next to you is snoring, please do give them a poke."

There was scattered laughter, and several students shook their drowsy neighbors. Ix liked her immediately.

"I'm Tormaline Telle, head instructor at Candle Corps Academy. You're all here because you have the aptitude to become Flames of Candle Corps one day, should you choose. But first you must learn how to control the powers you possess—and, much more important, you must decide how best to make use of them.

"A few introductions. In the front rows, we have our instructors, professors, and some of the captains of Candle Corps."

Ix craned her head toward the group of people in stunning black coats. Some looked stern and solemn, as if they were taking this all very seriously, but others were smiling and waving, and one wizened old man had fallen asleep with his mouth wide open and a cat on his chest. Ix didn't see Captain Kel, but she spotted Healer Mella in the crowd. The woman flashed her an encouraging smile. Though it was somewhat dampened by the glare Ix was getting from Vice-Captain Wystorm.

Telle went on. "In the middle seats, we have our Sparks, the second- and third-years—too rowdy, simmer down!—and in the last rows, our Embers, the fourth- and fifth-year students."

The Embers were even louder than the Sparks, whooping and hollering.

Telle banged her lectern again, but she was smiling. "As head instructor, my door is always open. I love teaching. I love counseling students. I especially adore handing out awards. I do not like having to discipline troublemakers. Those of you who are here to learn, I'm sure we'll get along swimmingly. Those, on the other hand, who think joining Candle Corps is a license to break the rules . . ."

Her gaze swept over the Novices, and Ix shivered as they met eyes.

". . . be warned that I won't hesitate to expel any students who tarnish the name of this storied institution."

Ix felt like she'd swallowed a Dire Frog. *Candle Corps or exile*, Kel had said. If she was expelled, she wouldn't just be banished from the school. She and Aunt Tara would be banished from the whole kingdom. It was a frightening thought . . . especially since Ix had never been particularly good at following rules.

Telle's voice turned warmer. "To serve as a Flame is a sacred trust. Candle Corps is as old as the kingdom of Spinar. We work under the blessing of the throne but never at its whims. Our only loyalty is to protect the balance of our world and keep the Nightmares at bay. Remember: you are what stands between the kingdom of Spinar and the darkness of the Labyrinth."

The Dreamlight flames flickered and seemed to glow brighter for a moment. Ix felt a hot, sharp glow inside her, too. *Longing*, she thought—to belong here, like Captain Kel thought maybe she could.

Head Instructor Telle cleared her throat. "And now, before I lose you to dreamland again, I'll hand it over to Head Councillor Alexis Moongrave and the Elder Flames for the initiation."

Ix's warm feelings died. "Initiation?"

"I know," Ollie whispered, misunderstanding Ix's surprise. "I can't believe we have to show our Dreamlights in front of the entire Elder Council. I'm so nervous."

Not half as nervous as Ix, who had never even tried to conjure a Dreamlight, let alone succeeded.

Her palms were already sweating. She was going to fail the initiation, and then she was going to be detained, right in front of everybody.

All at once, the lights went out. Ix's gasp was drowned out by a much louder scream.

"You knew that was going to happen, Beatrix," said the dry voice of the tall girl who'd come through the mist with them.

"But it was so sudden, Nora!" Beatrix protested.

Ix felt Hanky ooze out of her pocket and climb up into her collar, curious.

"The Elder Flames," Ollie hissed.

Eight glowing lights had started moving across the stage. At first Ix thought they were just flames suspended in air, but then she realized they were figures in long dark robes, with cowls pulled low over their faces. The hems of their intricate robes swept across the floor, sending a hush through the entire crowd.

It was dark like the dead of night. Silent like the world under a blanket of snow. Like all the light and sound had been devoured.

The bobbing flames stopped at center stage.

"Beatrix Bianchi," a woman's voice rang out. "You are called before the Elder Flames."

"I don't want to be first," Ix heard Beatrix moaning. But then came timid footsteps as the girl made her way onto the stage. The woman who had spoken reached out, handing Beatrix something. Ix wondered if she was Alexis Moongrave.

"I'm ready," Beatrix said.

The Elder Flames all closed their hands, extinguishing their Dreamlights. This time there was only a moment of total darkness before a single pinprick of light bloomed onstage—a bright flame a handspan high, flickering above Beatrix's palms.

"May your Dreamlight shine ever true," the woman in the cloak said.

Like a spell was broken, the audience started clapping and cheering. Beatrix wobbled off the stage, and the eight Elder Flames lifted their lights again.

"What just happened?" Ix whispered to Ollie.

"The Elder Flames gave her a special candlewick that draws out a person's Dreamlight power. All you have to do is hold it, and your Dreamlight will rise. Then you've officially joined Candle Corps."

There was no more time to ask questions. The hush had fallen over the audience again as a dark-haired boy named Andre Navarro was called before the Elder Flames, and then tall, ghostly pale Nora Crane.

Ix felt lucky she wasn't afraid of the dark, as they were plunged into pitch-blackness each time. She'd hoped Darien, at least, would have as little potential as he had manners. Unfortunately when his flame leapt into the air, it was the highest one yet.

"Valerie Wystorm," Alexis Moongrave called.

Ix leaned close to Ollie. "I've heard that name before—on a vice-captain."

Ollie shrugged. "There are a lot of Wystorms at Candle Corps. Valerie's family is legendary. They've held a seat on the Elder Council for generations."

Ix craned her head toward the pretty girl with rosy cheeks and blond curls who stood before the Elder Flames. Her candle flame shot a full foot high, but the girl's face still looked sour and pinched.

"That was amazing!" Ix whispered to Ollie. "Why does she look so unhappy?"

"Well, Valerie would probably be the strongest student this year, except for . . ."

"Morrigan Bea!" the Elder Flame called.

Whispers erupted across the auditorium as Morrigan took the stage. Even in the dim light, Ix caught a flash of her red hair. Morrigan tossed it off her shoulder, looking utterly at ease. Almost before the lights went out, a giant reddish flame shot up from her wick like a bonfire. Morrigan tipped her head back to keep from singeing off her eyebrows.

Strangely, there was only scattered applause. Between the lukewarm cheers, Ix could hear people muttering.

"I can't believe they let another girl from that monster family in."

"Don't look at her."

"Nobody's safe with the Bea Wolves around."

In the back row, a tall boy with brown skin and short black hair brought his fingers to his lips and whistled loudly, as though trying to drown out the whispers.

Morrigan scowled at everyone, including the Elder Flames, before stalking off the stage.

Ix wanted to ask Ollie what a *Bea Wolf* was, but he was being called forward. "Oliver Pembrook." His flame had a soft golden glow, and there was something gentle about it that made Ix want to hold her hand over it. Ollie blushed at the cheers and applause as he left the stage to join the rest of the Novices.

Ix was the only one left.

"Ix Tatterfall," Alexis Moongrave announced.

Legs like jelly, Ix dragged her feet all the way up onto the stage. From up close, she caught a glimpse of Alexis Moongrave under her cowl. She had brown skin and long gray hair, and her eyes crinkled in a smile behind her wire-rimmed glasses.

Ix wiped her sweaty palms against her overalls before taking the wick. It was so thin and slippery it felt like it might slide right out of her hand.

"Ready?" the woman asked.

Ix wasn't, but she nodded anyway.

All the lights went out. Even though she knew the audience was out there, Ix suddenly felt totally alone. Her heart pounded so loud she was sure the Elder Flames could hear it.

One second passed, then two. Nothing happened.

Ix felt that nervous grin creeping onto her face as whispers raced through the dark room. She concentrated on the wick, begging it to light. After agonizing seconds, a single wisp of smoke rose, followed by a flame so tiny she could barely see it.

Alexis Moongrave pinched her glasses and bent forward, her nose inches from Ix's hand as she squinted at the flame. Ix could hear stifled giggles from the audience.

One of the robed figures snorted. "There's never been a Novice who performed so poorly at the initiation," the man scoffed. "Can such a minuscule Dreamlight even be considered worthy of Candle Corps?"

Ix wanted to run off the stage in shame.

Alexis Moongrave laid a warm hand on her shoulder. "Nonsense. A Dreamlight—no matter how small—is proof of a Novice worthy of Candle Corps. Perhaps you'll grow into it," she told Ix. And then, loud enough for everyone to hear, added, "May your Dreamlight shine ever true."

"Thank you," Ix mumbled, miserable.

The only person clapping was the same boy who had whistled for Morrigan Bea. "Don't sweat it!" he called, giving her a thumbs-up.

Ix felt herself shrinking inside. Just once, she wanted to fit in. But here she was again: Ix the weirdo, the anomaly. Ix the outcast, already a joke before school even started. She was tempted to check her pockets for stray Belittle Worms—tiny gray inchworm Nightmares that clung to your clothing like burrs. Having one on you made your self-esteem shrivel up till you felt two inches tall. The one day Arthur Vance had actually made her cry, she'd found a Belittle Worm tucked into the cuff of her jacket.

No such luck this time. If Ix felt minuscule, it was all her own thoughts.

Ix hurried back to join the other Novices. With a *whoosh*, the Elder Flames vanished from the stage, and the Dreamlights burst back to life in the candelabras.

"Don't worry about it," Ollie told her. "It's an old ritual—no one really puts any stock in it." Hanky seemed to agree, squirming encouragingly in her pocket.

But the rest of the Novices were giving her a wide berth. Valerie Wystorm was whispering furiously behind her hand. Darien Winters held up his fingers, shrinking them to nothing with a snicker.

Only Morrigan Bea met her gaze. "At least you made an impression," she said.

Ix pulled her hood up to hide her face. That wasn't the impression she'd been hoping for.

11

THE MYSTERIOUS MORRIGAN BEA

It was past two by the time the initiation ended. Ix felt like she might fall asleep on her feet, or maybe on the elbow of the suit of armor standing next to her in the crowded hallway. The Inkling in her pocket had drifted off. Last Ix looked, it had wrapped itself in her actual hanky, only one little arm sticking out.

Someone tapped her shoulder. Ix jumped.

"There you are. I lost you in the crowd."

It was the tall boy who'd whistled for Morrigan and clapped for Ix. He looked to be about fifteen, with sharp fox features and a welcoming smile.

"Ix Tatterfall, right?" he said, offering his hand.

Ix nodded, reaching out tentatively to shake it.

"I'm Tempest Valerian. Captain Kel asked me to keep an eye on you. Come on, I'll take you to your room." Students were disappearing down the hall, but Tempest turned the other way, toward an arch with gargoyles on either side. "The South Wing isn't far. I'll show you the back way, up the Kneazel-Crooks."

The Kneazel-Crooks turned out to be a column of very steep stairs winding up into the dark, dimly lit by hissing Dreamlight flames in glimmering lanterns. Ix's bag banged against her knees as they climbed. Halfway up, the flame over their heads went out all at once, plunging them into darkness. Ix gasped.

"No need to worry," Tempest said. "It's a Blackout Bat. They eat the Dreamlight flames, when they can get at them. Usually come right off if you clap."

Tempest clapped twice, and the light puffed back into the lantern. Now Ix could see the culprit. It was a tiny Nightmare bat as long as her thumb, with velvety charcoal-black fur, hanging upside down from the light. Tempest clapped again, and it let go, flapping over to perch on Ix's shoulder. Ix laughed.

"See? Totally harmless," Tempest said, scratching its tiny belly.

Tempest seemed to know a lot about the keep. As they started off again, Ix studied him, noticing the four little tufts of white flame embroidered on the shoulder of his coat.

"Are you Captain Kel's vice-captain?" she asked.

The boy chuckled. "Flattering, but no. I'm an Ember, fourth-year. I've got two more years at the academy before I become a Flame."

"Is Captain Kel here? I didn't see him at the ceremony." Ix only had about a million things to ask him.

"He's away on a mission. What mission, I have no idea." Tempest shrugged. "Most of the Flames get their orders from the Elder Council, but Captain Kel has a reputation for going off on his own." He shot her a knowing look. "I heard you crossed paths with him in the Labyrinth."

Ix's guts squirmed like they were filled with Nervy Worms. "He told you that?"

"Actually you did, just now," Tempest said. "All the captain told me was that he'd met a girl with *interesting* powers, and I should watch out for you."

Expulsion. Exile. Imprisonment. Every horrible thing Ix had come here to escape flashed through her mind. "Please don't tell anyone," she begged.

Tempest lifted his hands. "I didn't mean to scare you. I am literally the last person who would ever turn you in. I've been to the Labyrinth loads of times—not always with permission."

"And you're still here?" Ix asked, remembering Head Instructor Telle's speech about *rule-breaking*.

Tempest grinned. "My first year, Instructor Cadence threatened to camp outside my door if I didn't stop sneaking out."

He hopped over an uneven step and spun to face Ix, hands clasped behind his back.

"The Valerians are one of the founding families of Candle Corps. Did you see the woman who looks like me in the front row of the auditorium? That's my sister, Torrent Valerian, and she *is* a vice-captain. And if you meet the Elder Flames again, you'll meet Tyrese Valerian, my father. The North-Northwest Wing on the very top floor, if you could find it and blow the dust off the plaque, would say *Dedicated to Evorance Valerian*. And if you found the oldest statues in the oldest, dustiest corners of the castle, a lot of them would probably look like me and say Valerian, too."

"That's amazing," Ix said. Nobody in her family had ever done anything important—as far as she knew, anyway.

Tempest sighed. "It can be a lot to live up to. My father wants me to carry on the family tradition—become head captain, maybe even Candle Corps' official emissary to the king. But I've got my sights set on joining Captain Kel's squad. He's been deeper into the Labyrinth than anyone. People say he's determined to get to the very center, to Death's Door."

Ix shivered. Just like her father.

They reached the top of the stairs and clambered out into a common room full of students and scowling gargoyles and big squishy couches. The Blackout Bat flapped off Ix's shoulder, indignant to be in such a bright place.

"Anyway, don't worry," Tempest finished, mussing her hair. "Whatever rules you break, I promise you I have broken them all first. Now, come on. I'm sure your roommate's dying to meet you."

She hadn't heard anything about a roommate! After that embarrassing Dreamlight performance, she'd been hoping to hide out in her room alone, maybe forever.

Her sense of doom grew with every door they passed, until they reached the very end of the hall. "Here we are," Tempest said, knocking sharply.

The door jerked open just a crack. "What?" said a very cranky, very familiar voice.

Tempest smiled. "I've got your roommate here."

"I thought I got a room to myself," the person on the other side snapped.

"Novices don't get single rooms."

"*You* did."

"As always, I am the exception that proves the rule," Tempest said. "Now open up and meet your roommate. I picked a good one for you."

The door swung open. Just as Ix had feared, on the other side stood Morrigan Bea. She had traded her skirt and sweater for button-down pajamas, and her wild hair was trapped in a messy braid, but her annoyed expression was exactly the same.

Morrigan's eye twitched. "You again!"

"Great, you already know each other," Tempest said. "Captain Kel wanted me to keep an eye on both of you, so I figured this was the most convenient."

"For you, maybe," Morrigan muttered.

"Anyway," Tempest said, clapping Ix's shoulder. "Everybody gets the morning after the initiation off, but your teacher will expect you at noon for orientation. Don't be late. And if you have any questions, I'm sure Morrigan will be more than happy to answer them—she's old hat around here."

Ix had a lot of questions. But Morrigan didn't look happy to fill her in. In fact, she looked kind of murderous as Ix slipped into the room. It was just big enough for two beds, under cozy patchwork quilts, and two desks. A tall window of bubbly old glass looked out on the castle courtyard. One door led to a closet, the other to a bathroom with a clawfoot tub.

"Ugh! That Tempest." Morrigan slammed the door so hard everyone in the entire wing probably heard it. She'd definitely woken Hanky, who wiggled in Ix's pocket. "I swear he does these things just to irritate me."

Ix dropped her bag on the floor, letting the Inkling ooze down and scamper into the dark space under the bed. "He seemed pretty nice to me."

"Well, he's not. He's insufferable. And a busybody." Morrigan grabbed a few notebooks off the desk and shoved them roughly into a drawer. "But he's also a prodigy whose Dreamlight power already rivals that of the Flames. That's why Captain Kel takes him along sometimes on his trips into the Labyrinth." She rounded on Ix, her hands on her hips. "You, on the other hand, I don't get at all. Especially after that speck you made at the initiation."

Ix winced, embarrassed all over again. "Thanks for reminding me."

"Why did Captain Kel bring you into Candle Corps? And what were you doing in the Labyrinth that night, anyway?" Morrigan demanded.

Fresh off being tricked by Tempest, Ix was careful how she answered this time. "What did Captain Kel tell you?"

"That you had your reasons. And that it's none of my business. But since I'm stuck with you, I think I'm entitled to know." Morrigan stomped forward until she and Ix were practically nose to nose. "So what's the big secret? Who are you?"

"I'm no one," Ix insisted, backing up until she hit the wall.

"You think I'm going to believe that?"

Morrigan's hair stuck up with bits of frizz. Suddenly Ix remembered how Morrigan had looked in the Labyrinth, the red flames blazing around her like wolf ears and a tail. And what the students had been whispering in the auditorium.

"You first," Ix said. "What are the Bea Wolves?"

Morrigan jerked away like she'd been stung. Her green eyes flashed. "Fine. Keep your secrets, Ix Tatterfall."

Morrigan dug around in her desk until she found a stick of chalk. With a loud, angry screech, she drew a line across the floorboards, right down the center of the room.

"That's your half, and this is my half. I don't need to know anything about you, and you don't need to know anything about me. Don't talk to me, don't sit with me—don't even look at me. Just stay out of my way."

With that, the redhead threw herself onto her bed. She shot Ix one last scathing look as she blew out the candle.

There was just enough moonlight filtering through the clouds

for Ix to dig out her own pajamas. Ix thought about apologiz-
ing. But the way Morrigan was bristling under her quilt said if Ix
bothered her again tonight, she was getting the chalk crammed
down her throat.

Oh well, Ix thought, crawling into bed. She'd have tomorrow.
And the day after that. They were roommates, after all. Morrigan
couldn't ignore her forever. Still, she made a mental note to ask
someone else about the Bea Wolves.

The last thing she felt was Hanky curling up in the crook of her
neck. At least she wasn't totally alone.

12

THE CURIOUS CAT

Ix had barely closed her eyes when she felt curls of mist on her face. Her first panicked thought was that she'd ended up in the Labyrinth, jumped from her bed on her very first night at the academy. But the mist felt different than usual.

Ix blinked, sitting up in the dark. There was no moss or choke-weed or spotted mushrooms, no high stone walls towering over her. A second later, she realized why. The Grinning Cat was watching her from where he lay halfway through a tear into the Labyrinth. The mist poured out around his body, and an eerie glow lit the giant cat from behind. He'd wedged himself partway into Ix's dream tonight.

"Smiles," Ix said, surprised. "What are you doing here?"

"My Mistcats told me something interesting today. They said you'd gone off with the fireflies. I had to see it for myself."

"Fireflies?"

"Your so-called Candle Corps," Smiles said, licking his teeth. "They burn bright and they wink out fast." A tiny bit of glowing dandelion fluff drifted through from the Labyrinth, and Smiles snuffed it out with his claws.

Ix had been so busy avoiding Candle Corps for her own reasons, she hadn't even stopped to wonder what the Sorrows thought of them. Chaos didn't look displeased with her exactly, but he'd also never gone to the trouble of visiting Ix in a dream before.

Suddenly it all hit her at once. Ix was trapped here at Candle Corps. She didn't even know where her father's crystallized body had ended up. She couldn't count on Candle Corps to help him. She needed to do it herself. Then if the worst happened, and she and Aunt Tara were banished, at least they wouldn't have to leave Nathan Tatterfall behind.

"I need to learn to use my Dreamlight powers so I can save lost souls."

"Dreamlight powers. Hmm . . ." Smiles tipped his head, amused.

"What did you really come here for?" Ix asked, crossing her arms.

"So suspicious." The cat chuckled. "I just came to reminisce a little. Do you remember the first time we met?"

"Of course," Ix said. She'd only been six the first time she followed a little blue-and-white Mistcat and found Smiles at the other end. She hadn't even known he was a Sorrow then.

The cat waved a lazy paw. "That wasn't the first time we met," he said, as though reading her mind. "You came into the Labyrinth as a baby once—nothing but a tiny, babbling creature that still moved on four legs. I'd never seen human young before. At that age, you're no fun for a Sorrow."

Ix's breath caught. She had no memory of that, but she imagined a tiny dark-haired baby crawling through the Labyrinth. Babies were no fun for Sorrows because they didn't yet understand things like greed, and wrath, and despair. Those things came later.

"I put you in my mouth," the Grinning Cat admitted.

"You tried to eat me?" Ix was horrified.

"Goodness, no! Eating a human—what a disgusting thought."

He worked his tongue a few times, as if to get the taste off. "I was simply carrying you. I planned to spit you into the nearest doorway into the Labyrinth and make you some other Sorrow's problem."

That still sounded pretty bad to Ix. Even if babies weren't particularly interesting to Sorrows, there was nothing to stop a Creak-o-dile from gobbling her up.

"Before I could, I heard a human calling frantically for his child. Don't mistake it for kindness—honestly, it was less work than the alternative. I spit you out into a patch of Pillow Flowers, and the pollen instantly lulled you to sleep. I even tore a convenient hole back to the Waking World in the mist beside you, in hopes that you would both disappear."

"What happened?" Ix asked breathlessly.

"The man came, and he picked up his young, and then he walked right by the portal I'd made and headed into the Labyrinth. I'll never forget what he said. *As long as you are with me, little wishling, Death will surely come for us.*"

Ix's heart swooped. "Death?"

The man Smiles had seen must have been her father. He had called Ix *little wishling*, because she was his wish-come-true. But why would he have been looking for one of the Sorrows—especially the most powerful of them all?

The cat's giant amethyst eyes glittered. "Apparently your father took you into the Labyrinth looking for the Soul Reaper."

"You never told me this before," Ix accused.

"Why would I?" Smiles looked bored. "It's not an especially interesting story—well, except for the end. And your father certainly never found Death. The Soul Reaper had already disappeared by then."

Ix shivered, rubbing at her goose bumps. "Then why are you telling me now?"

Smiles's striped body shook with mirth. "Because people do not end up in the Labyrinth over and over by mistake.

"The fireflies are creatures of the Waking World. They wink in and out of the Labyrinth, but they belong on this side." The cat swirled his shiny claws into the mist as the darkness of the Labyrinth started to swallow him up. "Are you sure you're really where you belong?"

That was the one thing Ix was never sure of.

"Something to think on," the cat suggested, his grin glinting as he disappeared completely. "Sweet dreams."

13

THE DEVIOUS DOORWAY

Ix awoke the next morning with drool on her pillow and something tugging on her hair.

"Whaaaa?" she mumbled, surging up and sending Hanky splatting onto the blankets.

The Inkling had been yanking at her, she realized. Bright sunlight streamed through the window. There was no sign of Morrigan. Ix squinted at the clock: 11:40.

Orientation started at noon.

"I'm late!" Ix cried, leaping up and digging frantically through her bag. At least everything she wore was either black or purple, so whatever she grabbed would match.

"Someone could have woken me," Ix complained to Hanky as she crammed her feet into her shoes. The Inkling gave a very irritated and huffy shake. "You're right, you did. You coming along today?"

Hanky just oozed back into the dark space under the bed.

"Lucky you," Ix grumbled, stifling a yawn as she rushed out. She now had exactly ten minutes to get . . . *somewhere* in the giant Covenant Keep.

The hallways were deserted. Ix panicked until she heard voices up ahead. It sounded like Darien Winters and the boy who'd gone after him in the initiation, Cole Cunningham.

"I heard Valerie Wystorm has a room all to herself in her family's wing," Darien was saying. "Naturally, my father will be hearing about this."

"If anyone deserves their own room, it's you," Cole agreed. Already auditioning to be Darien's number-one crony.

Ix made a face. There was no way she was asking Darien for directions, but she could follow them to orientation. She crept behind them down the passageways.

"If they at least let us stay outside the dorms . . ." Cole was saying.

The rest was muffled behind the thunk of a closing door. Ix poked her head around the corner and found herself in front of two identical doors standing side by side.

Odd, she thought. But there was no time to dwell on it. She took her best guess, grabbing the heavy brass handle of one and pushing it open.

Suddenly she felt like someone had given her stomach a hard yank. The cracks in the wood of the door widened into a jagged face, the mouth splitting into a gleeful grin.

A Nightmare! It wasn't a door at all she'd grabbed, but a Nightmare pretending to be one.

The door dragged Ix forward, through the opening. With a creaky laugh like a saw, it spit her out somewhere else.

"No!" Ix cried. But it was too late. The door had vanished, leaving a bare stone wall. And worse, she was somewhere she'd never seen before.

Dreamlight flames burned low in the windowless hallway, throwing shadows over eerie-looking busts with their faces shorn away. Ix swallowed. She had no idea where she was or how to get back.

Ix picked a direction and started walking.

There was something deeply unsettling about this place. The air was heavy and cold, and dozens of dark velvet curtains hung along the walls. Ix pulled one back and found an oil painting underneath, bound in silver chains. It was old. And battered. The frame was barely holding together, as if something had been trying to get out.

The painting jerked, banging against the wall. Ix backed away. Something bad was sealed inside there. She could feel its malice.

A chill like an icy breath prickled on her neck. Followed by a whisper—a strange voice hissing in the dark.

"Hello?" Ix called. The only sound was the shiver of her own breath. Her mind must be playing tricks on her.

The whisper came again, louder. Right behind her.

HERE!

Ix whirled around and found herself face-to-face with a narrow red door. It was set deep into the wall, its hinges black with rust. Ix's ears buzzed. She was certain that's where the whisper had come from. Someone was calling to her from the other side.

She reached for the gnarled iron handle. Then someone seized her shoulder.

"What do you think you're doing?"

Ix whirled around. "Vice-Captain Wystorm!" she spluttered.

Vice-Captain Wystorm looked, if possible, even more livid than the last time they met. Her fingers sank like talons into Ix's shoulder. "That's one of the doors that leads into the Central Tower. It's forbidden for anyone below captain class. Much less a Novice on her first day."

"I didn't mean to," Ix insisted. "I don't even know how I got here. I got tossed through this fake door, and then someone was whispering—"

But the vice-captain wasn't listening. "I knew you'd be trouble. I'm marching you straight to the Elder Flames, and they'll expel you on the spot—"

"I'm sure there's no need to go that far."

A fair-skinned man with sandy hair and wire-rimmed glasses had come up behind them. He wore an easy smile. Ix noticed he had a number of scars—jagged, pale grooves like claw marks that slashed all the way down his neck until they disappeared under his high-collared sweater. It looked like something had tried to slice him open—and almost succeeded.

Vice-Captain Wystorm's eyes narrowed. "Swann."

"It sounds like an honest mistake with the Devious Doorway," Swann said, giving Ix a reassuring look. "It plays that prank on a few new students every year."

The vice-captain scoffed. "I suppose I should have expected such leniency from you. Someone with Nightmare sympathies." Still, she let go.

Ix's shoulder throbbed from her tight grip. She gulped as Vice-Captain Wystorm bent so they were eye to eye.

"I'm watching you, Tatterfall. You will slip up, and when you do, I'll see to it you get exactly what you deserve." She strode off, leaving the threat hanging in the air.

"So you're Ix Tatterfall," the man said kindly. "I'm Elyan Swann. Don't worry too much about that. Every student gets a few disciplinary marks." Ix noticed he didn't say *On their first day*. "Come. I'll take you to orientation—I'm a bit late myself."

Ix hurried to keep up with his long legs. "Thank you, Instructor Swann."

"Professor Swann, please. I earned that doctorate, and I've got the bad eyesight to prove it." He chuckled and then pushed his glasses up his nose, studying her blank expression. "A little young for academic jokes. Good to know."

"Are you a Flame of Candle Corps?" Ix asked, curious. He wasn't wearing the coat.

"No. Though most of your teachers are members of Candle Corps, I'm strictly an educator. I'll be teaching the fundamentals: history, arithmetic, government, and literary arts. Probably not your most interesting class," he added, noticing her grimace, "but you never know what's going to come in handy."

Ix seriously doubted math would help her with Nightmares. It never had before. He seemed nice, though, unlike Vice-Captain Wystorm.

"What did she mean . . . *someone with Nightmare sympathies*?" Ix asked, hoping it wasn't a sore subject.

Swann sighed. "Cassandra Wystorm is a traditionalist. Someone who believes all Nightmares should be banished from the Waking World. People like that tend to think only a certain kind of person belongs at Candle Corps—not me, or you either, from the sound of things," he added, with a smile. "But I'd like to think we all do our part to change their minds."

14

VOICES IN THE DARK

They were very late by the time Professor Swann ushered her into orientation. All the Novices turned to stare as Ix slid into her seat, wishing she could get the big, nervous grin off her face.

"Let's strive to be on time in the future," Instructor Cadence clucked, plonking a teetering stack of textbooks onto her desk. The one for Professor Swann's class was as thick as a paving stone.

Ix had liked Professor Swann immediately. But it seemed like not everyone felt the same.

"I can't believe I have to take lessons from someone without a speck of Dreamlight energy," Darien muttered to Cole. Ix's stomach lurched when they laughed.

Morrigan rammed her foot into the back of Darian's chair, shoving him forward into his desk with a breathless "Oof!" and then "Ugh!" as a cluster of Inklings splattered all over his nice white shirt. The disgusted look on Darien's face as they oozed down and skittered away made Ix feel a little better.

She was still thinking about it when Instructor Cadence dismissed them. "Is there a lot of that here? Looking down on people without Dreamlight power?" she asked Ollie as they wedged through the crowded halls, Sparks and Embers chattering around them.

Ollie wrinkled his nose. "Only if your last name is Winters.

There are a lot of people without Dreamlights here, since the families of most of the captains and high Flames live at the keep. Like Professor Swann."

"What do you mean, like Professor Swann?"

"He's Captain Kel's husband."

Ix thought again of the professor's scars. Captain Kel had scars, too—scars that looked like they might have been made by the same sharp claws. She wondered what had happened.

Ollie seemed to notice her troubled look. "Don't worry about the Winterses," he said. "Supposedly, they're descended from the royal family. One of their ancestors gave up his claim on the throne to lead Candle Corps, but before he could take over, Candle Corps voted to be led by a council instead. My cousin Annika says the whole family never really got over it."

"But it was a long time ago, right?" Ix asked.

Ollie shrugged. "Some people never forget what they think they're owed."

They'd reached the dining hall. It was already full to bursting, students laughing and talking excitedly as they filled their trays with sumptuous stews and stuffed pies and flaky pastries. Ix's stomach growled. But even that wasn't enough to make her go in.

The cafeteria. The bane of outcasts everywhere.

Ix looked around for somewhere to sit. Morrigan had a table to herself, but she gave off approach-and-die energy. The other Novices were already avoiding Ix like her woefully inadequate Dreamlight powers were contagious. She could see Tempest waving her over, but she was too self-conscious to sit at his table with others from the Ember class.

Ollie seemed to be hesitating, too.

"Are you going in?" Ix asked.

Ollie's shoulders scrunched up to his ears. "I usually eat while I'm studying. Besides, I don't want to get in your way of making friends."

"But we could be . . . friends," Ix said, trailing off. Ollie had already scampered off, heading toward the library. She hoped he was just shy and not that he didn't like her already.

Ix ate tucked up in a corner, lonely and pretending she couldn't feel everyone's eyes on her. The food was good. But she would have traded it all for some company.

She was dead on her feet by the time she trudged back to the South Wing that night. She'd gotten lost again and had to backtrack all the way around the Duskwatch Tower, and her foot throbbed from tripping over a Stubbed Toad. Those annoying little Nightmares liked to lie in wait around dark corners and then roll right into the middle of your path for maximally painful toe stubbage.

Morrigan was already tucked up in bed. She glared at Ix and jabbed her thumb at the desk, where Hanky was turning excited little somersaults.

"I don't know how you tamed that thing," Morrigan said. "But it better stay on your side of the room."

"Hanky's not hurting anything," Ix protested, cupping the little Nightmare in her hands. The Inkling waved its sticky arms, wearing Ix's polka-dot handkerchief like a scarf. At least someone was happy to see her.

The day's events kept churning in Ix's head. She didn't want to ask Morrigan. But she didn't know who else to ask.

Ix turned over in bed. "Hey, Morrigan. Have you ever heard a strange voice whispering to you in the keep?"

Morrigan snorted. "Yes. Right now. A roommate I never wanted, blathering at me while I'm trying to go to sleep." Then she pulled the quilt over her head and rolled away.

Feeling unsettled, Ix blew out her candle and fell into an exhausted sleep.

Hours later, Ix shot up in bed, gasping for breath. Something fluttered against her face. It was a little Blackout Bat, its wings flapping wildly as it clung to her hair. Ix untangled the Nightmare and blinked blearily at it.

"You scared me," she whispered. The bat chittered, hanging upside down from her thumb. "What are you doing in here, anyway?"

That's when Ix noticed it wasn't alone. There were a few extra Inklings in her bed tonight, and some Starlight Spiders dangling from the window. She'd have to be careful; she didn't need anyone asking why the Nightmares were congregating in her room.

She had a feeling Morrigan would go full Seething Serpent on her if Ix woke her up. Luckily, her roommate was still fast asleep. As quietly as she could, Ix slipped out of bed and tiptoed down the hall, heading for the arch that led into Tempest's secret stairway. She'd just take the bat to the Kneazel-Crooks and get back to bed before—

Ix stopped. There was a whisper of wings up ahead—a whole cloud of Blackout Bats flitting around the dark archway and hanging from the curtains, as if something had spooked them. A moment later, she understood why. There were voices coming from the Kneazel-Crooks.

Ix peeked inside. She couldn't see anybody, but she could hear two people speaking in low, urgent voices down below.

"—we're lucky no one was hurt," one voice was saying.

Ix froze. It was Vice-Captain Wystorm. The worst person imaginable to catch Ix out of bed in the middle of the night. She wiggled her fingers until the little Blackout Bat took off.

The vice-captain sounded grave. "I've never seen Nightmares acting like that. I'm taking a squad into the Labyrinth to hunt for any more with those strange green eyes."

Green eyes? Like the Nightmares Ix and Morrigan had fought in the Labyrinth. She knew she should go back to her room, but . . .

Ix crept down another step.

"Is it true what Captain Rossi said?" The second voice was Instructor Cadence's. "An entire pack of Fiends devoured . . . only scraps left, as if something had swallowed them whole?"

Ix's blood ran cold. Raggedy Jack had been eating Nightmares and *looking for more friends.*

Instructor Cadence's voice was tight with worry. "But we should be safe here, in the keep," she insisted.

Vice-Captain Wystorm scoffed. "Don't count on it. Dangerous things have gotten into Candle Corps before. Some have even been invited."

"You're that worried about the Tatterfall girl?"

Ix sucked in a breath at her name. She pressed herself against the stone wall, listening as hard as she could.

Wystorm's voice turned venomous. "Her father was a willful rule-breaker. And he's been in the Crystal Sleep for exactly ten years—that can't be a coincidence."

Ten years? It didn't mean anything to Ix, but Cadence made a surprised sound in her throat.

"I'm just saying," Wystorm finished, "I'd keep an eye on that one."

"I keep an eye on all my students," Cadence said firmly. "And I'll thank you to leave the patrolling of the dorms to me from now on . . ."

Ix heard the clap of footsteps as the instructor began to climb the stairs. Heart racing, she slipped up the steps, scattering the Blackout Bats.

She got back to her room without being seen. But it was a long time before she managed to fall asleep.

15

THE ACCIDENTAL UNSEALING

Life at Covenant Keep moved faster than Ix ever could have imagined. It felt like one minute, she'd just arrived, and the next she was up to her elbows in homework, furiously erasing the splotch Hanky had left on her answer sheet.

Every morning Morrigan woke Ix by banging around in her dresser drawers like she was rooting out an infestation of Wriggle Roaches. She hadn't crossed into Morrigan's side of the room, but her socks were getting closer to the chalk line—partly because Morrigan fumed and glared at them like she wanted to set the whole black-and-purple-striped pile on fire.

Much harder than handling her new roommate was getting anywhere on time. Ix had the sense that Covenant Keep didn't like her any more than Morrigan did. Some doors wouldn't open for her no matter how hard she yanked at the handle. Twice suits of armor had almost dropped their halberds on her, and when she walked the halls alone, all the paintings rattled and clanked in their chains.

She heard the strange whisper again, too, mostly at night—a distant voice beckoning, like it was seething up from the very heart of the keep itself. Ix couldn't make out much. But it always seemed to end with the hissing promise, *Soon.*

Ix had more immediate concerns, like the Devious Doorway. The more nervous you were about getting lost, the more likely the doorway was to find you. But knowing that just made Ix twice as nervous! The crafty Nightmare had already tricked her three times. She'd gotten into the habit of following people closely through doorways, just to make sure they ended up in the same place.

"You can't be that excited for Nightmare Theory," Ollie said as they headed into the Firstlight Tower, Ix nearly trodding on his heels. "You always say you need to bring toothpicks to prop your eyes open."

Nightmare Theory was taught by Instructor Felding, a very wizened, very bald old man who gave long, rambling lectures on the possible origins of the Labyrinth and seemed constantly perplexed to find students behind him, as if he'd been lecturing for an empty room. A Bupkis Bird sat on a perch on his desk, interrupting class to shout out dire predictions.

"Nightmares! Calamity! The end of the keep!" it shrieked every time Ix passed.

"Bupkis Birds just talk nonsense. It doesn't mean anything," Ollie assured her.

"And yet, it doesn't shout about anyone else destroying the keep," Ix grumbled.

She was a little jealous of Hanky, who didn't like being confined to her pocket and mostly spent the day snoozing in the socks under her bed. The Inkling also liked exploring—though as often as not, that ended with Hanky skidding under the door, on the run from the South Wing's big floofy tabby.

Her favorite class was Nightmare Creatures and Maladies. They spent most of class learning to identify Nightmares that commonly slipped into the Waking World and, more importantly, how to get rid of them. For their first class, Instructor Cadence even brought in a beaten copper jug that held a gleaming scorpion with a long double stinger. She let them crowd around and run their fingers over its pearly green-black scales.

"This is an Unscorpity," Instructor Cadence explained. "When these creatures escape the Labyrinth, they attach to people and make them suspicious of even their close friends." Instructor Cadence pinched the scorpion expertly below the stinger, shuffling it back into the pot before anyone got stung. "Learn how to deal with Nightmare creatures and perhaps someday you will be one of Candle Corps' Balefires traveling the kingdom, curing people of Nightmare maladies."

Ix liked the thought of becoming a Balefire. If she didn't get drummed out of the academy first. Vice-Captain Wystorm seemed to be lurking around every corner, just waiting for Ix to break the rules. And she couldn't stop thinking about what she'd overheard in the Kneazel-Crooks, about Jack and about her father. She had a thousand questions for Captain Kel, but she hadn't seen him even once.

One morning, a week in, Ix woke up to Morrigan's shriek as she pulled open the closet doors.

"What are you doing in there?" Morrigan demanded.

Ix blinked her groggy eyes. "In where—oh." It took her a second to realize she'd been sleeping in the closet, sprawled over their lumpy shoes.

She must have slipped into the Labyrinth the night before, just for a moment. Back in Brittlewick, Ix had gone into the Labyrinth once or twice a week, and it was hard to stop.

She had dropped out in a lot of weird places before—the pumpkin patch, her aunt's trunk of winter coats, even the hollow of an old tree. Compared to that, her own closet wasn't so bad.

Morrigan's face said otherwise.

"If you're trying to scare me, it won't work," Morrigan said.

Ix decided not to mention her shriek. "I'm not. I'm . . . you know. Picking out my shoes. By feel," she added, wincing as she pulled a chunky boot out from under her head.

"Just when I think you can't get any weirder," Morrigan grumbled, snagging a sweater off a hanger and stalking away.

She kept shooting Ix suspicious looks as they got ready for class. Suddenly Morrigan whipped around.

"You know, this has been bothering me since the beginning," Morrigan said, stomping over the chalk line. She reached for the silver lock on Ix's overalls.

Captain Kel's words rang in her head. *Don't let anyone look too closely at that lock.*

Ix froze, petrified. "That's—I can explain—"

Morrigan seized the lock and snapped it open. "You don't have to lock it when you're not in the Labyrinth. Stop looking like it's your first day."

"Right," Ix stammered. But her heart didn't stop thudding for a long time.

By the end of the second week, Ix was hopelessly behind. Especially in Dreamlight Defense, taught by Captain Akari Ito.

Sparks of Dreamlight trailed after the stern captain as she walked the rows, her black hair shimmering in a tight knot.

All week, Captain Ito had the Novices practice making Dreamlight flames. Everyone's was different, Ix had realized—some flickering and smoky, some bright as stars. Andre Navarro's burned so hot it set the curtains ablaze. Morrigan and Darien seemed to be vying for the strongest flames, but even Beatrix Bianchi could make something.

Everyone but Ix.

It felt like her initiation all over again. Sometimes, when she closed her eyes and concentrated hard, she thought she saw a flicker of *something*—a glossy sheen like a curl of fire. Only it didn't look like the bright Dreamlights on the walls. It was more like a tongue of rippling purple-black fire.

After class on Friday, Ix screwed up her courage and approached Captain Ito.

"Are some people's Dreamlight flames a different color?"

"In rare cases, they can be." Captain Ito sighed. "You saw Miss Bea's flames, didn't you? I assure you, there's no cause for alarm. Her powers are well in hand, and the red color is to be expected."

"Uh . . . right," Ix said, trying not to sound as confused as she felt. She hadn't been talking about Morrigan at all. She'd been wondering about the flame inside her. But now that she thought of it, Morrigan's Dreamlight in the Labyrinth had been red, and nobody else's had.

She wondered if it had something to do with the Bea Wolves. Unfortunately, she'd lost her chance to ask Ollie—he'd already scurried off to the library.

Ix trudged down the hall, watching Valerie Wystorm twirl her

Dreamlight effortlessly around her finger. They weren't supposed to make Dreamlights outside of class, but of course they all did, snuffing the little flames out quick and stuffing their hands in their pockets when a teacher came around the corner.

It seemed to be so easy for everyone else. So why not Ix?

She was in no hurry to catch up to Valerie and the rest of the Novices headed for the common room. Nor was she keen on heading back to her dorm, so Morrigan could glower at her. So instead, Ix let herself wander, thinking about that strange flicker she'd seen behind her eyelids.

Maybe hers had been the smallest flame ever recorded in the initiation. But Alexis Moongrave said it counted. Which meant she *had* to have Dreamlight powers in there somewhere.

With a deep breath, Ix closed her eyes. It was right there—the purple-black flame that seemed to ripple inside her. This time, she tried to let it grow, coaxing the flame higher.

Her hands tingled with the strange rush of power.

What was that?

Ix rubbed her palms against her overalls, trying to banish the odd feeling. Like she'd been scuffing her feet across the ancient rug and was now charged to shock somebody.

She was in a cobwebby back hallway with chained-up pictures and stoppered vases on tall stands. Suddenly one of the shadows detached itself from the wall, running toward her on long, skinny legs like a water-skipper.

It was one of the castle's Inklings. Another one leapt down from the raggedy drapes—and then another, and another. In seconds, a dozen little Nightmares were racing at Ix full tilt.

"Hey, wait!" Ix said, flailing in surprise as several Inklings leapt onto her legs. Her hand whacked into an expensive-looking vase that wobbled precariously on its stand. She spun around, barely catching it with both hands before it fell.

It felt like a jolt leaving her body. All that strange, tingly energy that had been gathering around Ix poured into the vase. The Inklings lost interest, oozing back into the shadows.

Ix jerked away, but it was too late. The fat stopper on the vase popped off, and a second later mist was pouring out of the jar, along with the creature that had been sealed inside.

Ix had just let loose one of the Nightmares.

"No, no, no . . ." Ix whispered frantically. Her heartbeat thumped in her ears as a shadow emerged from the mist. She saw the long, gleaming claws first, then the flashing black eyes, and then . . . *a fuzzy body*?!

A little gray sloth less than a foot long had dropped onto the stone floor. It headed right for her—one agonizing inch at a time.

Ix heaved a giant sigh of relief. This was a Nightmare called the Weighty Sloth. They could be dangerous when they got big, but it looked like this one had been sealed long enough to return to its friendly size. The Weighty Sloths clambered up on people's backs, causing the feeling of an ominous, crushing weight on their shoulders. The more slumped and defeated you became, the more the sloth grew, until finally the creature was so crushingly large you couldn't even get out of bed.

This one was tiny. But Ix couldn't leave it here. It might attach itself to a student or a Flame, and then there'd be all kinds of questions about where it came from, and Vice-Captain Wystorm would boot her out of Candle Corps so fast Morrigan would be chucking her stripy socks out their dorm window.

Ix glanced up and down the hall. One of the Doors to Nowhere still had a little curl of mist coiling out from the cracks. Maybe she could just slip the creature back into the Labyrinth. Then no one would be the wiser.

Ix crouched down and reached for the sloth. "Okay. Come on—hurry. Before somebody sees you."

The creature took her hand eagerly, pulling itself into Ix's arms. She almost stumbled under the weight. Suddenly it felt like so many things were bearing down on her. She took two wobbly steps toward the door and had to catch herself on the wall.

All her secrets about the Labyrinth were such a burden to carry alone. And Ix was so exhausted from always trying to fit in and failing. Maybe coming to Candle Corps had been a mistake.

The sloth in her arms blinked up at her with wide, glassy eyes. It was unfairly cute for something that was trying to crush her spirit.

She'd just take a quick break. A little nap. Surely Ix couldn't be expected to do all this by herself. That battered old trunk under the window looked comfortable—maybe she'd just crawl in there and never come out . . .

No! Ix shrugged the Weighty Sloth, which now felt more like a cannonball, higher in her arms. Her final steps were woozy, but at last she made it to the door. The mist was cold even through her boots as she opened it a crack—just wide enough to slip the creature back inside.

The Weighty Sloth was reluctant to leave Ix's arms, clinging to her with its sharp claws. Ix thought of all the things she had to do—finishing her letter to Aunt Tara, and practicing with her Dreamlight, and writing a five-page paper for Professor Swann's class. She was far too busy to lie around with a Nightmare sloth . . . even if she wanted to.

Thinking about tackling small things on your to-do list was the best way to dislodge a Weighty Sloth. Ix would get ahead in her homework—maybe she'd even clean her room! Wouldn't that surprise Morrigan.

The last thought was enough to shake off the sloth. It got down with a sleepy grumble and crawled through the opening. Ix slammed the door and hightailed it back to the South Wing before someone caught her sneaking around the very forbidden Door to Nowhere.

Not until she was back in her room did Ix think to wonder who had been opening a door to the Labyrinth in that old, unused corner of the keep. Even then, it wasn't nearly as concerning as her other worries. Ix had definitely unsealed a Nightmare. She had no doubts now that her powers were different from everyone else's. The only question was *why?*

16

THE SPIDER WEAVERS

A week later, all the Novices gathered for their first outing to Spindlecrook. Officially, they were going to get measurements taken for their Candle Corps coats, but after that they were free to explore the city as long as they came back by curfew.

Ix was practically vibrating with excitement. Spindlecrook was a secret Candle Corps town—the only one of its kind in all of Spinar. Everyone in it could see Nightmares or was connected to the Labyrinth in some way. Ix wondered if maybe she and Aunt Tara could have lived there, if they hadn't been so scared of Candle Corps finding her father.

Instructor Cadence led them through a butter-yellow Door to Nowhere in the East Wing that came out on a wide cobbled street in the middle of a bustling city.

"Lively, now!" Instructor Cadence called. "They're expecting you all at the Spider Weavers Works. First left, sixth right, under the watchtower and up the crooked staircase. You can't miss it."

More like, I'll never find it, Ix thought. She would have gotten lost in a heartbeat if Ollie hadn't offered to show her around.

As they set off, Ix tried to look at everything at once. The main street was lined with shops selling all manner of things. Crystal balls boasting GENUINE LABYRINTH MIST swirling inside. Poofy pillows that promised to capture the most beautiful dreams. Smelly candles to keep away Invisible Itch bugs. And so much food! Ix drooled at the sight of cinnamon funnel cakes, chocolate-covered bananas on sticks, and caramel popcorn dotted with Candle Corns, little black-and-white candy corns in the Candle Corps colors.

"Careful, those have a kick," Ollie warned her, when Ix bought a bag. Aunt Tara had been relieved to get Ix's letter, and when she'd written back, she'd sent some pocket money along.

"What do you mean?" Ix asked, tossing three in her mouth. Then she felt her eyes water as—*pop! pop! pop!*—fizzy caramel flavor exploded onto her tongue.

Ollie laughed at the look on her face. "Candle Corns burst in your mouth."

Ix knew that now. And she loved it! She offered some to Ollie, and they walked on together, the Candle Corns popping into buttery sweetness.

At first glance, the people of Spindlecrook didn't seem all that different from those in Brittlewick. But it was the little things that gave them away. One woman wearing all black was lugging a metal parasol to keep every speck of sunlight off her. Two men on the corner consulted strange pocket watches with multiple dials, far too complex to be marking time. And a lot of people wore glowing crystals that reminded Ix of Dreamlights—talismans to keep Nightmares away.

Ollie pointed out the Dreamchasers from the regular dogs.

"See the pointer there, with the curly updo? Those are the best for picking out Nightmares, and then they point their entire bodies at them like a weather vane. Oh! And that one over there, the basset hound with the long ears? They can't see Nightmares, but they can smell them. Bloodhounds can smell even the tiniest Malcont-Ant hiding in someone's shoe."

"We should have some Dreamchasers at Covenant Keep," Ix marveled.

Ollie smiled. "We do. In fact, I heard a rumor there's a captain who made his bulldog his vice-captain."

"It's not a rumor," said a voice behind them. It was Morrigan. Ix hadn't even realized her roommate was walking near them. "That's Captain Rossi you're talking about. His bulldog, Bella, is his vice-captain. He even made her a little Candle Corps coat, with a Soul Lock and everything, so she can go in the Labyrinth."

"Seriously?" Ix asked.

Morrigan shrugged. "I think it's more of an honorary position— Professor Swann says Co-Vice-Captain Weisgard is humoring him. But I've seen the tiny coat myself, when Captain Rossi hangs it on his laundry line."

Ix and Ollie burst out laughing. Morrigan looked like she wanted to join in. Then she seemed to remember she hated them.

"Whatever. I have places to be," she said, turning away and stomping off.

"I hope you know it's not you she dislikes. It's me," Ix told Ollie, as Morrigan vanished into a little shop selling apricot-artichoke tea.

Ollie gave a sheepish shrug. "I'm not really that good with people anyway. I like to read a lot, but when I get nervous, all that information comes spilling out, and people think I'm showing off or babbling . . . like before, with the dogs."

"I think everything you know is cool," Ix told him. "When I get nervous, I get this huge, creepy grin, like a total Nightmare." She gave him her best imitation of the Grinning Cat, which made them both giggle. "Maybe we could eat together in the cafeteria sometimes. It's less nerve-racking if you have a friend to sit with."

"There's always so many people in there," Ollie said, twisting his fingers together.

"You don't have to," Ix assured him. "But I promise to save you a seat."

"Thanks," Ollie said, looking relieved.

At last Ix and Ollie found their way to the Spider Weavers Works, where an old woman used a knotted cord to get their measurements. When they were done, they paused at the huge front window, watching men and women working at spinning wheels and giant looms.

"Wow!" Ix pressed herself against the glass, gaping at the Nightmare spiders and the arach-needleworkers spinning cloth.

Inside, Ix could see a muscled man with a hairy spider as big as a cat perched on his shoulder: an Iron Webber. They made the impassable giant spiderwebs she'd encountered in the Labyrinth a few times. The man looked to be making some kind of net. A few graceful figures with Starlight Spiders in their long hair churned out the most beautiful spider silk Ix had ever seen. And in the back, a cluster of people at looms wove a shimmering black cloth, Silver Orb Weavers dangling like pendants from their ears.

"That must be the Silverweave for Candle Corps," Ollie whispered.

Suddenly a door banged open. A familiar figure came hurrying out of the alley, stuffing inky fabric into her pocket.

"Healer Mella?" Ix said, surprised.

Healer Mella froze, as if startled to see them. "Ix, Oliver. I didn't know there were any students in Spindlecrook today."

"The Novice class is here to get measured for our coats," Ollie explained.

"Ah." Mella relaxed. "Silverweave is an amazing substance, isn't it? It naturally absorbs and stores light, which gives our coats that shine in the Labyrinth. But its true value is that it can contain Nightmares. We use it in the keep's strongest seals."

Ix blinked at Mella's coat. Up close, she realized it was covered in patches—squares of dark material sewn down with giant X cross-stitches. She hadn't seen that on any other uniforms.

"Did you come to get a new coat?" she asked.

Mella gave her a strange smile. "Oh, I'm far too attached to mine to replace it. I was just picking up a special order. I prefer to mend it myself—with this." She pushed her blond braid over her shoulder, conjuring a tiny glowing needle between her pinched fingers.

Ollie and Ix leaned in for a closer look.

"You've no doubt seen swords and the like, but this needle is my Shadow Render." Mella coiled her finger through the little tail of thread that dangled from the end.

"It's so tiny," Ix marveled.

"Bigger isn't always better when it comes to Shadow Renders. It's all about having the right tool for the job. This needle can do a great many things. Stitch a wound. Bind a Nightmare into a painting's canvas. And of course, patch a coat." Mella stroked a black square of fabric fondly. "Six patches so far. I guess I'll have to wait until there are two holes to patch it again, so I don't end up with seven." Then she seemed to catch herself. "You'll have your own coats soon. Be sure to take good care of them."

"We will," Ix and Ollie promised, waving after her.

They were deep in conversation about which teacher gave the most grueling homework, heading back to the main street in search of more food, when a dog started baying.

"It's the Dreamchaser hound!" Ollie pointed across the street to where the long-eared dog was sitting back on its haunches, howling. "I wonder if he smells something."

"It's not just the dog," Ix said. All the cats had jerked up, too, their backs arched and their fur standing on end. And they were all looking in the same direction.

A strange ball of mist had gathered at the end of the street, getting bigger and bigger. The one-eared tabby cat on the wall next to them hissed as the mist slithered up the cobblestones. And then all the cats were running, vanishing down the alley.

Ix's heart pounded. "Something's coming," she whispered.

17

MONSTERS IN SPINDLECROOK

The mist glowed a sickly red. Then creatures burst from it, flooding into Spindlecrook. The street filled with shrieks and screams as people started to run. Ix saw a brown-and-white mastiff dog pulling a woman and her baby stroller to safety, away from the clomping feet and the lashing tails of the creatures that had come through.

Ix gasped.

"Warty Hornswoggles!"

They were Nightmares from Wrath's domain. They had hairy, warthog-like snouts and bodies, with reptile legs and long, hairless rat tails. They tore down the street in a rage.

Ix had never seen Nightmares pour out of the Labyrinth like this, much less in broad daylight. What was even stranger was the Warty Hornswoggles themselves. In the Labyrinth, they were grumpy and territorial, but they only got all puffed up and angry if you provoked them. She'd never seen them attack first. Now they were knocking over tables, biting at people, and chasing after anyone who ran.

"We have to get out of here!" Ollie shouted.

Ix had just turned to run when she noticed a commotion across the street. "Look!" she cried. Two other Novices, Nora and Beatrix, were trapped on top of a café table. Beatrix shrieked as the Warty Hornswoggles surrounded them, snorting viciously and snapping at their feet.

"We have to help them," Ix said.

Ollie nodded in agreement. "But how?"

"Can you make your Dreamlight flame really hot, like when Andre set the curtains on fire?" Ix asked. "Warty Hornswoggles don't like fire. I'm going to distract them, and while I do, you rescue Nora and Beatrix."

"I'll try," Ollie said, lifting his hand and calling a Dreamlight. It started out a gentle golden, but then got brighter and hotter, until it felt strong enough to give Ix a sunburn. "Wait, what about you?" Ollie asked, as they raced toward their classmates.

"Don't worry about me," Ix said, shooting him a grin. "Running from Nightmares is my specialty. That, and riling them up!"

Ix broke away from Ollie, waving her arms over her head. "Hey, Warties! Bet you can't catch me!" She purposefully scuffed her feet on the ground, like she was going to charge. Warty Hornswoggles hated to be challenged.

The Nightmares turned away from their ravaging. Ix's stomach gave a sudden horrified swoop. They all had electric-green eyes, just like the Nightmares Jack had controlled in the Labyrinth. Now she knew why they were acting so strangely.

Ix didn't have time for another thought. The first Warty Hornswoggle pawed the cobblestones. Then the whole pack was after her, dodging Ollie's bright fire as they tore down the street.

Ix ran. She might have been able to calm regular Nightmares and lead them back into the Labyrinth. But creatures controlled by Jack—

Ix was in trouble. Big trouble.

She burst out of the alley and careened around a corner, nearly tripping over the curb. The angry snorts were right behind her now. She wasn't even going to be able to slip into the Labyrinth and escape.

Snorty mouths chomped noisily at her back.

Then something slammed into Ix and tackled her to the ground, knocking the breath out of her. Nails scrabbled against her arm, and a little bit of slobber splattered her face as the creature sat on Ix's back. And barked.

"Good girl, Bella!" called a deep, gravelly voice. "Now guard!"

The big scary beast on Ix's back was a very jowly bulldog with a bit of drool hanging from its mouth. Ix lifted her head to see a man in a Candle Corps coat striding toward her, two spider weavers at his side. He was a stocky middle-aged man with tan skin and a salt-and-pepper beard. Ix had never seen him before, but the dog on her back was wearing a little Candle Corps coat, which probably made this Captain Rossi and Honorary Vice-Captain Bella the bulldog.

"The Nightmares are being controlled," Ix yelled from beneath her slobbery savior. Bella growled at one Warty Hornswoggle and nipped at another.

"Spread out on my command," Captain Rossi shouted.

The two spider weavers ran to opposite sides of the street.

That's when Ix realized they had something in their hands—a giant gleaming net they stretched across the path of the charging Nightmares. It looked exactly like the one she'd seen the man with the Iron Webber twisting.

The Warty Hornswoggles hit the net like a wave. Their force pulled the two spider weavers a few feet down the cobblestones, but then the creatures started to slow down, slumping on top of each other in a big, snuffly pile.

"Grab the net, Weisgard!" Captain Rossi shouted at the last man—Vice-Captain Weisgard, Ix guessed. Between the four of them, they managed to wrap it over the whole pack of Nightmares, the Warty Hornswoggles going still one after another.

For a moment, Ix worried they were dead. Then she heard the snorty snores. They'd just fallen asleep, lulled by the web.

Captain Rossi turned to Ix, dusting off his hands. "You all right, girl? You can get up now."

At first Ix thought he was talking to her. But it was actually the bulldog. A fact Ix figured out when Bella scrabbled off her, running over for pets and praise. Captain Rossi was only too happy to give it, cooing and scratching the dog behind the ears.

"Those mean, nasty Nightmares didn't hurt you, right, girl?" he said, ignoring everyone else.

"You get used to it," Vice-Captain Weisgard sighed as he gave Ix a hand up, pushing dark hair out of his lanky face.

Ix heard a crash. Then a very worried Ollie skidded around the corner, Nora and Beatrix right behind him.

"You're okay!" Ollie said, relieved. Then he let out a very loud "Oof!" as Bella the bulldog took one look at him and tackled him to the cobblestones. Ollie laughed helplessly as the honorary vice-captain slobbered all over his face.

Captain Rossi chuckled. "You're a couple of Novices, aren't you? You must be the Pembrook boy. Bella can always tell the students from Dreamchaser families."

"Well, it's . . . very . . . nice . . . to meet her," Ollie managed, scrambling to his feet before the bulldog licked his glasses right off.

Vice-Captain Weisgard looked them over with a critical eye. "All academy students are being gathered at the gate. Hurry back."

"But those Nightmares—" Ix protested.

"Are well in hand," Captain Rossi promised, waving them off. "Leave the rest to us, kiddos. Bella's more than a match for these puffed-up punks."

Ix dragged her feet as she followed the others back. She was uneasy, thinking about the Nightmares' electric-green eyes. But it didn't seem like Captain Rossi was interested in hearing anything more.

Beatrix sniffled as Nora recounted how they'd ended up chased by the Warty Hornswoggles. "Thanks for helping us out, Ollie . . . and Ix." Nora added Ix's name a little reluctantly, but Ix couldn't really blame her. Ollie had scared them off with fire. She just ran.

"Sure," Ollie said, flushing a little. "I wonder what all those Nightmares were doing in Spindlecrook, though."

No one had an answer. But when they reached the gate, where Instructor Cadence was gathering the Novices, Ix noticed that there were claw marks on the yellow door that led back to Covenant Keep. Like something had been trying to get in.

THE RULE OF SEVEN

The attack at Spindlecrook was all anyone was talking about the next day. In their Dreamlight Defense class, all the Novices clustered around Captain Ito, clamoring that she teach them to conjure their Shadow Renders. Captain Ito waved them off, utterly unconvinced.

"Conjuring Shadow Renders is a second-year lesson. I'm not teaching advanced battle skills to a group of Novices who can't even control their Dreamlights. Watch the curtains, please, Mr. Navarro."

"But what if the Nightmares get into the keep?" Beatrix wailed after class. All the Novices had gathered in the common room, trading wild theories about the Warty Hornswoggles that had run amok. "How are we supposed to defend ourselves?" Beatrix wanted to know.

"We don't," Nora said, wiggling her fingers at Beatrix. "Novices get eaten first. Maybe the Nightmares were in Spindlecrook looking for a snack."

"Or maybe they're already here," Andre said, popping up behind Beatrix with a fake growl.

Beatrix shrieked and hit him with a pillow.

"I don't think it's fair that *one* of us already knows how to make a Shadow Render," Valerie huffed, glaring at Morrigan.

Morrigan raised her eyebrows in surprise at finding herself the center of attention. Then a rush of red power surrounded her. Just for a second, Ix saw the knifelike claws and the wolfish ears Morrigan had in the Labyrinth. Beatrix gasped, and Andre toppled backward off the couch.

The flames vanished as Morrigan uncurled her fist, looking smug.

"I didn't realize the claws and tail were your Shadow Render," Ix blurted out. "How do you make it do that?"

"You can't *make* a Shadow Render do anything. Everyone's has a natural form—a shape it wants to take. This happens to be mine."

"It's so cool," Ollie said, eyes sparkling.

Morrigan's cheeks flushed. She almost looked pleased, until Darien brushed past them, lip curled in disgust. "Cool for a monster, anyway."

Morrigan scowled.

"Come on. We'll be late to class," Valerie said. They all gathered up their books and hurried in different directions, so no one would end up walking in a group of seven.

Only Professor Swann seemed determined to go on like nothing had happened. As soon as the bell rang, he launched right into a long, yawn-worthy lecture about the founding of Candle Corps over five hundred years ago. It was especially rambling and hard to follow because he kept getting distracted trying to shoo an insistent tabby cat off his desk.

Ix liked Professor Swann. But today she was restless, staring blankly at the diagram of Covenant Keep in her textbook and idly doodling a bat into one of the eight towers. There were also eight doorways in the main hall. Eight Elder Flames on the council. Everything in Candle Corps came in sets of eight. Well, except one thing.

Before she realized it, she'd raised her hand.

Professor Swann brightened. "Yes, Ix? You have a question about the mausoleum for Candle Corps' founders underneath Duskwatch Tower?"

"Not . . . exactly," Ix admitted. "I've been wondering. If the number seven's so unlucky, why are there Seven Rules?"

The rest of the class perked up, too.

"Ah, one of my favorite paradoxes," Professor Swann said with a knowing smile. He'd given up and scooped the tabby cat into his arms, tickling it absently under the chin. "But I'm afraid we can't blame this one on the founders. It's said that when they first established the rules for safeguarding souls, there were eight of them."

Ix leaned forward in her seat, eyes wide. She'd never heard of an eighth rule before.

Professor Swann glanced around, as if surprised to have everyone's attention. "The eighth rule was something so dangerous and taboo, the Elder Flames of Candle Corps became concerned that even the knowledge of it would lead people astray. So the rule itself was stricken, never to be written or spoken of again."

"But what was it?" Darien Winters pressed. He was so curious he'd even forgotten to sneer.

Professor Swann blinked behind his glasses. "I have no idea. That is far, far before my time. But . . ." He waved a finger excitedly. "Though it's no longer recorded anywhere, the rule itself still exists. And whatever it warns against is still forbidden. The original rules were carved into the foundation of the Central Tower. Though the rocks are buried too deep to be unearthed, we still walk over them, strengthening those seals every day."

Ix's mind whirled as she tried to imagine something so terrible it couldn't even be written about.

Someone knocked on the doorframe. Ix turned to see Captain Kel.

"Looks like we have a visitor." Professor Swann let the cat leap away and leaned on his desk with a friendly smile. "What can we do for you?"

"I'm here to borrow one of your students." Morrigan was already rising from her seat when Captain Kel said, "Ix Tatterfall."

Morrigan sat down hard. Ix rose nervously to her feet. She could feel Morrigan's hot glare on the back of her neck. She trotted out into the hallway, the other students whispering at her back.

Kel led her down a few corridors before pulling back a velvet curtain to reveal a narrow staircase descending into the dark. Ix clung to the creaky railing as she followed him down the steps. "Where are we going?"

"There's someone I thought you'd want to see more than me. And we'll be able to talk freely there, without being overheard." He glanced back at the dark passageway, and Ix bit down her next question, jumping over a gap in the stairs to keep up.

Captain Kel led her through the twisting catacombs until they reached a heavy stone door that looked like it belonged in a tomb. And inside was—

"My father!" Ix cried, running to him.

19

THE CRYSTAL SLEEPERS

Nathan Tatterfall lay on a granite slab draped in rich purple cloth. Around him lay five more silent figures glittering under crystal shells. Six of them in all.

Ix's father looked just as serene as he always had in Aunt Tara's house, but it was different seeing him here, in the eerie light of the Dreamlight flames and surrounded by other bodies. Ix squeezed his arm.

He was cold. He'd never felt cold before. Or so very far away.

Ix could just make out smudges of features on the other figures in the Crystal Sleep. At least one woman wore the Candle Corps uniform. They were all as still as corpses.

"Mella looks in on them," Captain Kel said, as though he wanted to comfort Ix but wasn't sure how. "She hasn't found a cure yet, but she does what she can."

After ten years, Ix knew there wasn't much you could do except polish the crystal now and then. And keep the spiderwebs off.

Ix got to her feet. "Healer Mella said what's happening to them might have something to do with what's happening to the Labyrinth?"

"It's a theory." Kel crossed his arms. "But something has been wrong with the Labyrinth for a while—and it's been getting worse.

Souls aren't passing through the way they should. The Sorrows' domains are bleeding into each other. And the boundaries into the Between World are weakening."

Ix shivered, thinking about the Nightmare attack in Spindlecrook. And that night when the Labyrinth had gushed dozens of souls into Chaos's realm. Every year, it felt like more and more creatures were escaping the Labyrinth—not just little ones, but big things like the raging Infurious.

Captain Kel shook his head. "The Soul Reaper, who's supposed to keep the other Sorrows in line, hasn't been seen in years. And now strange things are starting to appear in the Labyrinth—things no one has ever seen before."

"Like Jack," Ix whispered.

Kel nodded. "I've been in and out of the Labyrinth, searching for information about him. I didn't find much. And there's no mention of him in Candle Corps' records. I'm afraid the truth of what's happening to the Labyrinth must be in Death's domain, and we'll have to get there to set things right. We've already lost too many people . . . very good people," he added softly. Then he shook himself and laid a reassuring hand on Ix's shoulder. "But none of that is yours to worry about."

But Ix *was* worried, about that and so many other things.

"I don't think my Dreamlight powers are like everyone else's," she blurted. The rest spilled out of her all in a rush: how she'd barely been able to light the wick at the initiation, and the darkness inside her where her Dreamlight should be.

Captain Kel frowned, rubbing at his chin. "I could tell there was something different about you from the moment I saw you slip into the Labyrinth. Your power is different from anything I've

ever seen. That's why I gave you this." He pointed to the lock still
clipped to Ix's overalls strap. She'd forgotten it again.

"It's a Soul Lock, right?" Ix said, remembering what Ollie had
told her. "You said not to let anyone look at it too closely."

"Because that one is fake—just a normal silver lock," Kel said.
"Most people are in grave danger if they enter the Labyrinth without a Soul Lock. The deeper in you go, the more likely your soul
will peel right out of your body. I'm not sure why that doesn't happen to you."

That sounded horrifying, and not at all comfortable. Ix chewed
her thumbnail, thinking. "Morrigan's powers are different, too,
right?"

"They are." Kel leaned against the wall with a sigh. "Her family
is sometimes called the Bea Wolves because one of their distant
ancestors is said to be a Nightmare creature that left the Labyrinth—
a powerful and terrible wolf that transformed under the full moon.
That was hundreds of years ago, but the family's Nightmare powers still tend to manifest as wolf traits."

Ix gaped at him. Morrigan had Nightmare powers! Her night-
marish roommate was an actual Nightmare.

Captain Kel gave her a look, like he knew what she was thinking. "Members of the Bea family are in danger of succumbing to
that Nightmare power. You've seen the very thick Soul Lock on
Morrigan's uniform?" Ix nodded. "That's because over the years,
many of the Bea Wolves have lost themselves and run off to become Nightmares in the Labyrinth."

Ix swallowed hard. It must be awful to know you could lose
yourself to your powers.

"Then Morrigan's family . . ." she began, but Kel shook his head.

"The rest is Morrigan's story to tell."

"But you think my powers could be like hers? That I could be part Nightmare?" Ix had no idea who her mother was—only that Candle Corps wouldn't have approved of her. And they definitely wouldn't have approved of a Nightmare.

"I don't know what your powers are, or where they come from. But I do know you're in the right place to find out." The captain dropped a hand on her head. "Maybe joining Candle Corps wasn't really your choice. But I do believe you belong here. Maybe we can even learn something from you."

A warm feeling rose in Ix's chest. No one had ever told her that before—that she belonged anywhere.

"Your teacher is going to start wondering if I kidnapped you," Kel teased, smiling. "For now, we should get back."

Ix squeezed her father's crystallized hand one more time. He was colder here. But also more real. Like maybe she could get him back.

As they slipped up the stairs and out the velvet curtain, Ix realized she'd forgotten one important thing.

"I remembered something about Jack," she told Captain Kel. "When Terror screamed, his mask split open, and I saw his face. Just for a second. He wasn't a Nightmare inside that scarecrow. He looked like a human soul."

Captain Kel's eyes narrowed. "That's very troubling indeed."

Ix made it back to class just in time for Professor Swann to dismiss them. Captain Kel stayed behind to talk to his husband, closing the door against prying ears.

In the hallway, Ix found herself cornered by the other Novices.

"What did Captain Kel want with you?" Valerie asked, her face pinched.

"Probably trying to figure out how a fluke like you ended up in Candle Corps," Darien suggested.

Ix squeezed her textbook to her chest. "He wanted to see how I was fitting in. Since he's the one who recruited me."

"You expect us to believe *you* were recruited personally by a captain?" Darien demanded.

Morrigan pushed her way through the crowd and leveled a hot glare at Darien. "She's not lying. I know getting picked on merit is a foreign concept to someone whose daddy gets them all their invitations, but it still happens."

Beatrix and a few others snickered. Darien's face twisted into a scowl.

"*Merit*," Darien spat. "If that's what you call it when a loser captain picks out loser students. I changed my mind. You and that no-talent fluke are perfect to carry on the legacy of the Wrecked Captain. He doesn't have a squad anymore, right? Or even a vice-captain? Because he's too afraid he'll get them killed or scarred up like his husband."

There was a collective gasp. Ollie clapped his hands over his mouth. Ix stared at the surprised faces.

"You take that back!" Morrigan demanded. Her hands balled into fists, and unless Ix was mistaken, little bits of reddish energy were crackling in her wild hair. She surged forward and grabbed Darien by the collar, shoving him against the wall. "Captain Kel is the bravest, most selfless Flame in all of Candle Corps. And more powerful than you could ever hope to be," Morrigan hissed. "Apologize for what you said."

Now it definitely wasn't Ix's imagination. The blazing wolf ears rose above Morrigan's head, and it looked like those giant claws were about to erupt from her hands. Ix stared, remembering Captain Kel's words.

Members of the Bea family are in danger of succumbing to that Nightmare power . . .

"Morrigan—" Ix started.

"Do it. I dare you." Darien's lips twisted in a smirk. "My father says you're the last of your cursed line. Good riddance, I say."

"You're dead!" Morrigan shouted.

Suddenly a figure draped himself across the pair of them, grabbing Morrigan under one arm and Darien under the other. "What are you Novices getting up to in the hallway? Fighting with Shadow Renders is strictly prohibited, you know."

"Tempest!" Morrigan said, at the same time as Darien hissed, "Valerian."

Tempest's voice was as cheerful as ever, but his eyes were sharp. "So? Anybody want to fill me in?"

Ollie and Ix shared a look. The other Novices scattered, mumbling excuses.

"We were just having a friendly chat," Darien said, trying to shake off Tempest's arm.

"Morrigan?" Tempest asked, eyebrow raised.

"Yeah, friendly chat," she ground out.

Tempest didn't look like he believed them for a second, but he gave a big smile. "Well, I adore a friendly chat," he said. "You have lunch next, right? I'd love to ditch and catch up with my new under classmates."

Tempest hooked an arm around Darien's neck and led him toward the cafeteria, cheerfully talking his ear off.

"Did I ever tell you about the time my whole Novice class got infested with Noise-Canceling Ear Slugs? Instructor Cadence yelled herself blue telling us how to get them out, but of course, no one could hear her . . ."

Ollie trailed after them, throwing nervous glances over his shoulder. Ix and Morrigan followed a few steps behind. Morrigan still looked like she wanted to yank out Darien's tongue, but at least her red flames had faded.

Ix nudged her elbow. "Thanks. For standing up for me."

Morrigan huffed. "Don't read into it. I just can't stand that guy."

"Neither can I." Ix bit her lip. Then she whispered, "Is it true? What he said about Captain Kel?"

Instantly, she wanted to take it back. Morrigan rounded on her, eyes blazing.

"How can you ask that? Darien doesn't know anything. And neither do you."

Then she stalked off, shoulders hunched up to her ears, leaving Ix wondering why she always put her foot in her mouth.

20

THE WHISPER AT THE RED DOOR

After classes on Friday, Ix decided to explore the cobwebby secret stairways in the East Wing with Hanky. Her footsteps echoed in the empty hall.

"It's just you and me today," she said to the little Inkling hanging out of her overalls pocket.

Ollie had been handpicked by Healer Mella to learn more about healing arts, and his first lesson in the infirmary was this afternoon. Ix wanted to be happy for her friend. She *was* happy for her friend. But there was also a stubborn feeling of jealousy burning in her gut like a bad stomachache.

It wasn't fair. Everyone else was getting better at controlling their Dreamlights. And Ix wasn't. Aunt Tara always said the only thing that mattered was whether you tried your best. That all the most important things about a person were deep down inside. But Ix was tired of having deep-down-inside talents. She wanted right-on-the-surface talents, like everyone else.

The only thing Ix had a knack for was accidentally unsealing Nightmares. Like the Ornery Owl that had popped out of a sealed jar in the library while she was just stacking some books. Or the nest of Sleepless Mice that scurried out of a teapot and infested the entire Novice dorm. Ix spent all night pretending she had no idea why everyone had insomnia, while she caught them all one by one. At least she had two keep cats for help—a pair she'd named Pickles and Peanut Butter, because they were perfect together.

Ix scuffed her shoe against a wrinkly rug, frustrated. Even if she *could* find her father's soul, she'd never be able to lead him out of the Labyrinth if she couldn't summon a Dreamlight.

She had a feeling the key was that strange dark flame inside her. But every time she reached for it, she got the tingly buzz she'd felt right before she released the Weighty Sloth.

"What I need is somewhere I can practice—alone," she told Hanky. "But where can I go that I won't unleash Nightmares on everyone?"

Hanky tugged on Ix's braid, waving a spindly arm toward the hallway.

"Here?" Ix asked, doubtful. The Inkling shook its head, pointing behind her.

Something rattled on the wall. Ix spun around to find the Devious Doorway behind her. That's what Hanky had been pointing at. It didn't bother pretending to be a regular door this time—its craggy face was already stretched across the wood, the teeth of its wide smile rattling together as it stared at her.

"You're trying to tell me something?" Ix guessed. Its jagged eyes kept cutting over to the brass knob. "You want me to go through?"

If a door could nod, that's what this one was doing.

Ix hesitated. It could just be trying to trick her again. On the other hand, Hanky was still waving excitedly. Ix opened the door slowly, ready to be tossed unceremoniously through. But this time, the door only opened a crack. Through the gap, she saw hawthorn trees and a field of swaying silver-leafed plants.

Outside!

The Devious Doorway had made a path to the forest outside the keep. Ix's heart leapt. That was exactly what she needed. She couldn't unseal anything out there.

She pulled her head back in, staring at the grinning door. "You're saying you'll make a doorway outside for me?"

The door creaked its teeth together in agreement.

She couldn't go out in the daytime when someone might spot her. "Will you meet me tonight after dark?" Ix asked, excited.

The door shook and rattled in a nod before disappearing.

"Good exploring, Hanky," Ix said, reaching down and tapping its arm in a little high five.

That night, Ix waited until everyone was asleep before creeping out of her room and down the Kneazel-Crooks. Hanky kept a lookout up on her shoulder, holding on to her twiggy pigtail. She found the Devious Doorway waiting for her just outside the South Wing.

"Thank you," Ix whispered to the Nightmare as she slipped out of the keep.

The cold night air raised gooseflesh on Ix's arms. The red-and-gold trees that looked so pretty during the day shone eerily in the dark, their rustling leaves hissing overhead. The high walls of Covenant Keep rose at her back. A field of tall silver plants stretched out in front of her, the long stalks swaying in the light of the hangnail moon.

Hanky rolled down into her palm, making a worried question mark.

"It's fine . . . probably," Ix told the Inkling, tucking it into her pocket. "There shouldn't be anything dangerous this close to the castle."

There didn't seem to be a path, so Ix waded into the silver plants. They were taller than she'd realized, almost as tall as she was. Her heartbeat sped up as she lost sight of the keep. She could hear the leaves rustling, the feet of tiny creatures skittering through the stalks. The darkness closed in around her. Ix pushed down her fear, concentrating on her hands.

A Dreamlight—that was what she needed right now.

A teeny-tiny pinprick appeared on the end of Ix's finger. But when she tried to make it bigger, darkness flickered behind her eyelids, and the spark of light went out.

Something leapt from between the silver stalks, right at Ix. Ix gasped. It was just a Mistcat, its blue-gray body twining around her legs. Its intelligent eyes fixed on the glow that had suddenly appeared in her hand.

In her fear, she had indeed called something. But it definitely wasn't a Dreamlight. It was more like a *Dark*light. A purple flame hovered over her palm. The Mistcat seemed totally mesmerized, flicking its tail as it watched Ix's hand intently. Even Hanky had stuck its head out of her pocket, fascinated. It reminded Ix of the way souls looked when they were drawn to Dreamlight.

Ix stared at the Darklight in her hand and reached for more. It felt like it was trying to form something, as though there was a shape it wanted to take. The exact way Morrigan had described her Shadow Render.

The purple light wavered in Ix's fingers, stretching out almost like a grasping arm. Now that she wasn't fighting it anymore, the strange buzz was gone. This felt right. It felt . . .

Swish!

Ix lost her concentration at the sudden sound. The purple light vanished, and the Mistcat leapt in surprise, bolting back into the rows of plants.

Crunch.

The noise came again. It sounded like something slicing through the plants.

Swish. Crunch.

Ix crept forward through the silver stalks, holding Hanky close. The sound was just ahead now. She crouched down, peering through the saw-edged leaves.

There was someone in the garden—or something. Metal glinted in the moonlight as a figure in a dark cloak lifted something high, then sliced down through the silver plants. It was a sickle, like the one Jack used.

Ix covered her mouth to stifle a gasp. The figure paused.

"Who's there?" a soft voice hissed.

Beneath the hood, Ix couldn't tell if it was Jack, or even whether it was a person or a Nightmare. The sickle glinted as they spun around, the dark cowl staring toward Ix.

"I know you're there," the figure warned, taking a step toward her.

Ix froze, too terrified to breathe.

A yowl split the air as the Mistcat raced past the figure's feet. The sickle came down, quick as a whip, and Ix watched in horror as it sliced through the end of the Mistcat's tail.

The Mistcat hissed in pain and fear and took off. Heart crammed all the way up her throat, Ix leapt up and raced after the Nightmare, fleeing into the field.

"Stop!" the voice rasped.

Ix heard the whoosh of the sickle at her back. And then the *crunch, crunch, crunch* of the plants shoved aside as the figure came after her.

Ix kept tripping on the broken stalks, scrambling up from her knees. Hanky clung to her overalls strap. Moonlight glinted off the sickle. The figure was right behind her. With one last leap, Ix grabbed the Mistcat and dove forward, vanishing into the Labyrinth.

It wasn't the comforting glow of Chaos's realm on the other side. When she stumbled out, she was in a part of the Labyrinth she'd never seen before. A hot wave of air rushed over her cold skin, the sky an eerie red glow.

Wrath. She'd accidentally jumped into the most dangerous domain of all.

Rusty chains swayed in the air above her, clanking. The giant spiderweb of an impassable Iron Webber blocked the passage in front of her. Ix backed away until she hit the metal wall, cut with rivets and ugly grooves.

Then she heard the growl.

At the end of the passage stood a giant, bristling Jimber-Jawed Hound. It looked more like a gargoyle than a hound, with a thick gray body and huge fangs protruding from its jaw like tusks. Ix had never seen one before. But Smiles had warned her that if she did, it would be the last thing she ever saw.

The creature charged, its lumbering body thudding down the passage. Ix looked desperately at the walls and the chains. She was trapped.

THIS WAY!

The whispery voice seemed to be yelling right in Ix's ear. She turned, spotting a hole in the iron web just big enough for her to pass. Ix raced for the gap.

STRAIGHT DOWN THE PASSAGE!

Ix had no time to question the voice, running down the hallway with the skittering claws of the Jimber-Jawed Hound right behind her. She threw herself under the web and slid out the other side.

NOW FIND ME!

A patch of mist waited just ahead—an escape from the Labyrinth. She tried to concentrate on the Novice dorms and her nice safe bed. But the pull of the whisper was stronger. She slid through the mist and came out deep in Covenant Keep, near the Central Tower.

Ix's stomach lurched. She recognized this hallway—the creepy busts and the paintings under velvet curtains. She had been here before, on her first day. And she knew what that whisper was, so strong it had found her all the way in the Labyrinth.

The red door.

She hadn't imagined it then. And she wasn't imagining it now.

The Dreamlights were dim around her. Pulse thrumming, Ix approached the narrow door. She could feel Hanky tucked up tight in her pocket, shivering in fear.

"What are you?" Ix asked the door.

I'm . . . waiting . . . Such a long, agonizing wait.

Ix heard the whisper stronger here. Like it was hissing up through the cracks of the stone, trying to claw its way into her head.

The one I've been waiting for . . . is it you?

Ix was right in front of the door now. Her heartbeat was so loud it sounded like it was pounding on the red wood. Almost without thought, her hand reached out for the handle . . .

LET ME OUT!

The force of the words nearly knocked Ix into the wall. Hanky scrambled up onto her shoulder, tugging urgently on her braid. Ix stared at the door. There was some kind of Nightmare locked up down here. Something more powerful and terrifying than Ix had ever encountered. Something that *wanted out*.

And Ix had nearly helped it escape.

"I won't let you out," Ix told the door. "And I'm never coming back here. So leave me alone." She clutched Hanky tight as she hurried away.

Still, she couldn't help looking back at the door one last time. Too late, she realized she had taken exactly seven steps. She stepped backward fast.

Never keep things in groups of seven.

She'd broken another rule. Seven steps, and then she'd looked at a forbidden door. If it really was bad luck, she was toast.

You can't escape me. The whisper followed her as she fled into the dark. *You **are** the one. And my wait is almost over.*

21

THE WEEDS OF MISERY

A month in, Ix finally felt like she was getting a handle on everything at Covenant Keep. Except Morrigan.

Everything Ix did seemed to get on Morrigan's nerves. Morrigan didn't like her overalls or her creepy jack-o'-lantern grin or how she left her socks all over the floor. She didn't like Hanky's colony of Inkling friends living under the bed or the way Ix sometimes crawled into the closet to study because she thought better in the dark. It didn't seem like there was much about Ix that Morrigan *did* like.

Morrigan was easily the best in Captain Ito's class, sitting back and watching the rest of them struggle to control their Dreamlight while her red flames flickered around her like a lazy, satisfied tail. She aced every one of Instructor Felding's quizzes and even had the answers to all of Professor Swann's fiddly history questions. She acted like it all came so easy to her. But Ix had seen her studying long past midnight, scribbling away next to the crackling candle until she fell asleep over her books.

"Why don't you tell everyone how hard you work?" Ix asked. "They'd probably like you better."

Morrigan flipped her hair. "I'm not interested in people liking me. In fact, I don't care what they think about me at all."

But Ix knew that was a lie. If she really didn't care what anybody thought, she wouldn't try so hard.

Sometimes she wondered what it would be like to be friends with Morrigan. But that was probably impossible. Morrigan was a top student, and Ix was scraping by in everything but Nightmare Creatures and Maladies. Morrigan's Dreamlight was a wildfire, and Ix's was barely a spark. The only thing they had in common was how much they *didn't* like Darian Winters, and how much he despised them.

Oh. And being total outcasts.

Ix pressed her sweaty palms to her new coat, buzzing with anticipation. Ahead of her, all the Novices stood in two rows in their shining black Candle Corps coats, lined up outside one of the Doors to Nowhere. She and Morrigan and Ollie were in the very back, as usual.

For the first time, Ix was entering the Labyrinth *not* as a rule-breaker, but as an official member of Candle Corps.

Yesterday their finished uniforms arrived from Spindlecrook. Ix had stared at herself for a long time in the mirror, studying the single white flame embroidered on the shoulder and the shiny black fabric that hung down to her striped socks. She looked so different from the scraggly scarecrow Arthur Vance used to chase through the pumpkin patch.

Ix still thought about banishment sometimes, especially when she felt Vice-Captain Wystorm's gaze on the back of her neck. But somehow, against all odds, Ix was starting to feel like maybe she belonged here at Covenant Keep.

And now she looked the part. Or at least she hoped she did.

"Once we're inside, we're going to *stick together*," Instructor

Cadence said. "Absolutely no playing around with Dreamlights or attempting to call your Shadow Renders."

A couple of students groaned in disappointment.

Instructor Cadence waggled her finger. "An untried Shadow Render can be twice as dangerous as a Nightmare. Why, I once knew a Novice who tried to conjure his Shadow Render to cut down a handful of herbs. A Fright Bat flew up in his face, and he lost control and wound up nearly eaten by a giant Creak-o-dile. Ah, there you are, Tempest. I was just telling the students about when you were a Novice."

Tempest laughed as he jogged up to them. "But did she tell you the part where, inches from its massive creaking jaws, I managed to block its bite with a chokeweed vine?"

"I most certainly did not!" Cadence said. "We are going into the Labyrinth on a simple mission to collect some plants for Healer Mella. There will be absolutely no nonsense, horseplay, or shenanigans! That goes double for our volunteer from the Ember class."

She stared hard at Tempest.

Tempest nodded, but as soon as Cadence's back was turned, he shot Ix and her companions a wink.

Morrigan reached over and snapped Ix's lock shut. "One of these days, your soul's going to pop right out of your body."

Instructor Cadence sliced her key cutter into the Door to Nowhere, then ducked into the misty entryway, motioning for them to follow. Ix held her breath as she stepped over the threshold. No matter how many times she slipped into the Labyrinth, it always felt like coming home. It wasn't nearly as dark as she expected, which meant they hadn't entered Terror's domain. They were in one of the other quadrants. And Ix had a feeling she knew which one.

A Joy-Sucking Mosquito buzzed right by her ear. Morrigan slapped at her neck.

"Ah, Misery," Tempest said as he closed the door behind him. "Everyone's favorite quadrant." Ix laughed, but Morrigan just ground her teeth.

"Welcome, Novices," a voice said. A broad-shouldered man with tan skin and wavy black hair was coming toward them through the wild, bog-like patch they'd come out in. His uniform was spotless, his boots polished so brightly Ix could almost see herself in them.

"Captain Calloway," Cadence greeted.

"I've cleaned the surrounding area of Tormentulas and Woe-begone Woolies," Calloway boomed. His normal speaking volume seemed to be set at near-yell. "I also chased off a few Moaning Ghouls, but those could come back. I trust you Novices know how to handle yourselves."

Some students nodded, while a few mumbled under their breath.

"I can't hear you!" he shouted.

"Yes, Captain Calloway," everyone said together, louder.

"Big talk from a man whose pants are tucked into his socks," Tempest mumbled under his breath.

The captain's eyes zeroed in on them.

"Just figuring out groups," Tempest announced, louder, grabbing them around the shoulders. "I'll take these three troublemakers."

There was a mad scramble among those left. Beatrix, Nora, and Andre snagged Instructor Cadence, which left Valerie, Darien, and Cole to join Captain Calloway. The first group would be gathering Blubber Blossoms. The second was after Pepper Puffs. And Ix's group was somehow going to get ahold of Lickety-Split Weeds. Before they set off, Captain Calloway gave them each a very enthusiastic high five. Ix wondered if her hand would ever stop throbbing.

"Captain Calloway seems intense," Morrigan said, once they were out of earshot.

Tempest laughed. "He is. But he knows his stuff. They call him the Lodestar. He's the number one in Candle Corps for rescuing souls."

Ollie pushed his glasses up, glancing around. "Any Lickety-Split Weeds will probably be near the edges," he said. He pointed toward the far side of the wild patch, where an oozing green bog gave way to scraggly crabgrass and depressing gray stone walls.

"I hate it here," Morrigan said, slapping at her neck again.

"Nobody likes Misery," Ollie agreed, frowning as the toe of his boot slid into a patch of Bummer Muck. Once you got a little of that on you, it was hard to shake it off. Ix tugged at her jacket, damp and uncomfortable.

It was always a little too hot or a little too cold in Misery's domain. The light was sort of greenish, and almost all the plants were poisonous but not deadly. There was Itching Ivy, Nausea Nettles, and even Blister Mushrooms, which were white and filmy and exploded with pus when you touched them. Even if you didn't touch anything, you were always damp, and gobs of slime oozed from the Snot Moss hanging all over the trees.

It wasn't one thing that made Misery so awful—it was a hundred tiny things, each more irritating than the last, until you couldn't stand it. Misery had a way of sneaking up on you. Unlike Terror, with its sudden frights and jump scares, Misery wore you down.

The way to deal with Misery's domain was to keep laughing or humming cheerfully and never let yourself fixate on all those little discomforts. And when something was really getting to you, it was best to close your eyes and take a deep breath—as long as you weren't in front of a Pepper Puff, of course.

Tempest was absolutely in his element, making Ix and Ollie laugh with more Novice stories Instructor Cadence definitely wouldn't approve of.

Morrigan, on the other hand, was clearly letting it get to her. "Ew!" she cried in disgust as a giant gob of Snot Moss splattered her shoulder.

"No harm done," Ix said, wiping the worst of it off with her sleeve.

"It'll wash right out," Tempest added. "Don't sweat it."

Morrigan looked livid. And a little sweaty. But she was cut off by Ollie jumping up and down excitedly.

"That's them, right?" he said, pushing his floppy curls out of his face. "Those are the Lickety-Split Weeds!"

They'd learned about Lickety-Split Weeds last week. The plants looked a little like thistles, with shaggy purple flowers and jagged leaves. But Lickety-Split Weeds could pull themselves out of the ground and scuttle away on their roots, which was where they got their name.

"I think we should just tackle them head-on," Morrigan said.

Tempest clicked his tongue. "That sounds like a good way to get a face full of dirt."

"Maybe we could chase them up to the edge of the bog?" Ix suggested.

"Only if you want to take a swim with the Loathing Leeches."

"What if—" Ollie broke in, then stopped, looking unsure.

Tempest bumped his shoulder. "Go ahead, Ollie."

Ollie bit his lip. "What if we ambush them? Maybe Ix and I could sneak around the back, and then you and Morrigan could scare them toward us when they run."

Tempest laughed. "Perfect! I dub it Operation Weed Seize," he declared, making them all groan at his bad joke.

Quiet as they could, Ix and Ollie snuck around behind the patch of Lickety-Split Weeds. In the distance, Ix could hear the sound of four people sneezing uncontrollably. Someone in Valerie's group must have set off the Pepper Puffs. Captain Calloway was honking like a goose with a head cold.

Ollie and Ix crouched behind a mold-infested stump. Ollie waved, giving the signal.

"Now," Ix heard Tempest say, at the same time as Morrigan yelled, "BOO!"

They both jumped out and lunged for the patch of Lickety-Split Weeds. The flowers wiggled free and made a run for it. Ollie and Ix fell over each other trying to leap out at the same time and both ended up going face-first into the dirt and Snot Moss. They didn't catch anything, but they did scare the weeds badly enough that they all scuttled back toward Morrigan, who swept the whole lot up in her coat.

"You got them!" Ix shouted.

"Nothing to it," Morrigan said.

A second later, the plants had all curled in on themselves. The tops of the flowers popped off, and Morrigan let the roots scamper away to bury themselves and grow again. She tucked the heads into the pouch Instructor Cadence had given them.

"Operation Weed Seize succeeds," Tempest joked, pulling Ix and Ollie to their feet. Ollie tried to clean some Snot Moss off his glasses, but his shirt was equally slimed. Ix shook a glob of Bummer Muck off her sleeve.

Morrigan gave her a smug look. "No harm done, right?" she said, echoing Ix's words. "It'll come right off."

"And in the meantime, try to stand as close to Captain Calloway as possible on the way home," Tempest suggested.

Ix and Ollie took one look at each other and then burst out giggling at the thought of pristine Captain Calloway all covered in slime.

Ix was starting to think they'd actually pulled it off, when suddenly she heard it—the most frightening sound in the entire Labyrinth.

It was like a wail of wind at first, racing down the corridors and chasing all the mist away until there was no escape. The walls of the Labyrinth shook and shuddered, pounding with a hundred bristling legs, followed by an earsplitting shriek. The cry of Despair, the All-Consuming Centipede.

Ix's stomach plummeted to the soles of her feet.

Despair was the most dangerous of the Seven Sorrows, so uncontrollable that even the other Sorrows avoided it. It swallowed up human souls and Nightmare creatures alike, hurtling mindlessly through the maze whenever it awakened.

And it was headed right for them.

22

A TOUCH OF DESPAIR

"Stay together! Link arms and run for cover—don't let anyone end up alone!" Instructor Cadence yelled into the howling gale.

Stubby trees bent nearly in half with the force of the wind. Nightmare creatures of all kinds were fleeing around them—Burpy Toads hopping out of the bog and the Lickety-Split Weeds scuttling away like cockroaches. Through her whipping hair, Ix could see a whole knot of shaggy sheep-like Nightmares called Woebegone Woolies huddled together under the trees. When Despair came, the only rule was to never, ever be alone. Alone, you stood no chance against the All-Consuming Centipede.

Ix might have stood there forever, rooted to the spot, if Tempest hadn't grabbed her arm.

"Come on!" he yelled, pulling Ix with one hand and Ollie with the other. Morrigan followed close behind, her hand clenched into Ix's coat. Tempest dragged them to the wall and pushed them behind a crumbling chunk of stone. Across the way, Ix saw Captain Calloway tucking Valerie's group behind a clump of twisted trees.

"Oh no!" Ollie pointed, his face grim.

Instructor Cadence's group was in trouble. They had been in the very center, nearest the bog. Beatrix was sobbing, clinging to Nora's jacket, while Instructor Cadence heaved desperately at Andre, whose boot was stuck fast in the mud.

The pounding feet of the centipede were so close the rocks buzzed under Ix's fingers. Despair screeched horribly, and Morrigan threw her hands over her ears.

Cadence finally wrestled Andre free, but it was too late. Two giant feelers had appeared as the centipede barreled toward them through a ragged fissure. Tiny creatures flew up from its feet and were immediately devoured. The All-Consuming Centipede had no eyes, no face, just a wide-open mouth. Despair ate everything.

Ix sank to her knees, dizzy. She felt like she would never get up again—just curl into a ball and give up on everything. What was the point against a creature like that? What hope did anyone have?

And then suddenly Captain Calloway was striding into the center of the wild patch, giving Cadence and the Novices time to escape. The previously finicky man was heedless of the muck and mulch that splashed on his uniform as he reached into the air and pulled out his Shadow Render, a shining glaive. His Candle Corps coat glowed like a beacon, and a ball of light rose over his head, his Dreamlight flame blazing for all to see.

Hope, Ix remembered, throwing her arms around Morrigan and Ollie, while Tempest sheltered them against the crumbling wall. That was the only thing that countered Despair. The light of Candle Corps was the light of hope.

Suddenly Ix remembered what Head Instructor Telle had said at the initiation.

You are what stands between the kingdom of Spinar and the darkness of the Labyrinth.

"Here, you great beast!" Captain Calloway yelled. He whipped the glaive over his head and struck at one of the squirming legs.

Despair wailed, the sound so powerful the captain was thrown back. He fought his way forward through the gale.

"This way," he called, spinning the glaive. Ix realized he was stepping backward, leading Despair away from them, deeper into the Labyrinth.

"It's working," Morrigan cried.

Suddenly a whole section of rotting bank crumbled under the centipede's great weight. The bog at the center of the wild patch began to churn, slowly, and then faster and faster, little bits of sticks and plants spiraling down as it tried to suck everything in.

"It's a sucking sinkhole!" Ix shouted in horror.

A scream pierced the air.

It was Beatrix. As the sinkhole grew, the Brickle Bushes where Beatrix's group was hiding were ripped away. Beatrix fell into the sinkhole, pulling Nora with her. They flailed as the muck and the mud and the misery tried to pull them under. Cadence had just managed to grab hold of Andre before he, too, was swept away.

The Sorrow's head turned toward the screams.

"Eyes on me, you great lump of a Nightmare!" Ix heard Captain Calloway yell.

"I've got to help them," Tempest said, rising.

He hurtled out from behind the rocks, a glowing Shadow Render leaping to his hands. For one moment it looked like nothing more than a stick, the kind Ix had pretended was a sword when she was little. But then it stretched out until it was as long and thick as a walking stick.

"Whoa," Ollie whispered.

Morrigan gripped the stone wall as Tempest dropped next to the roaring sinkhole, stretching his Shadow Render out to Beatrix. He dragged her out of the muck and passed her along to Instructor Cadence. Then he threw himself down on his stomach, his staff stretching even longer and thinner as he reached for Nora.

A sudden chill ran down Ix's spine. Something wasn't right.

Her head whipped around, toward the tail of the centipede, which had just come through the opening in the walls.

Only it wasn't just the centipede. Something was riding on top of Despair. A raggedy scarecrow, dancing on his pick-apart feet and laughing his scratchy laugh.

"Jack," Ix whispered.

"What?" Morrigan demanded, spinning around.

"What is that thing?" Ollie asked in horror.

Ix looked around desperately. They had to warn everyone about Jack—

She had just taken a breath to shout when the scarecrow leapt, landing on top of the crumbled wall they were hiding behind.

Ix's scream died in her throat. Jack looked down at them from his torn eyeholes, and his jagged smile grew wider.

"Just the tender little fleshies I was looking for," Jack said, almost purring. "Now, which one of you is the little mist-slipper the cats whisper about? Hmm?"

Ix couldn't breathe. Her chest constricted like she'd been caught by a Squeezing Dread Snake. *Mist-slipper.* He meant her.

23

THE SHADOW SICKLE

Ix's heart thudded as Jack loomed over them.

"Get back," Morrigan snarled, reddish claws bursting from her knuckles. She swiped at the scarecrow's feet, but Jack dodged easily, holding his hat to his head. Then he lurched forward all at once, putting his sackcloth face right into Morrigan's.

"More a wolf, this one," he said, mostly to himself. "Let's become friends later, hmm?"

Jack's gangly arms shot out, flinging her away. Morrigan yelled as she landed in a nest of slithering chokeweed.

"Morrigan!" Ix screamed.

Jack tottered a little, rounding on Ix and Ollie in an off-kilter lean. Ollie was shaking like a leaf, but he had his hands up, his fingers glowing as he called his Dreamlight. Ix could feel that strange power flickering to life inside her, too, the darkly shining flame.

"What do you want with us?" Ollie demanded.

"*One* of you," the scarecrow corrected. He tapped his bony fingers made of odds and ends on his chin. "But which one. Oh, I know!" He loomed over them, drawing his rusted sickle from his belt and swinging it back and forth. "An itsy-bitsy fleshie crawled up the Labyrinth spout. And now it's time for Jackie to flush the sneaker out!"

He drew the sickle across his own neck and then put his face right into Ix's.

"It's you, isn't it," he hissed. "You know the secret of slipping through the misties, and you'll teach it to Jack."

Ix's head was buzzing, and so were her hands.

"Leave her alone!" Ollie yelled. His Dreamlight flared, and he threw himself forward, shining the light directly into the scarecrow's face. Jack hissed and swung at Ollie. Ix barely managed to push him out of the way of the sickle, both of them tumbling into the dirt.

Morrigan let out a yell. The chokeweed was closing around her neck. Ollie scrambled over to her, fighting the slithering weeds as Ix rose to face the scarecrow.

"Irritating," Jack seethed. "IRRITATING. So very irritating! Why does *nobody* want to be my friend?"

He lunged forward and grabbed Ix. Ix fought desperately, scrabbling against his bits and pieces of fingers as Jack curled his fist into her coat and lifted her completely off the ground. His jagged mouth curved into a smile.

"Well, we'll have time, won't we? I've never had a fleshie inside before."

He tipped his head back, his mouth opening wide. Ix suddenly remembered exactly where Jack kept his friends.

She clung to Jack's arm, tearing at the scarecrow's iron grip. Then she noticed something: a tiny flicker of purple light on her fingers. That same feeling she'd had when she called the Darklight, like there was a shape this power was meant to take.

Ix shrieked. It was half a battle cry, half a scream of terror. Then she raised her hands and conjured her Shadow Render.

The weapon that sprang to her hand was a long, curved blade on a polished wooden handle. A hand sickle, Ix realized. Just like Jack's.

The blade glowed in the greenish light. Ix couldn't help feeling there was still something missing, like it wasn't quite finished. But right now, she'd take anything with a sharp end.

Ix swung the hand sickle as hard as she could. It sliced through a few of Jack's fingers. A bent nail and a pair of sticks tied together with wire tumbled to the dirt. Jack howled and dropped her, and Ix scrambled away.

"Not fair!" Jack whined as he danced backward. "But I'll still have my way."

Ix held the sickle in front of her. She felt Ollie join her on one side and Morrigan on the other, but they were horribly outmatched against a creature like Jack.

Then a warm Dreamlight blossomed just over Ix's shoulder, and another one above her head. More and more flames burst to life around her. Captain Calloway and the centipede had disappeared, but all of Ix's classmates were on their feet, holding out their hands and creating Dreamlight flames around Ix and Morrigan and Ollie. Tempest was exhausted and covered in muck, like he'd taken a swim. But he was smiling as he raised his hand, adding his own powerful flame.

Instructor Cadence strode toward them with her Shadow Render in hand. It looked like a shovel rather than a weapon, but the way the woman carried it over her shoulder, Ix had no doubt it could get the job done.

"Phooey on that screeching centipede," Jack lamented, taking two clattering steps backward. "All the pains I took to wake it up, and it couldn't even clear one room of fleshies."

"Get back, Nightmare," Instructor Cadence warned, stepping in front of Ix.

Jack took a step back, like he was about to run, then suddenly dove forward, tackling Cadence to the ground.

The woman swung out with her shovel, but Jack didn't stay to fight. After bowling Cadence over, he ran right past her, diving down a side passage and disappearing into the Labyrinth.

"I hope that's the last we see of that thing," Cadence grumbled, brushing herself off. "Are you all right? Ollie, Ix, Morrigan?"

Ix nodded shakily. Somehow, she and Ollie had escaped with little more than Jack's horrifying handprints on their coats.

Morrigan was scuffed-up and dirty. But she was almost glowing as she met Ix's eyes and said, "I guess you weren't totally useless this time."

Ix grinned. "Can't you just say we were all awesome together and we should be friends?"

"No, because I'd have to barf afterward," Morrigan shot back. Then she smiled. "But I guess just this once, since we faced death together. Thanks for having my back." She looked between Ix and her sickle and Ollie, who had rescued her from the chokeweed.

"Anytime." Ix grinned.

Then the other students crowded in around them. Andre stared at Ix's Shadow Render. "How did you do that?" he asked in awe.

"Can I see it?" Cole asked, ignoring Darien's dirty looks. Even Valerie seemed a little stunned.

"That was a very impressive feat," Instructor Cadence agreed. "I've heard of students manifesting their Shadow Renders for the first time because of extreme danger, but I've never seen anything quite like that."

Ix fumbled the sickle, grateful when it flickered out and disappeared.

Instructor Cadence clicked her tongue. "You're very lucky. Many people find their Shadow Renders harder to call in the Labyrinth."

"Right. Lucky," Ix mumbled, as Cadence turned away to look after the others.

If anything, that strange power had come easier here. There was no doubt about it now. Ix's powers weren't Dreamlight powers at all—they were all Nightmare. And if she wasn't mistaken, she was much more powerful inside the Labyrinth.

She put it out of her head as Tempest slumped over Ollie's and Morrigan's shoulders, mussing a very slimy hand in Ix's hair. "My favorite Novices. I knew there was something special about you."

Ix wrinkled her nose. "Did you just rub Bummer Muck in my hair?"

"This is just regular old muck," Tempest promised.

Tendrils of mist had crept back into the passage by the time Captain Calloway returned, limping slightly. "Miserable as usual round here," he groused. "Take us back to the castle if you would, Instructor Cadence."

Cadence patted her pockets—and then again, with more urgency, pulling all the quills from her hair. Her face was ashen.

"It's gone. My key cutter. I must have lost it in the bog."

But Ix went cold, remembering the way Jack had tackled Cadence.

"I don't think she lost it," Ix whispered to Ollie and Morrigan as Captain Calloway cut a doorway in the mist and led the class back into the keep. "I think Jack took it."

"But why would he want it?" Ollie asked.

"And what did he want with you?" Morrigan added, looking worried.

Ix had an idea. But she didn't like it very much.

24

THE GARGOYLE COURTYARD

A few days later, Captain Kel came to see Ix. Professor Swann shot him a look, as if to make it clear he didn't approve of his class time being used for secret meetings, but Ix couldn't get out of her seat fast enough.

"I heard what happened in the Labyrinth," Kel said as they climbed down the rickety stairs to the catacombs. "I'm glad you're all right."

"You didn't hear everything." Quickly, Ix told him the things she knew hadn't been in the official report: about the missing key cutter and what Jack had said. "I think he was after me. He wanted to know how I travel through the mist."

"So do I," Captain Kel joked, but his smile was thin. He looked as if he hadn't slept much. "If you're right, all I can imagine is that Jack's trying to get out of the Labyrinth."

That's what Ix had been thinking, too.

"What if he's trying to come here?" she blurted out. "Do Nightmares ever attack Covenant Keep?"

"Only once, in all the time I've been here." Captain Kel's eyes grew distant. "One night, not long after I'd been made a captain, all the Doors to Nowhere started shaking, and a great rift opened in the Central Tower. Nightmares poured into the castle. It took everything we had to hold them back. We never figured out exactly what happened, but it was a time of great upheaval in the Labyrinth. I guess that was about a decade ago."

Ten years. That was as long as Ix's father had been crystallized. As long as his soul had been lost.

Ix remembered what the Grinning Cat had told her, the story she'd been trying very hard not to think about. The night Nathan Tatterfall had taken baby Ix into the Labyrinth.

As long as you are with me, little wishling, Death will surely come for us.

Ix still had no idea what that meant. But Death hadn't come for them. In fact, the Soul Reaper had disappeared.

Captain Kel must have seen her worried look. He squeezed her shoulder. "Don't worry. Covenant Keep has stood for five hundred years, and it's got at least a few more centuries in it. You're safe here, Ix."

Ix bit her lip, not sure how to tell him that wasn't what she was worried about at all.

She was still preoccupied as she trudged to Nightmare Creatures and Maladies that afternoon. The classroom was empty. A piece of paper had been plastered to the chalkboard that read:

MEET IN THE GARGOYLE COURTYARD

FOR HAZARDOUS NIGHTMARE CLEANUP.

ATTENDANCE IS MANDATORY!!

Ix blinked at the sign. *Hazardous Nightmare cleanup?* She wasn't sure if that sounded extremely fun or extremely unfun. Either way, she was late.

The rest of the class was already gathered by the time Ix arrived, puffing and out of breath. There was no teacher in sight.

"What's going on?" Ix asked Morrigan and Ollie, sliding between them.

"Apparently some kind of infestation came through one of the Doors to Nowhere last night," Morrigan said. "Also, Instructor Cadence already marked you tardy."

Ix deflated—but then perked up as she looked around at the rows and rows of fierce gargoyle statues. They looked so real she half expected them to spring to life, their stone wings rippling as if ready to take off.

"Does that mean there's some kind of Nightmare here?" Ix asked.

"Probably," Ollie hazarded, "and it must be dangerous. Instructor Cadence went to get us protective gear."

Cole kicked a rock away from one of the statues. Then he bent down, frowning.

"I think I found something. But it's just a slug."

"Cole Cunningham, don't you dare touch that!" Instructor Cadence warned, hustling up in a huff. "And for goodness' sakes, watch your feet—there are more of them."

Their teacher wasn't alone. Healer Mella followed, carrying an armful of thin gloves, which she handed around. Ix slid hers on and instantly felt like she'd plunged her hands into a bucket of ice.

"They're freezing!" she exclaimed.

"They should be," Mella replied. "I've treated them with Icily-

Lilly extract. And you are to keep them on at all times. That's how dangerous this Nightmare can be."

Now that Cole and the others had backed away, Ix had a clear view of the Nightmare creature stuck to the gargoyle's clawed foot. It did look a little like a slug, but instead of a tail, it had oozing tendrils that clung to the stone. It reminded Ix of a mix between a flower bulb and a gooey eyeball.

Delicately, Cadence turned the creature so they could all get a better look. "These are the larval form of the Memory Eater."

There were a few gasps. Beatrix jerked back like she was afraid of being bitten.

"Ooooh! Would it have eaten Cole's memories if he touched it?" Andre asked. Cole went pale.

Cadence sighed. "At this size, no, but it would have sampled one—which would be a very unpleasant experience. They can be safely handled in their larval state, if they're *not* agitated."

"It's full-grown Memory Eaters that are extremely dangerous." Healer Mella ran a finger along the slithering slug. "These little ones look like they haven't begun to feed yet. Once they do, they're insatiable."

Cadence clapped her hands together. "We're going to calmly, and *quietly*, and quickly find all the Memory Eater larvae in this courtyard. When you've got one, bring it to the crate here." Cadence laid the first slug gently in a wooden crate, burying it a few inches into the cold dirt inside.

"This doesn't seem like a job for Novices," Darien Winters complained. Ix wasn't sure if he meant because it was dangerous or because it was beneath him.

"More hazardous Nightmare cleanup and less complaining,"

Instructor Cadence suggested, before swooping off to the other side of the courtyard, where Beatrix's first larva had slipped out of her hand and was bouncing over the stones.

There were Memory Eater larvae all over the courtyard, like the world's grossest scavenger hunt. Ix made a face as she plucked at the slimy tendrils of a slug that had crawled into one gargoyle's ear, like a ball of wiggly earwax.

"What makes full-grown Memory Eaters so dangerous, anyway?" she asked. "Aside from the obvious, I mean."

Ollie's eyes lit up, like they did when he was remembering something he'd read. "Memory Eaters are creatures of Despair. They start by eating memories from the souls trapped in the Labyrinth, and when that isn't enough, they'll try to escape to feed off people directly. Like these ones, I guess," he added, squinting at the wriggling slug in his fingers.

"That's right, Oliver." Healer Mella had approached, hands clasped behind her back. "What's most dangerous about these Nightmares is that they're never sated. The more they devour, the larger their appetites become. The biggest Memory Eater ever captured was taken down in the Waking World. It was too powerful to send back into the Labyrinth, so it's sealed here, in the keep."

"Who caught it?" Ix asked, amazed.

"Captain Kel," Morrigan said, sounding a little proud. "He went to the town of Mistmorrow all by himself and defeated the Memory Eater single-handedly."

Mistmorrow! That was the next town over from Brittlewick. A shiver crawled down Ix's spine, imagining one of these creatures, bloated and grown to enormous size, chasing people down and sucking out their memories.

"Sounds suspicious to me," said a bored voice. Ix hadn't realized Darien was right on the other side of the statue, plopping Memory Eaters carelessly into the crate. He snorted. "I mean, we're talking about the same captain who failed so hard he almost washed right out of Candle Corps." Darien shot Morrigan a nasty smile. "I'd think you of all people would want him gone, *Bea Wolf*."

"You shut up!" Morrigan warned, gripping one of the little slugs.

Darien sniffed. "This again? How long are you going to defend someone who clearly only puts up with you out of guilt?"

Too late, Ix saw it happening. As Morrigan got angrier, the sparks of her bright red Dreamlight jumped over her skin. There was a soft sizzle as they hit the larva.

"Look out!" Ix lunged forward, trying to grab the Memory Eater. Her hands closed around Morrigan's just as the creature squirmed to life.

A rounded mouth like a leech's opened in the fleshy skin. Ix gasped as the tiny needle teeth pierced right through the thin gloves, closing around her finger—and Morrigan's.

Suddenly images were flooding into Ix's mind. *A woman with wild red hair just like Morrigan's, standing at a dark window.*

This was a memory, but not hers. The Memory Eater was tasting one of Morrigan's memories, and Ix was along for the ride.

The red-haired woman looked serene and peaceful, until the clouds moved away, revealing the giant full moon. Then she started to change. Her mouth twisted with fangs, and her fingers contorted into gleaming claws.

"Run, Morrigan!" she screamed. Then the memory faded into nothing but running footsteps, a thudding heartbeat, and darkness.

When Ix came back to herself, it was to find Healer Mella kneeling beside her, waving a strong minty-smelling vial under her nose. Ix coughed, sitting up. Instructor Cadence had retrieved the wriggling larva and now stood over them, looking very exasperated.

"Are you both okay?" Ollie asked.

Cadence was having none of it. "Ix and Morrigan. You two get in more trouble than my last four Novice classes combined—and one of those classes was Tempest Valerian's!"

Ix blinked at Morrigan, still reeling from the memory she'd just seen. "Was that . . . ?" she asked.

"You saw?" Morrigan's face crumpled. "Instructor Cadence, I don't feel well. I'm going to lie down." Morrigan didn't even wait for an answer before running away.

Ix gaped after her. Instructor Cadence traded looks with Healer Mella, then rubbed her temples like she'd had a run-in with a Skull Thumping Beetle.

"Carefully, *please*," she begged the class. "Finish searching for larvae carefully."

Morrigan didn't come back to that class, or the next one. She wasn't in their dorm, either, when Ix trudged up the stairs at the end of the day.

"Maybe she just needs some space," Ollie suggested.

"Maybe," Ix mumbled. But she couldn't get that flash of Morrigan's memory out of her head. She wouldn't want to be alone with a memory like that.

Maybe Morrigan didn't want to be friends. But Ix did. And she was going to prove it to Morrigan—if only she could find her.

25

THE BEA WOLVES

Ix walked the length of the castle twice looking for Morrigan. She checked everywhere—even the parts she usually stayed away from, the secret passages and the corridors with the chained-up paintings. She covered her ears against the insidious whisper, like a cold breath on her neck.

This way . . . it beckoned. Ix felt her feet try to turn toward it, but she shook it off.

I'm not looking for the red door, she reminded herself. *I need to find Morrigan.*

Dusk was falling when Ix finally climbed up to check the belfry. She found Morrigan perched on the edge, her bright red hair a shock of color against the purple sunset. Her legs dangled over the courtyard below.

Ix sat down next to her, careful not to upset all the Blackout Bats hanging upside down beside the old bronze bells. Morrigan tensed as their shoulders bumped, but she didn't pull away.

"I don't really know what I saw," Ix said honestly. "I can try to forget it, if you want."

Morrigan was quiet. Then she shook her head. "No. I've been trying to forget it too long already." She leaned back, sighing. "That was my mother. Reagan Bea."

"Your mother?"

There was a ghost of a smile on Morrigan's lips. "She was Captain Kel's vice-captain. He and Professor Swann have known me my whole life. Which is awful, by the way—they're so smug. They love to reminisce about how I used to run away from Inklings and get my head stuck under their coffee table." Morrigan wrinkled her nose, and Ix laughed.

"Doesn't sound so awful to me."

"We'll dig up some embarrassing baby stories about you and see how you like it," Morrigan grumbled. Then she took a deep breath.

"You probably know, the Bea family is descended from Nightmares. The original Bea Wolf was a creature of Wrath, and that anger runs in the family. My mother had Dreamlight powers even stronger than mine—Nightmare powers, too. But she was always in control. Of her power. Of her temper. Of everything.

"Back then, Captain Kel's squad was a frontline team. They went farther into the Labyrinth than anyone. One night, about three years ago, when they were in so deep they were almost to Death's domain, the Labyrinth started rumbling and spitting out souls and Nightmares everywhere."

"I've seen something like that," Ix whispered.

"Everything in the Labyrinth went wild. Captain Kel and the rest were cut off from the mist, cornered by a pack of Jimber-Jawed Hounds. My mother transformed to save her squad. But she couldn't save herself."

"What do you mean?" Ix asked.

Morrigan shrugged miserably. "When a Bea Wolf overuses their power, before they lose themselves completely, they can transform into a Nightmare wolf, like the very first Bea. For a short time, they're enormously powerful. But that control never lasts, and then they're lost to the Labyrinth forever.

"After my mother transformed, Captain Kel spent months searching for her. And he actually found her and brought her back. We all thought it was a miracle. But she was . . . different after that. Jumpy. Fearful. And so angry. At the next full moon, she transformed once and for all."

Ix remembered the flash she'd seen of the red-haired woman erupting with fangs and claws. That must have been the moment the Memory Eater was tasting.

"I ran to Captain Kel for help. He wanted to face my mother alone, but I insisted on going back with him. Elyan—Professor Swann—came along to look after me. I thought we could save her. I didn't understand how powerful the pull of the Nightmare power would be."

Morrigan took a shuddering breath.

"Professor Swann was covering me when he got those scars. And Captain Kel was protecting both of us when my mother got him." She touched the spot on her jaw where Captain Kel had his scar. "He probably would have been fine if he'd gone all out—but it was my mother, his vice-captain. He hesitated. And she escaped into the Labyrinth."

"Oh, Morrigan." Ix didn't know what to say. She squeezed Morrigan's hand hard. "Is she still lost in there?"

"No," Morrigan sniffed. "All the Bea Wolves go through Death's Door in the end. The Flames stopped seeing my mother a couple years ago. And Captain Kel never took another vice-captain or a squad after that."

She wrapped her arms around her knees.

"I thought they'd hate me—Captain Kel and Professor Swann—but they've been looking out for me ever since. I go stay with my grandmother sometimes, but she renounced her Dreamlight power and blames Candle Corps for everything. I have to pretend like none of it exists when I'm with her. That's why I like being here."

"I like it here, too," Ix whispered. She'd spent so long trying to disappear in Brittlewick, never feeling like she could be her real self. Secrets had made Ix special, but they had also made her very lonely. She and Morrigan were more alike than she'd thought.

Morrigan swiped the back of her hand against her wet eyes. Suddenly she looked angry.

"It's my fault. Everything that happened. And since it happened right here, everybody knows about it." She shook her head. "You don't know what it's like. To have people whispering about you. To be different from everyone else. Dangerous."

"Actually, I do." Ix took a deep breath. "Because I have a secret, too. I think I'm part Nightmare."

Morrigan had shared her story with Ix, and Ix wanted to be brave enough to do the same. Quickly, before she lost her nerve, Ix told Morrigan everything. Not just the new things, about her Shadow Render and her Nightmare powers. But the old things, too—about being an outcast, about never fitting in, about her father trapped in crystal and how much she wished he would wake up. She never realized how much lighter she'd feel, saying those things aloud.

In return, Morrigan told Ix how Professor Swann and Captain Kel had practically adopted her after she lost her mother. Captain

Kel was training her to control her Nightmare power, and he let her tag along on missions sometimes. And Professor Swann had her over for dinner once a week and took her shopping at the market in Spindlecrook, where he liked to stop in every little teashop to try unusual teas.

They talked until the sunset faded and the stars winked like Dreamlights in the sky. A few Blackout Bats floated down to land on Ix's shoulders, their tiny wings tickling her until she and Morrigan giggled too much and they all took flight in a rush.

"We should probably go find Ollie," Ix said at last. "He promised to save us dessert."

"Not dinner?" Morrigan asked.

Ix grinned. "Who wants dinner when you can have Candle Corn?"

Morrigan rolled her eyes. "You're corny and he's sweet."

"And you're zingy," Ix said. "So we're perfect together—like pickles and peanut butter."

Morrigan made a face. "You'd better be talking about the cats and not a sandwich," she grumbled, needling Ix with her toes.

Ix felt a lot better. But she had one more secret. One that scared her so much, she hadn't even told Captain Kel.

"I think I'm the reason bad things keep happening. Maybe my power that draws in Nightmares draws other things, too. Like Jack." Ix pulled her knees up to her chest. "Do you think they'll kick me out of the academy?"

"Not unless they kick me out first," Morrigan said hotly. "And if Darien Winters or anybody else gives you a hard time, you send them my way, and I'll show them what a *real* Nightmare is."

Ix laughed a little wetly, blinking back tears.

Suddenly Morrigan threw her arms around her and hugged her hard. Ix's mouth fell open. It was the last thing she'd expected from standoffish Morrigan. When Morrigan let go, her cheeks were pink.

"Don't read into it. If you could see your face, you'd have done the same thing."

"So, Nightmare girls forever?" Ix asked, grinning.

"Too corny," Morrigan said, but she was grinning, too.

26

THE SECRET OF THE SILVERWEAVE

Fall had arrived in all its glory. Out the window of the common room, Ix watched the blazing orange leaves on the hawthorn trees flutter down, while little Lovelorn Moths clung to clusters of ruby-red berries.

At last, Ix was actually improving at her classes. She and Morrigan and Ollie made a good team in Nightmare Creatures and Maladies, and she could conjure her Shadow Render whenever she tried, now that she'd mastered the trick of using Nightmare energy. Captain Ito said she'd never seen a Novice improve so fast. Ix sort of felt like she was cheating, but it was worth it for the sour look on Darien's face.

After that night in the bell tower, she and Morrigan had told Ollie everything. Ix had worried about revealing that she might be part Nightmare—what if he thought she was dangerous? What if she *was* dangerous? But Ollie had just smiled at her, his eyes bright behind his glasses.

"I figured it was something like that," he said, pointing to where Hanky was making a little nest in her hair. "Nightmares don't like just anybody, you know."

"You're not afraid of me?" Ix asked, to be sure.

Ollie shook his head. "Whatever you are, you're still the same person to me. Besides, it's like Head Instructor Telle told us on our first day. It's not about what power you have. It's about what you decide to do with it."

"Thanks," Ix said. Suddenly, everything felt lighter.

As the days grew colder, the trio took to spending afternoons studying in the sunny library that filled three floors of the First-light Tower and was perpetually overrun with lazy, lounging cats. The high shelves spilled over with books—massive encyclopedias of Nightmare creatures and tiny cobwebby diaries with firsthand accounts from the Labyrinth's early explorers. And some books that weren't books at all, but actual Nightmares sealed into dusty old tomes, the pages shut tight by silver padlocks.

"I can't believe Professor Swann expects us to read three whole chapters on the founding of Spinar this weekend," Ix groaned.

"I'd take eight times that much reading over Instructor Cadence making us memorize all these plants," Morrigan complained. She had pushed her books aside and was wiggling her fingers unwisely at Pickles the cat under the table. He lashed his black-and-white tail in excitement. "How are we supposed to tell them apart?"

"It's easy if you know the trick," Ollie said, setting down a stack of books and dropping into the chair next to Morrigan's. The second he did, the pudgy orange tabby, Peanut Butter, flopped into his lap. "See the saw-edged leaves on this one, how the edges look ragged? That's silverweed, the stuff they weave into our Candle Corps coats. If you cultivate it by starlight, it absorbs light and shines in the Labyrinth. Healer Mella showed me the field of silverweed she's growing out by the hawthorn forest."

Ix nearly did a double take, leaning over the illustration of the spiny plant. "Wait—I've seen this before! That cloaked figure I told you about—this is what they were harvesting."

"The one who came after you with a sickle, you mean?" Morrigan glanced at Ollie. "What can you do with it?"

Ollie's forehead wrinkled. "All kinds of things. These days, it's mostly used by spider weavers. What's cooler is what they *used* to do with silverweed." He flipped the pages excitedly, stopping on a drawing of gossamer silver threads. "When Candle Corps was first founded, the only way they could get into the Labyrinth was to force the soul out of the body. Instead of Soul Locks, they used silverweed threads to tether the soul to something in the Waking World, so it wouldn't get lost."

"Ow!" Morrigan yelped. She'd forgotten about Pickles until he chomped her fingers. The cat jumped up into Ix's lap, purring and very pleased with himself. "And that actually worked?" Morrigan asked, sucking on her sore thumb.

"Not always," Ollie admitted. "Some souls never came back, but since they were tethered to this side, they couldn't get through Death's Door, either. It says their bodies turned to eternal stone."

Ix's stomach lurched. "That sounds like the Crystal Sleep," she whispered. "Maybe whatever's happening now is the same thing that happened back then. Maybe those souls are stuck somehow. Tethered to something." Her stomach twisted, thinking of her father down in the catacombs.

"It's more than that," Morrigan muttered. "If you can force a soul out of a body, that means someone could have done it on purpose."

They were all quiet, turning that over in their heads. Ix stared down at the encyclopedia, open to a drawing of one of Death's apparitions. Its ghostly hands clutched a wicked-looking scythe.

A hand dropped suddenly onto her shoulder. Ix nearly jumped out of her skin. But it was just Tempest, leaning over them with a friendly smile.

"What are my favorite Novices whispering about?"

Ix snapped the encyclopedia shut, much too suspiciously. "Nothing."

"Lamenting how much homework we have and how scary the teachers are," Ollie said with his best innocent smile.

Ix was positive Tempest didn't believe them. But he chuckled anyway.

"Wait until you meet the instructors for the upper levels. Scarier than a pack of Warty Hornswoggles." He ruffled Morrigan's hair, making her scowl. "But I know a secret. After you see this, you'll never be afraid of them again. Come on."

Tempest knew all the best secrets of Covenant Keep. Today he led them to a door in the North Wing. The plaque read RECORDS ROOM.

"Isn't this off-limits?" Ollie asked nervously.

"Don't worry. No one ever comes here," Tempest said. "Besides, I've done everything you can think of and worse, and they haven't thrown me out yet."

He ushered them cheerfully into a room crowded with dusty inkpots and unsteady towers of parchment. Ollie sneezed, and a handful of paper shot into the air.

Tempest patted a big mahogany cabinet. "You know how if you're scared to speak in public, they say to imagine everyone in their underwear?"

"You want us to imagine the captains in their underwear?" Morrigan said, wrinkling her nose.

Tempest laughed. "No need. This is way better." Then he threw open the cabinet and showed them what he'd found.

It was a stack of dusty old logbooks filled with school portraits of all the previous classes of Candle Corps Academy. There were the captains and instructors as teenagers—all of them awkward and gawky, some with big gap-toothed smiles and most with bad haircuts. Ix forgot her worries as they paged through the books, laughing at the old black-and-white portraits.

"Is that what Captain Rossi looks like without his mustache?" Ollie exclaimed, pointing to a young man with a square jaw. "And look, it's baby Bella!"

Sure enough, young Aldo Rossi held a bulldog puppy, its long tongue hanging out of its mouth.

"Actually, that's his first puppy," Tempest said, leaning close to read the caption. "Lucrezia Belinda Rossi."

Morrigan rolled her eyes and cracked open another book. "Here's Instructor Felding back when he had a ponytail. And who's that with Healer Mella?"

Tempest craned over her shoulder to get a look. "That's her twin brother."

Ix squinted at the spindly letters under the drawing of two children, each holding a blazing Dreamlight. *Allison and Jacora Mella*, it said.

Ollie pushed his glasses up his nose. "I didn't know she had a brother."

"She doesn't talk about him much," Tempest admitted. "It's a sad story. Not long after becoming a Flame, he disappeared."

"In the Labyrinth?"

Tempest shrugged. "No one knows. Her Dreamlight power was

always stronger than his. Some people think he ran away."

Ix studied the drawing. The boy's face looked familiar, but she didn't know why. Maybe it was just that he looked so much like Mella.

Morrigan didn't seem to care. She flipped to the next page, cackling at the portrait of a girl with dark circles under her eyes and a tarantula perched in her whirly curls.

"Where's Captain Kel? He's got to be in here," Ix said. She flipped past young Instructor Cadence with a beehive hairdo and Captain Ito with a dozen rings and a cool rebel look, until she found it: the drawing of a boy with his dark hair slicked back from his stern face. He seemed to be glaring at the snooty boy in the portrait next to his, whose name read *Fallon Winters*.

"I think he combed his eyebrows for this picture," Tempest said with a grin. "Nice to know his expression hasn't changed in twenty-five years."

Morrigan snickered. "I've gotta show this to Professor Swann."

Tempest mussed her hair. "Don't get too smug. They'll do your student portraits, too. And then someday, some other kids will be making fun of you."

"Does that mean yours is in here, Tempest?" Ollie asked. Then they were all tugging at his coat, clamoring to see his portrait, until Instructor Felding stuck his bald head in and chased them out.

Between her schoolwork and her new friendships, Ix was finally starting to feel like she had the hang of things at Covenant Keep. There was only one thing that still troubled her: the red door.

She had tried to stay away from the Central Keep, taking the long way around even though she was always late for Professor Swann's class. But there was no escaping that whisper. Especially when it started finding her in her dreams.

CREEPING DREAMS

"Ix! Ix, snap out of it!"

Ix's eyes shot open. Morrigan was shaking her by the shoulders. Ix was in their bedroom, but she was on her feet, grasping for the handle of their door.

"What's happening?" Ix asked groggily. She couldn't quite understand why she was out of bed, or why Morrigan looked so alarmed.

Morrigan blew a messy curl out of her face. "You were sleep-walking," she said.

With sudden, horrifying certainty, Ix knew she'd been heading for the forbidden door, coaxed by the whispering.

She promised Morrigan six times that she was fine as she slipped back into bed and pulled Hanky against her cheek. But it was hard to fall asleep again with the memory of those whispered words in her head.

Soon, the voice had promised. *So very, very soon.*

On the day the first swirls of frost sparkled on the dorm window, Ix came back to find Morrigan scuffing out the chalk line on the floor with her sock.

"Just making it official," Morrigan said. "By the way, I'm supposed to invite you and Ollie to dinner tonight."

"Dinner?" Ix said blankly.

"With Captain Kel and Professor Swann." At Ix's surprised look, Morrigan blurted out, "It's boring. Just long history lectures no one cares about and bad tea that tastes like toothpaste. You don't have to come, if you don't want." But Ix could see her ears were red, like she was embarrassed that Ix might say no.

"I want to," Ix said quickly. After hearing all Morrigan's stories, she wouldn't miss it.

Morrigan snorted. "Just be sure you come hungry—they'll feed you until you explode."

The sun was just setting as Morrigan knocked on the captain's door on the west side of the keep. Professor Swann welcomed them inside. The rooms were cozy, with crinkly old maps pinned to the walls and piles of colorful patchwork quilts.

At first Ix felt out of place, as if she'd come to class without her homework done. But soon enough, between trying to find something polite to say about the pumpkin-peppermint tea (Morrigan was right, it was worse than toothpaste) and the hand-painted tea set (an heirloom from Captain Kel's great-aunt, who'd painted one cup for each of the castle cats), she entirely forgot to be nervous.

Ollie showed up with Tempest, who had invited himself along. So when Captain Kel arrived, he found all five of them crowded around the dinner table, jostling for elbow room.

Kel crossed his arms, fighting a smile. "I see the family's grown again."

Professor Swann chuckled and handed him a plate. "The more the merrier, right?"

"Yes—well, probably?" he amended, watching as Morrigan grabbed for the persimmon bread and Tempest held it over her head. Professor Swann rushed to the table, panicking that they would both end up in the soup.

Dinner was delicious, and there was far too much of it. Ix stuffed herself on black-berry cobbler and thick oat cakes drizzled with honey until she could barely move.

"I'll be heading out again for a while," Captain Kel told them as they lined up to go back to the dorm. "There are some things I need to investigate in the Labyrinth. But if you get into any trouble . . ."

"Not to worry," Tempest declared, winking. "Getting into trouble is my specialty."

"Not the kind of trouble I had in mind," Captain Kel called after them, before Professor Swann tugged him back inside.

Ix walked back with a buzzy, giddy feeling. As they headed up the stairs to their room, Morrigan nudged her in the ribs.

"You're smiling."

"I'm always smiling," Ix said.

Morrigan shrugged. "Yeah, but it doesn't look as creepy as usual."

With surprise, Ix realized she wasn't smiling because she was scared or nervous or lonely. She was just smiling because she was happy. The thought stuck with her as she brushed her teeth and crawled into bed. She rolled over, watching Hanky reach tiny little arms up to play with the Starlight Spiders dangling in the window.

"Good night, Morrigan," Ix whispered into the dark.

"Go to sleep already," Morrigan whispered back, tossing a pillow at her head.

Ix fell asleep smiling, wondering what beautiful constellations the Starlight Spiders would spin for tomorrow.

28

NIGHTMARES IN THE KEEP

Ix was in front of the red door again. Only she didn't know if this was real or a dream.

She had dreamed of the red door almost every night since Morrigan had shaken her awake. Twice in the last week, she'd even caught herself wandering back to that hallway, though she meant to be going somewhere else.

Now her hand hovered over the gnarled handle.

"Quite the conundrum, isn't it?"

Ix whirled in surprise. The Grinning Cat was lounging partway through a tear into the Labyrinth. At least that meant this was definitely a dream.

"The temptation of a locked door, I mean," Smiles continued with a wave of his claw. "You know you're better off not knowing what's on the other side . . . but when has a human ever been able to stand the agony of *not knowing*?"

"I'm not coming here on purpose," Ix protested. "And dreaming or not, that door is forbidden."

Smiles chuckled through his teeth. "Ahh yes, *forbidden*—what a quaint human concept. Don't you know the more forbidden something is, the more people want to do it? If they really wanted everyone to forget about that thing in there, they should have put it in a mop closet. Nobody likes to mop. Everybody likes a secret."

Smiles inched forward on his belly, his luminous amethyst eyes glowing. Ix knew she should try to shake the dream off. But he was right. The secret gnawed at her.

"What's down there?" Ix asked, glancing back to the door.

"Lots of things, I suppose." The Grinning Cat shrugged. "Bits and bobs, maybe a caged Nightmare or two. Stacks and stacks of papers, no doubt. You humans do love recording all the little stories you won't be around to tell when your firefly lives wink out. But below all those things . . . all the way in the basement . . ."

The cat reached out a giant claw, beckoning Ix closer.

"Whispering in the depths is something that never should have been taken from the Labyrinth."

"Is it some kind of Nightmare that's calling to me?" Ix shivered.

"Oh, *that* is far more dangerous than a mere Nightmare," Smiles said, his voice hissing through Ix's dream. "The thing locked behind that door is the truth. And though some would like to see the truth go free, there are always others who want it to stay buried."

"Is that why you're visiting my dream?" Ix jerked back, struck by a sudden thought. "Are you trying to use me to get to the truth?"

"Me?" The Grinning Cat laughed until he wheezed. "I don't care for the truth one way or the other. I'm simply . . . curious. Think of me as an amused third party."

Ix's gaze was drawn back to the door. The wood was so red it almost seemed to be pulsing, like a heart beating in the dark. Ix's fingers brushed the handle.

Smiles's eyes glittered. "Do whatever you want," the cat told her. "Or don't do anything at all. Or do precisely what everyone least expects. It'll be interesting whichever way it goes. But you should know, I came here tonight to deliver a warning."

"What's that?" Ix asked, breathless.

Smiles was all teeth in the dark. "You're not the only one thinking about that door."

Ix was wrenched out of her dream by the loud tolling of the keep's bells. She tumbled out of bed, still blinking the sleep from her eyes. Across the room, Morrigan threw back her covers and leapt up.

"That's the alarm bell!" she said urgently. "We have to evacuate."

Ix poked her head under her bed and grabbed Hanky. She'd barely snatched the Inkling before Morrigan pulled her to her feet.

"Wait. My boots—" Ix started.

"No time. Come on!"

Morrigan pushed them through the door. The hallway was crowded with students in their nightshirts and nightgowns. Ix spotted Novices and Sparks and Embers, all looking bewildered.

"Ollie!" Morrigan called, waving him over in his purple pajamas.

"Form lines and *stay together*!" Instructor Cadence called out, looking worried.

"What's happening?" someone shouted.

"There's been a possible Nightmare infiltration," Cadence said. "It's best everyone evacuates—just as a precaution."

Ix's mind spun. *A possible Nightmare infiltration*—on the same night Smiles came to warn her about someone else being after the red door. It couldn't be a coincidence.

Ix stuffed Hanky into her pocket and trailed the clump of

students following Instructor Cadence. When they reached the end of the hall, she waited for the group to turn right and then slipped off in the other direction, ducking around a corner.

A hand grabbed her striped pajama shirt.

"What are you doing?" Morrigan hissed. Ollie stood at her side, looking wide-eyed and anxious.

"Shh!" Ix begged them, peeking down the hallway to make sure Cadence was out of sight. "I think I know what the Nightmare is after."

"How could you possibly know that?" Ollie asked.

"I had a dream . . ." Ix began.

Morrigan shot her a skeptical look.

"Look . . . there's something I've got to do. Trust me, please?"

"Fine," Morrigan grumbled, "but if we get in trouble, I'm blaming this all on you."

Ix shook her head. "You don't have to come with me. It could be dangerous—"

Morrigan snorted. "Like I'd let you go by yourself."

"Face it, you're stuck with us," Ollie said with a smile.

Ix felt lucky to have such good friends—and a little scared of what she was leading them into—as they raced deeper into the keep, toward the very place Ix had been trying to avoid.

Together, they pulled back a false painting and slipped into the hidden passage behind it. When they scrambled out the other side, they were near the Central Tower. The red door was down the next hallway. The Dreamlights burned even lower than usual, and the air was so chilly Ix could see her breath.

Then she realized why. Right in front of them stood a Door to

Nowhere—and it was wide open, spilling mist into the corridor. Uneven footsteps clipped against the stones ahead. Ix crept up to peer around the corner. Her heart jumped into her mouth.

Jack.

The scarecrow swung his sickle back and forth as he ambled toward the red door. The velvet curtains flickered over the paintings as he passed.

Ix ducked out of sight, pressing her back against the wall. The stones were cold under her bare feet.

The three of them couldn't possibly take Jack on like this. They couldn't possibly take Jack on at all!

Ix wanted to turn around and run. But she couldn't stop thinking about whatever was behind that door. Smiles had said it was the truth. Ix had no idea what that meant. But she was certain that whatever it was, Jack absolutely couldn't be allowed to get it.

"We have to stop him," Ix said, dredging up all her courage.

"He's too powerful," Morrigan protested. "We can't defeat him by ourselves."

"Maybe we don't have to," Ollie whispered. "We just have to slow him down long enough to bring the captains here." He grabbed one of Ix's hands and one of Morrigan's. "I'll go and I'll bring backup as fast as I can. You use your Shadow Renders to keep him distracted . . . and promise you'll be okay."

Ollie's hands began to glow. Ix felt that soft golden Dreamlight warming her up from the inside, and suddenly she could breathe again.

"It's a promise," she said. Then she dug the little Inkling out of her pocket, tucking it into Ollie's collar. "Here—take Hanky with you."

"And hurry back," Morrigan whispered as Ollie slipped away.

Then she and Ix turned back to the hallway.

"Do we have a plan?" Morrigan asked, red flames blazing around her as she called her wolfish powers.

"Stop Jack from opening that door. No matter what."

Morrigan grinned. "That's my kind of plan."

Ix heard the rattle of Jack's hand on the door handle, shaking the lock. With a deep breath she hoped wouldn't be her last, she threw herself around the corner, Morrigan right on her heels.

29

THE BROKEN SEAL

"Jack!" Ix shouted.

The scarecrow spun from where he had bent over in front of the door. In place of the fingers that Ix had cut off, he now had a prickly stick and a corkscrew he'd been about to shove in the lock.

"The wolf cub and the nasty little fleshie," he greeted them with a wave. "Haven't got the key to this door, have you?"

Ix gripped her Shadow Render tight. "Back away from there."

"We won't let you take anything from this keep," Morrigan warned, crouching like she was ready to spring.

"Take . . . ?" Jack sounded confused. Then he jerked up, suddenly outraged. "What about *taking back*? Hmm? Reclaiming something stolen from me? It's down there . . . I can feel it!" Jack spun again, pressing himself excitedly to the door. "So close. Someone took something precious from me. And I'll have it back tonight."

Suddenly Ix could hear it again, that whisper that had been plaguing her. It was even louder than before.

Time grows short. Come to me. Come find me. Quickly!

Only Ix couldn't tell if whatever was down there was talking to her . . . or Jack.

Jack threw back his sackcloth head, cackling. He wrenched up the corkscrew, aiming for the lock.

Morrigan let out a wild battle cry. In a blink, she'd leapt onto the scarecrow's back and plunged one claw into his jacket. A lump of moldy straw and a few old bones fell out as Jack reached over his shoulder, ripping Morrigan off and tossing her aside.

"Naughty children should be in bed," he crooned.

The voice was still whispering in Ix's ear, telling her to hurry, but she forced it away. She swiped at Jack with her Shadow Render. The scarecrow danced nimbly away, waving his sickle.

"Pests do not make good playmates. Run along for now," Jack warned them, turning back to the door.

Ix pulled Morrigan to her feet. Morrigan swiped the back of her hand over her bleeding lip, conjuring her claws again. But Ix could see them flickering, more jagged than before. At this rate, they weren't going to last long enough for Ollie to bring reinforcements.

A faint rattle came from beneath the curtain. It was one of the keep's sealed paintings. Suddenly Ix had an idea.

"Distract him from the door. Just for a second," she told Morrigan.

Ix let her Shadow Render dissipate and concentrated all her Nightmare energy into her hands, like she had when she'd accidentally released the Weighty Sloth. Then she grabbed the closest thing: a faceless statue wrapped in silver chains. It only let out a little hiss. Whatever had been inside was long gone.

"Come on!" Ix begged, grabbing a painting instead.

As soon as she touched the gilt frame, Nightmare power gushed out of her until she was dizzy.

Something shivered on the canvas. A silvery translucent Wraith pulled itself halfway out of the painting, its ghostly head swiveling around.

Ix spun. Morrigan had blocked Jack's sickle with her claws, but her arms were shaking, the rusted blade inching closer and closer to her neck.

"Morrigan!" Ix screamed, throwing herself at another painting.

Something erupted from the canvas. Ix saw a flash of scales and fangs and four angry blood-red eyes. The Nightmare she'd unsealed was a giant Seething Serpent—a creature from Wrath's domain that grew larger the angrier it got. This one filled half the hallway.

Ix paled. She'd wanted a Nightmare. But maybe not *that* Nightmare.

Jack jerked in surprise, the threads on his jagged mouth going slack. The snake thrashed. Its giant head shot out, biting first at the Wraith and then at Jack.

Morrigan scooted back into an alcove, staring with amazement and horror at what Ix had done.

"No fair!" Jack moaned as he dodged the serpent, which was becoming larger and angrier by the second.

Ix backed up—right into another statue. It rattled and rattled on its stand, before a little Quiver Lizard fell out. It took one look at the serpent and transformed into a Howlamander before it even hit the floor. Ix threw her hands over her ears as it tore off down the hallway, shrieking at the top of its lungs.

Jack slung his sickle into his belt. He grabbed the giant snake by the jaws, holding back its gaping mouth. The dark holes of his eyes bore into Ix.

"You'll regret this," he promised.

A horrible shiver ran down Ix's spine. At first she thought it was because of Jack's threat. Then she heard Morrigan scream.

"Ix, watch out!"

Ix ducked just in time as the Wraith grabbed for her. The creature's pale fingers were twice as long as they should be, and its ragged cloak dragged against the stone floor. A creaky chuckle emanated from under the hood. Ix's blood turned to ice.

This was a Wraith that had been sealed for hundreds of years. Ix couldn't imagine how powerful it was when it was first captured.

Ix's back hit the wall. The Wraith loomed over her, stretching out its sickly white fingers. Ix desperately tried to call her Shadow Render, but her power fizzled in her palm. She'd used up all her energy breaking the seals. She slid down the stones, feeling the Wraith like a wall of cold about to consume her. Then suddenly a golden Dreamlight bloomed to life beside her, crackling with sparks.

"Ix! Morrigan!" Ollie shouted from the end of the hallway. And he wasn't alone.

Ix had never in her life been so happy to see a bulldog. Bella bounded toward her, her nails scrabbling over the stones as she put herself between Ix and the Wraith, snarling and slobbering at the same time.

The Wraith jerked back, surprised. Ollie scrambled to Ix's side and pulled her up as he gasped out, "I brought everyone!"

He really had. Figures in Candle Corps uniforms flooded the hall. Ix's heart leapt when she saw Captain Kel among them.

"Over here!" Morrigan shouted. "Hurry!"

"Somebody get ahold of that blasted snake!" Captain Rossi yelled.

Ix wrenched around. Jack had already disappeared. Only the Seething Serpent was left, bashing its body against the walls as it

sprang at Captain Kel. He jammed his sword in between the dripping fangs and forced the snake's massive head to the floor.

Captain Rossi's Shadow Render was a giant double-headed
battle-ax. He lunged forward, knocking the Wraith away from Ix
like it was nothing.

"Catch, Weisgard," he said.

Vice-Captain Weisgard held up a bag made of Silverweave. He
caught the Wraith easily and snapped a cord around the mouth of
the bag, tying it tight.

"Return it to the Labyrinth, or back to be sealed again?" the
man asked coldly.

Captain Rossi grunted. "Above my pay grade." He turned to Ix.
"How about a proper thank-you? This is the second time you've
been rescued."

"Um . . . thank you, sir—I mean, Captain!" Ix stammered grate-
fully.

Rossi let out a belly laugh. "Not for me—for Bella." He gestured to the bulldog, whose tail thumped excitedly against the
stone floor.

"Oh, of course, good Bella," Ix cooed, scratching the dog behind the ears. The honorary vice-captain took the opportunity to
give Hanky a big drooly lick as the Inkling oozed out of Ollie's
pocket.

Captain Rossi gave Bella's head an affectionate ruffing. "Who's
the best vice-captain in the whole kingdom?" he cooed. Behind
him, Vice-Captain Weisgard hauled the Wraith away with a long-
suffering sigh.

Captain Kel had managed to subdue the serpent. It curled in
on itself as its rage subsided, shrinking and leaving only a giant

shriveled snakeskin behind. Morrigan kicked free of the alcove, and Ix and Ollie ran to her, squeezing her into a hug.

"I'm fine," Morrigan coughed. "Geez, don't make a big deal out of it."

"Sorry." Ix let her go. She'd been terrified that she'd messed up by letting the Nightmares loose and that Morrigan was going to be devoured.

"Are you okay?" Captain Kel asked, his eyes dark and serious.

"Yes," Ix said, still jittery from the near miss. Morrigan gave a shaky nod.

"Good," Kel said, relieved. "Because you are all in a lot of trouble."

30

THE ELDER FLAMES

Ix stared up at the huge double doors to the council chamber, her stomach in knots.

She had never seen Captain Kel so angry. He hadn't listened at all to their side of the story, and when Ix tried to tell him Jack was after the door, Kel cut her off.

"I'm well aware, but the red doors are all locked and sealed. And it's a captain's job to protect them, not first-year Novices."

"But what's down there?" Ix pressed.

Captain Kel's mouth twisted. "Nothing you should have anything to do with. Don't go back there. Ever."

When they reached the chamber, Captain Kel and Captain Rossi went inside to report to the council, leaving Morrigan, Ollie, and Ix in the hall with Professor Swann. At least their teacher was also in his pajamas, with his hair going everywhere and his glasses halfway down his nose.

Ix shifted nervously from foot to foot. The stone floor was icy on her bare toes. She wished she'd been able to go back for her socks.

Ollie looked contrite. "Maybe we should have waited for help."

Morrigan was indignant. "We were just trying to keep Jack out of the Central Tower. What else were we supposed to do? Captain Kel didn't have to get so angry . . ."

Professor Swann sighed heavily. "He wasn't angry because of Jack. He was terrified for your safety—especially yours, Morrigan. You know better than anyone what could have happened if you'd lost control and the Nightmare power overwhelmed you."

The blood drained out of Morrigan's face. Ix's guts squirmed like she'd swallowed a foot-long Guiltipede. She hadn't even thought about the Bea Wolves when she'd let Morrigan face Jack alone.

Professor Swann bent down and squeezed Morrigan's shoulders softly. "I'm glad you're not hurt. But I'm also very disappointed that you would take that risk." The sad look on his face was worse than all the yelling Captain Kel had done.

Morrigan's eyes were pinned to the floor. Professor Swann dragged a hand through his hair.

"Well, what's done is done. I know you three meant well. All we can do is learn from it for next time."

As he said it, the double doors creaked open. Captain Kel slipped out, followed by Captain Rossi, with Bella the bulldog panting at his feet. Kel did not look happy.

"Morrigan and Ollie, you're excused for tonight," he told them sharply. "Though Head Instructor Telle has been informed of your infraction. Captain Rossi will escort you back to the dorm."

"Come on, kiddos," Rossi said, clapping them on the shoulders. "Bella loves a good nighttime walk. Your instructor is Julia Cadence, right? I'm sure she's ripping out her hair with worry by now. Bit of a panicker, that one."

"What about Ix?" Morrigan asked.

"The council will speak with her," Captain Kel said, looking even more serious than usual.

Ix paled, watching her friends be escorted away.

"I'm sure they won't mind if I stay with you," Professor Swann said, laying a comforting hand on Ix's elbow. "Best to get it over with."

Ix didn't miss the significant look he shot his husband. Or the way Captain Kel's lips thinned in response as he led them through the huge doors.

The room on the other side was dark and whispery. The moon and stars glittered through a huge skylight cut into the cathedral ceiling. Beneath it stood a half circle of eight high-backed chairs, filled with men and women in pajamas and dressing gowns.

Professor Swann whispered their names to Ix as they approached. She recognized Head Instructor Telle, with her long hair pinned up under a kerchief. The man with thick black hair and a blue dressing gown was Tempest's father, Tyrese Valerian. Ix was disappointed to find there was more than one Winter on the council: an old man with a sour frown and another in a captain's coat who seemed to have Darien's sneer. He gave Ix a nasty look as he smoothed his sleep-mussed hair out of his pale face.

"Two Winters?" she whispered, dismayed.

"Yes," Professor Swann explained, ever the teacher. "Argus Winters is Darien's grandfather, a long-standing member of the council. The other man is Darien's father, Fallon Winters. As Head Flame and leader of the captains, he gets the eighth seat. A custom that keeps the council from ending up with an unlucky seven members."

Ix studied the others, searching for a friendly face. The man with the neatly trimmed beard was Lukas Moreno. Next to him sat Aya Ito, Captain Ito's wizened mother. The blond woman with ivory skin and a nightgown so frilly it could pass for an evening gown was Penelope Wystorm. At the very center sat the head of the council: Alexis Moongrave.

They all looked very serious. Ix hadn't eaten anything in hours, but her stomach still went wobbly as Argus Winters rose from his seat.

"Ix Tatterfall. Did you enter Candle Corps Academy under false pretenses, knowing you had Nightmare powers?"

"No! At least, not at first . . ." Ix glanced at Captain Kel, not sure what she should say. His face was stony.

"Feel free to speak up, child," Tyrese Valerian said kindly. "Captain Kel has already admitted his part in this deception."

Ix fisted her hands into her nightshirt. "I thought my Dream-light powers were a little different. But the more I used them, the more I realized that maybe they were something else."

Fallon Winters scoffed. "Defying the council for another one of your little projects, Kel?" He propped his chin on his hand. "First Morrigan Bea, now this girl. When will you learn to leave the Nightmares in the Labyrinth, where they belong?"

Kel's eyes narrowed.

"Temper, Fallon," Elder Moongrave said mildly. "Perhaps we could leave the personal disagreements for another time."

Argus Winters banged his fist. "Fallon is right. This is why the council discourages admitting students from Nightmare lineages. They cause no end of problems."

"Exceptions have been made before," Aya Ito pointed out. "The Bea family, for example."

"Ah, yes, the Beas." Penelope Wystorm gave a derisive sniff. "And *that* has caused no trouble? It's hard to dismiss the danger of Nightmare power, with you both standing there bearing those scars."

Professor Swann flinched, pressing a hand over his neck. In his loose pajama shirt, his scars were more visible than usual.

Captain Kel gritted his teeth and took a half step in front of his husband. "Ix has Nightmare powers. She can't do anything about that. Where is she supposed to learn to control them if not at the academy?"

"A valid point, Captain Kel," Telle said, with a sharp look, "*if* you had brought her in properly and with the right precautions. Her teachers had no idea what powers she had. If that Seething Serpent had escaped, many students could have been in danger."

Guilt stabbed into Ix's heart. She hadn't really been thinking about anything except stopping Jack when she'd unsealed the Nightmares. She could have hurt her friends, or Tempest. Even Darien.

"Regardless of how this situation came about, the girl is here," Tyrese Valerian pointed out. "The only question now is what to do about it."

"There is no question," Penelope Wystorm snapped. "Obviously, she should be expelled. *Every* Nightmare descendant in this school should be expelled. Humans and Nightmares were never meant to coexist. It's time to go back to the old ways. Covenant Keep should be purged of all Nightmare creatures, and from now on, all Nightmares should be dispelled on sight."

"You can't!" Ix couldn't stop herself from protesting. Professor Swann's hands tightened on her shoulders. "What about all the harmless Nightmares—the ones who haven't hurt anybody?"

Penelope Wystorm's gaze pinched in disgust, trailing down to Ix's sleeve. Hanky had crawled out of her pocket and was dangling from her elbow.

"There are no harmless Nightmares," the woman said sharply. Hanky squirmed under her gaze. Elder Wystorm sniffed. "I wouldn't be surprised if you're in league with this Jack creature, trying to bring down Candle Corps."

Captain Kel gritted his teeth. "You can't be serious."

"Perhaps we have become a tad too permissive of Nightmares . . ." Lukas Moreno mused, rubbing his beard.

"The answer isn't to expel our own students," Captain Kel protested. "None of this is her fault. It's mine."

"We're all *very* aware of that," Argus Winters snapped.

The arguing voices started to overlap, but Ix wasn't listening. This was so much bigger than her getting expelled from Candle Corps. Bigger even than her and Aunt Tara being banished to the Scally Woods. Morrigan could lose her family, her only home. All the Nightmares that lived in the keep, the Inklings and the Blackout Bats and the fun-loving Devious Doorway—they could be eradicated. And it all would be Ix's fault, because she couldn't follow the rules.

Ix felt eyes on her. Fallon Winters was watching her closely, his gaze cold and calculating. Then he smiled. It wasn't a smile Ix liked very much. The man stood smoothly from his chair.

"I agree with Captain Kel," he said.

A stunned silence fell over the room. Ix got the sense Fallon Winters and Captain Kel had never agreed on anything.

The head captain's eyes glittered. "Expelling all Nightmares would be premature. The girl should be given a chance to prove her worth, and her loyalty to Candle Corps."

"What are you after, Fallon?" Kel growled.

Fallon Winters paced before the chairs, his hands linked behind his back. "The problems of the Labyrinth can no longer be ignored, now that they're spilling onto our side. Nightmares in broad daylight, souls being spit out—and now this Jack creature has attacked our own keep. Captain Kel has long insisted that the origin of all these troubles lies in Death's realm. Which has been beyond our reach . . . until now."

Fallon's gaze settled on Ix. "The Sorrows gather once a year on the bank of the River of Shades to drink the Elixir of Night. All Hallows' Eve—the only night when Death's realm can be reached without traversing the entire Labyrinth."

Professor Swann made a strangled sound. But it was Kel who spoke.

"You're not suggesting sending a Novice to the Banquet of the Sorrows? On All Hallows' Eve, when they're at their most powerful? She'll be devoured."

Ix swallowed hard. She knew a little about the banquet. Smiles had told her about it once as he lay on his stomach, lazily sticking his paws into people's dreams and stirring them up. Like a cat with his claws in a fishbowl.

The Elixir of Night is the only reason we tolerate each other, even for a short while. Infighting is strictly prohibited between the Sorrows on All Hallows' Eve. But that doesn't mean we don't have a bit of fun—some friendly ribbing, a little brawl, maybe an underling or two gobbled up. Misery's a bore, Wrath never keeps her temper, Greed takes the best of everything, and ever since Death disappeared, we're on the honor system for behaving. Which means it's always a wild night.

Captain Winters was undaunted. "If she has enough Nightmare power to break seals, then surely she could use the Shroud."

Whispers broke out among the councillors. Ix turned to Professor Swann. "What's the Shroud?"

Professor Swann shook his head.

It was Fallon Winters who answered. "The Shroud amplifies

Nightmare power to make the wearer appear to be a creature of the Labyrinth."

"It was locked up for a good reason." Aya Ito looked serious. "We barely recovered it after Evelyn Bea went scouting in Wrath's domain and lost herself to her Nightmare blood. The Shroud is too dangerous to use."

Fallon snorted. "Only because it requires someone with strong Nightmare power, and that's running quite thin these days. Even among the ill-fated Beas. But now, Captain Kel has brought us a perfect specimen. She could slip in among the Sorrows unnoticed."

Professor Swann couldn't hold his tongue anymore. "She's not a specimen. She's a child!"

Penelope Wystorm sniffed. "You have no voice on this council, *Professor* Swann. Please remember you're here as a courtesy."

"It seems to me that the issue here is one of trust," Lukas Moreno said, his eyes stern. "Can Ix Tatterfall be trusted? Can anyone with Nightmares powers, or even Nightmare sympathies"—his gaze flitted over Kel and Swann—"be trusted to uphold the mission of Candle Corps? Let the girl infiltrate the Banquet of the Sorrows and bring back the truth of what's happening in the Labyrinth. Then she'll have proven that she and all those like her deserve a place here."

Silence settled over the room. Neither Elder Wystorm nor Captain Kel looked happy, but they weren't objecting, either.

"You can't seriously be considering this," Professor Swann said, incredulous. "Sending a child into the heart of the Labyrinth alone? It's too dangerous—"

"I'll do it!" Ix broke in, pulling away from Professor Swann and pushing to the front.

"She seems to be volunteering," Fallon Winters said, looking very smug.

Kel looked between Ix and the council and seemed to realize he was fighting a losing battle. He rubbed a hand across his forehead. "There would have to be precautions."

"Tarryn!" Professor Swann snapped, horrified. Ix had never heard him call Captain Kel by his first name in public before.

Kel gave him a look, as if asking what else he was supposed to do. "I'll be standing by in the Labyrinth," he said. "With people I trust."

"Naturally," Fallon Winters said with a dismissive wave.

All eyes turned to Alexis Moongrave. The ancient woman peered down at Ix through her half-moon glasses. "I have deep concerns about all of this. But before the council makes a decision, I must know. Do you truly understand what is being asked of you, young Novice?"

Ix understood the only thing that mattered. This was her only chance to save herself, and Morrigan, and all the Nightmares she loved in Covenant Keep.

"I understand," Ix said, lifting her chin. "I'm not afraid of the Labyrinth, or the Sorrows."

Alexis Moongrave sighed. "That is perhaps the most foolish thing ever said to me. And I am old enough to have heard a great many foolish things."

Fallon Winters clapped his hands. "Then it's settled. On All Hallows' Eve, Ix Tatterfall will enter the Labyrinth and infiltrate the Banquet of the Sorrows."

Ix gulped, feeling like she'd just volunteered to walk right into the jaws of a monster.

31

ALL HALLOWS' EVE

The only thing Ix was allowed to tell her friends about the Elder Council's decision was that she'd agreed to complete a task for them on All Hallows' Eve. The only thing the rest of the Novice class knew was that Ix had broken some serious rules the night the keep was attacked, and now she was being punished. Darien Winters kept shooting her smug looks, talking loudly about how some people just weren't Candle Corps material.

Even if Ollie and Morrigan hadn't suspected the council's task was something dangerous, Professor Swann's concerned frown every time he looked at Ix, and the way he kept worrying his quill until the whole feather popped off, would have given it away.

"You really won't tell us anything?" Morrigan pressed. It was late, long after they both should have been asleep. The Starlight Spiders shone in the dorm window.

"After," Ix promised. If she told Morrigan that both their futures—and those of all the Nightmares at Candle Corps Academy—were on the line, the fiery girl would definitely do something reckless. And Ix didn't want anything to happen to Morrigan.

During the day, it was hard to ignore the stares. Novices and Sparks and even some Embers whispered in the hallways as she passed.

"I heard she's the reason the Nightmares attacked."

"Maybe she broke the rules."

"Or she's working for them."

"She's the one the scarecrow was after in the Labyrinth, too," Ix overheard Nora telling a clump of eager Sparks. "And get this—she's friends with the Bea Wolf."

"Don't listen to them," Ollie told her. "Once the All Hallows' Eve festival is over, everyone will forget it and move on."

Ix really hoped that was true.

Even though she wasn't going to be able to enjoy much of the celebration, Ix spent the week helping put up the decorations. After a grueling morning scooping the guts out of dozens of pumpkins, Ix, Ollie, and Morrigan took a break with Tempest. He passed out a handful of ice pops he'd filched from the kitchen as he led them up to the top of the battlements. They sat with their legs slung over the edge of one of the keep's inner walls.

Morrigan's tongue was very blue. Ix wondered if hers had turned purple. Ollie's pop was sour lime, which he insisted he liked, though he kept squinching up his face.

"Isn't it too cold for ice pops?" Morrigan asked. Her scarf whipped around her in the crisp breeze.

Tempest shrugged. "I like it. Chills you right down to the bone."

Below them, in the Inner Ward, Ix could see one of the Ember squads practicing drills. Captain Calloway paced along the wall, calling out the names of Nightmare beasts in his booming voice.

Tempest pointed with his drippy ice pop. "Captain Calloway's the instructor for Advanced Labyrinth Movement—pretty much Candle Corps PE. I have nightmares about his drills."

"My cousin says only the strongest Embers get selected for his squad," Ollie said, pushing up his glasses. "Will you be in that squad next year, Tempest?"

"He's been trying to recruit me," Tempest said. "But I'll pass. I'm going to be Kel's vice-captain."

"I thought Captain Kel didn't have a vice-captain anymore," Ix said, with a glance at Morrigan.

"Eh. I'll wear him down. Besides, no way am I ending up with Calloway. My sister, Torrent, was in his squad, and I have it on good authority that he won't let anybody on a mission if their room isn't clean."

"Guess you're out," Morrigan teased Ix. Ix stuck out her purple tongue. She was trying to keep her side of the room clean, now that there weren't really sides anymore. But the floor was just where socks wanted to live. Plus, a mess gave Hanky extra hiding places.

"They're actually really strong. But they're picky about appearances, too." Tempest fluffed a hand through his hair, perfectly imitating Captain Calloway below. "Neat minds—neat movements—neat uniforms," he said dramatically.

Ollie laughed, choking on a bite of ice pop. His eyes went wide as it stuck in his throat. Morrigan slapped him on the back. The chunk of ice pop flew out and tumbled down to splatter on the pristine shoulder of Captain Calloway's coat.

Ix gasped. So did the Embers. Ollie's eyes went wide as saucers. Tempest poked his head over the wall to get a better look.

"*Tempest Valerian!*" came an angry shout from below.

Tempest cursed. "Rats. He saw me. Run, kids—save yourselves!"

So they ran, Ix and Ollie and Morrigan scrambling over each other, vaulting down the stairs and through the halls until they collapsed in a pile in the common room, out of breath from laughing.

Tempest caught up with them in the last few minutes of lunch. He slumped onto the table, bemoaning his punishment. "Captain Calloway made me polish his trophy case while he told me how he got every single one."

"It could've been worse," Morrigan said. "He could've made you clean your room."

"I'm so sorry," Ollie said. "But thanks for getting us out of it."

"Ah, don't thank me." Tempest waved carelessly. "I tried to throw the blame on you four times. Captain Calloway refused to believe that polite, well-mannered Oliver Pembrook would do such a thing."

Ollie flushed.

"Hey, look," Ix said. Out the window, she could see two people in the courtyard—Captain Kel and Fallon Winters. They seemed to be arguing. Fallon Winters jabbed a sharp finger into Captain Kel's chest as he spoke. Kel looked like he wanted to snap it off.

"What do you think they're fighting about?" Ollie asked. His voice was hushed, like he was afraid of being overheard.

Ix had a pretty good idea. Morrigan fixed her with a suspicious look. But it was Tempest who said, "They don't need much of an excuse. They've despised each other a long time."

Ix had gotten that sense in the council, too. "What happened between them?"

Tempest stole a peanut butter tart off her plate and popped it in his mouth, realizing too late that she'd smeared pickles on it.

"You know Captain Winters is Head Flame," he said, grimacing. "I'm pretty sure he only took the job to get his portrait in the front hall and boss everybody around. But Captain Kel's not all that good at following orders." He bent close over the table. "This is supposed to be all hush-hush. But Torrent told me some of the captains got drunk one night and let slip that Captain Kel was everybody's first choice for Head Flame, before . . . things changed."

He threw a quick look at Morrigan before continuing.

"Captain Winters never forgave him for that. He's in charge, but Captain Kel's opinion still carries a lot of weight around here. He'd probably like nothing better than for Captain Kel to disappear on one of his trips into the Labyrinth."

Outside, Kel spun on his heel and walked away. They all ducked so he wouldn't spot them. Fallon Winters stalked off in the opposite direction, seething. Once Winters was gone, Tempest pushed up from his seat.

"Well, I've spread enough castle gossip for one day. I have a few things to get ready. See you at the festivities tonight." Tempest gave them a mysterious wink as he headed off.

Ix's stomach dropped like she'd swallowed a Sinking Stone. She'd almost forgotten. She wouldn't be around for tonight's fun.

A few hours before the party, Ix and Morrigan put on their costumes. Morrigan wore a raggedy red-and-black dress and perched in front of the mirror fighting with her wild curls.

"Here, let me," Ix offered, clipping the spiny horns into her hair to complete the Fiend of Wrath.

"Well?" Morrigan demanded, spinning a circle. She'd put on dark eyeshadow, and her lips sparkled. She looked spooky and pretty at the same time.

"The costume's good, but it's the glare that really sells it."

Morrigan snorted, looking at Ix's all-black outfit. "And what are you supposed to be? A giant Inkling?"

"Actually, I'm going as a Wraith." Ix snagged the silver cloak off her bed, pulling the hood low over her face. "Ooooo," she moaned, raising her hands under the dangling sleeves.

"Hanky's more terrifying than you are," Morrigan told her, dropping a tiny orange crepe paper witch hat onto the Inkling's head. The little stick arms waved in approval.

Someone rapped at their door. It was Ollie dressed as a Blackout Bat, with fake fangs and swooping wings attached to his wrists.

"Are you ready? Everyone's headed down. They sent me back so I wouldn't be the seventh."

When they entered the castle ballroom, Ix was amazed by the transformation. Strings of Dreamlights crisscrossed the ceiling, and carved pumpkins and gourds grinned at her with jagged smiles. Everybody was in costume—Wraiths and Moaning Ghouls and all manner of Nightmare—each one wilder than the last. Ix spotted Darien Winters by the punch bowl in the black-cowled robe of an Apparition of Death.

"Shame," Morrigan muttered. "If he really wanted to scare people, he should have just come as himself."

Ollie took the seat next to them, followed by Professor Swann. He wore a shaggy coat and a pair of ears on a headband that made him look like a friendlier-than-expected Woebegone Woolie. Ix hadn't caught sight of Tempest yet, but his costume was sure to be unbeatable.

Ix tried to soak up all the laughter and fun and excitement of the party as they traded scary Nightmare stories over pumpkin pie and maple sugar candies. She wanted to stop inside that moment:

with Morrigan throwing
her head back laughing as
two Inklings fought over a
teaspoon, and Ollie gasp-
ing in surprise at the sight
of somebody's pet tarantula
out exploring the table,
while Professor Swann of-
fered everyone a sip of his
spicy cinnamon-chili tea.

All too soon, Captain Kel tapped her on the shoulder.

"It's time."

Professor Swann shot his husband a very disapproving look as
Ix got up to follow him out of the hall. They walked farther and
farther into the keep, far enough that Ix caught flashes of the forbidden red doors down the branching corridors.

Fallon Winters and Healer Mella, along with several captains,
stood waiting outside a Door to Nowhere. Mist was already curling up from the cracks.

"The Shroud," Captain Winters said, holding out a folded
cloth. It was gauzy and grayish white, and so thin it felt like spider's thread. Maybe it was, Ix thought, remembering the spider
weavers of Spindlecrook. When she shook it out, she saw it was
a long cloak with a hood meant to hang all the way over her face.

She wormed her way out of the Wraith cloak and slid the
Shroud over her shoulders. It was a strange feeling, like a layer of
mist settling around her and prickling on her skin.

Ix felt her nervous grin stretch over her face. "How do I look?"
she asked Captain Kel.

"It only works on Nightmares," the man said bluntly, though he laid a comforting hand on Ix's shoulder. "But I imagine you'll fool them all. Are you ready?"

No! Ix thought. No one was ever ready to face the Sorrows. But she just drew a deep breath.

"Ready."

"Good luck," Healer Mella said.

Fallon Winters opened the Door to Nowhere. "All of Candle Corps is counting on you," he murmured as Ix followed Captain Kel through. "Try not to disappoint."

32

THE TEMPTATIONS OF GREED

M ist swirled around Ix. With her next step, she was inside the Labyrinth. White stones smooth as marble rose above her. Everything was sinuous and curving. This was Greed's domain.

There didn't seem to be any Nightmares around, except for little pools of water filled with Miserlilies and jewel-bright Malicious Fish. Ix realized why as Captain Ito strode toward them, gripping her thin, curved Shadow Render sword.

"I've scouted the area and chased off a few Narcissusnakes," she told Captain Kel. "There's a pack of Phantasms nearby that look to be heading for the banquet. Miss Tatterfall can slip in with them."

Ix shuddered. Narcissusnakes had a poisonous bite that made you obsessed with your looks, helpless to do anything except stare at your reflection until you wasted away. Greed had always been her least favorite part of the Labyrinth.

"Thanks for the assist, Akari," Captain Kel said. Then he bent down so he and Ix were face-to-face. "It's not too late to change your mind. We can figure something else out."

Ix appreciated the offer, but she'd already made her decision. "I can do this," she told him. Morrigan and all the Nightmares were counting on her.

Captain Kel cracked a gruff smile. "If anyone can, it's you." He gave her shoulder a quick squeeze. "I'll trail you for as long as I can without being spotted, and Captain Ito will be here in Greed's realm, in case you come back this way. Healer Mella is on standby in the castle. And Ix—" He looked at her very seriously. "If there's any trouble, just get out of there. It's All Hallows' Eve, so the Labyrinth is thick with mist and doorways tonight. If you're in danger, escape however you can. Promise me."

"I promise," Ix said, swallowing hard. She'd accidentally hugged Terror once—she didn't need a repeat.

"This way," Captain Ito beckoned, pointing Ix down a curling pathway cut into the wall. "The Phantasms are just ahead."

Ix took one last long look at Captain Kel and then set off down the passageway. Almost immediately, she felt her guts squeeze with gnawing hunger. At the same time, a bent apple tree sprouted from a crack in the wall. Globes of fleshy red apples hung enticingly from every branch. Ix swallowed down the growl from her stomach.

Greed's realm was the only place in the Labyrinth you ever felt hungry or thirsty. All the trees dripped with delicious scents to entice you to bite into fruits crawling with parasites. The more beautiful something seemed, the more dangerous it was.

Some sleepwalking souls were pulled into Greed's domain by mirages of gold and jewels and riches, while others saw illusions of success and power. Ix had seen those souls from time to time, staring into the great mirror walls that sprang up through the twisting corridors. Their eyes glazed over as they stared at something in their reflection only they could see.

The longer you spent ensnared in Greed, the harder it was to shake off.

Think of all the things you're grateful for, Ix reminded herself. *All your happinesses from large to small.* That was the only way to fortify yourself against the insatiable hunger of Greed.

Up ahead, she heard light footsteps and muffled voices. The Phantasms. Ix hurried to slip in among them.

Phantasms were human-shaped Nightmares that dressed in colorful cloaks. Instead of flesh, their bodies were made of a shiny substance almost like mirror glass. When you looked into their eyes, their featureless faces would start to morph and change, until they had stolen a face from your memory to wear while they taunted you.

At least half a dozen Phantasms walked and skipped gleefully down the path. Silent as a shadow, Ix slipped in behind the very last one. She held her breath as the eyeless indents in its face swept over her, but the Phantasm didn't raise the alarm. The Shroud was working.

At the head of the line, a lanky Phantasm in a red cloak led the way. Ix peered around the figures, trying to see what they were following. It looked like a black mark on the ground, though it was strangely crooked.

"I would trade every soul I've sipped upon for a mere taste of the Elixir of Night," one of the Nightmares said excitedly from the center of the pack.

"There's more than one Phantasm pinned to the Masked Charlatan's wall for that offense," the leader in the red cloak warned. "Greed doesn't kill his underlings. He never lets anything go. Be careful, or you'll join his collection, tacked up like a Blood-Sucking Butterfly."

The Phantasms laughed. Ix huddled deeper into her cloak.

"Ah, our escort," the leader hissed.

That's when Ix realized what they had been following. It was a giant crack in the Labyrinth floor. She could see more of them splintering the white stone around her. They looked brand new, like they'd split open just for All Hallows' Eve. And they all led toward a dark fissure in the wall ahead. There was no mist curling over the threshold. Just deep, swallowing darkness.

A chill ran up Ix's spine like spider legs. She was breaking another rule tonight. *Never follow a crack with your feet, for cracks can become pathways to the darkness in your heart.*

Something hovered in front of the entryway. When she got closer, Ix realized it was an Apparition of Death. They were the Grim Reapers that worked only for Death itself and obeyed no other Sorrows. A dark cowl covered the dark space under the hood, and the ragged edges of its robe floated above the ground. It gestured to the fissure with its gleaming scythe.

It was welcoming them to the heart of the Labyrinth. To Death's domain.

Ix followed the line of Phantasms as they disappeared into the dark. Right on the threshold of the door, the Apparition of Death swooped down suddenly, putting its empty cowl right into Ix's face. She sucked in a breath so fast she felt the Shroud stick to her wet lips.

The faceless darkness stared into her. Suddenly Ix knew with utter certainty that even if the Shroud could fool all the other Nightmares in the Labyrinth, it couldn't fool the Apparitions of Death.

The Apparitions were the ones that collected troubled souls, measuring their greed, and misery, and terror, weighing up their deeds in life and deciding where in the Labyrinth they should start. Peaceful souls went right to the threshold of Death's Door. Others were doomed to wander the Labyrinth until they found their way or were devoured.

Ix felt like her soul had been laid bare. She'd been found out—and as soon as the Apparition revealed her, she'd be ripped apart by the Phantasms.

The Apparition of Death lifted its scythe. Ix stopped breathing. Then the figure bowed its head to Ix, gesturing to the passage beyond.

Was it inviting her in?

Suddenly her father's words came back to her. *As long as you are with me, little wishling, Death will surely come for us.*

Maybe the Apparition thought she belonged there, in Death's realm. Ix wondered if she was the only person who could have made it through this passage tonight.

She wasn't going to waste this chance. Ix hurried through the door before the Apparition changed its mind.

She had made it to the center of the Labyrinth.

33

THE BANQUET OF THE SORROWS

Ix followed the Phantasms into Death's realm, joining a long line of Nightmares flooding through the cracks and fissures into the center of the Labyrinth for All Hallows' Eve. Something whispered around her ankles. When she looked down, Ix found she was crossing through a thick patch of dark bell-shaped flowers.

Death Delphinium, she realized with a shudder. She'd seen them once in a book Ollie had borrowed from Healer Mella. The flowers grew in a ring around the edges of the Soul Reaper's domain, and it was said they could trap human souls. They were known as Death Bells because, according to legend, only the souls of the dead could hear them ring.

With the Shroud over her, none of the other Nightmare creatures seemed to notice Ix, and she was quickly swept along with the crowd. There were Wraiths in their silvery translucent robes, Moaning Ghouls rattling their chains, and roving packs of Fiends with cloven hooves to match their horns. Most of the Nightmares were human form, but there was also a smattering of Fright Bats wheeling above. Ix even spotted a Grinning Cross-Fox all the way from Chaos's domain.

Through the crowd, she caught glimpses of Death's realm. It was dark, lit only by the eerie light of ghostly purple flames that floated in the air. The walls of the Labyrinth shone like they were made of polished obsidian. Everything felt heavy and quiet and hushed.

Apparitions of Death drifted overhead, invisible against the darkness until the purple flames caught their scythes, which flashed like sickle moons.

Corpse Weed crept along the edges of giant coffin-like slabs of rock. Here and there, Ix spotted bone creatures darting through the weeds. Lizards that were nothing but skeletons ran up the walls, rattling all the way. A pair of Jimber-Jawed Hounds snapped at a Bone Rat darting between their paws.

A Wraith floating high above the rest raised a lantern, beckoning them forward. "The Banquet of the Sorrows is begun!" the creature cackled.

An excited cheer went up through the Nightmares. As they paraded through the dark corridors of Death's hall, Ix was suddenly reminded of the All Hallows' Eve parades back home in Brittlewick—all the people dressed as Nightmares, holding lanterns and candles as they walked the streets just like this. Tonight, the veil that separated the Between World and the Waking World was at its thinnest. As many Nightmares as were headed into Death's realm, many more would be escaping the Labyrinth to wreak mayhem and terror.

As they walked on, they began crossing tiny trickles of water that ran between dark stones. It was the River of Shades. Down the way, Ix could just see the outline of a creaky wooden boat that had run aground. A skeletal figure stood at the bow, watching them pass.

"Don't get trapped on the wrong side," one Phantasm teased

another as they darted by. "The Ferryman's river rushes back at first light, and any Nightmare left in Death's realm will have to pay the price or never return."

For the first time, Ix realized there was no mist around her. In fact, she hadn't seen any mist at all in Death's domain. Just the jagged fissures they'd come through, cracked open by the Apparitions.

She gripped the edges of the Shroud with clammy palms. No mist meant no quick escape if things went wrong. But there was no turning back now.

The dark corridors had opened into a patch of wild growth, a clearing covered in shivering white Ghost Grass that swayed without a breeze. Most of the Nightmares were peeling away, disappearing down side paths where Ix could hear raucous celebrations. At the center of the clearing, atop a hill, a ring of purple flames floated around a spring that shone like the night sky.

This was the Midnight Pool that burbled up once a year with the Elixir of Night. Only the bravest Nightmares dared to sit on the hillside—Fiends with spiraling horns so giant they must be hundreds of years old and powerful Wraiths that glowed with energy to the tips of their ragged cloaks.

Three figures sat at the very top already, including a giant striped cat. That was where Ix needed to be. She pressed her elbows into her sides, making herself as small as possible as she crept up the hill. A Jimber-Jawed Hound growled half-heartedly at her before settling back down. Ix cringed, but she made herself keep going—closer and closer, until she could peek out at the Sorrows and hear them talking.

"What is taking the others so long?" a tall figure with a deep, oily voice complained.

Ix had never seen him before, but she knew he must be Greed, the Masked Charlatan. He had blond hair slicked back under a top hat, and his face was entirely hidden by a white mask. In his pitch-black suit, his body blended into the dark, except for the white gloves that made his glowing hands look like they were detached from his body. As Ix watched, he dipped a fancy, jewel-encrusted goblet into the Midnight Pool and drank deeply.

Beyond him, Terror, the Eyeless Child, sat on a slab of rock, spinning a plain pewter cup in their hands. Their wild hair drifted around them, and their huge empty eyeholes glowed in the fire-light. Chaos, the Grinning Cat, lounged beside the spring with a cauldron. He lapped at it with his tongue, giving them all a toothy smile.

The Masked Charlatan tapped his gloved fingers against his goblet impatiently. "How dare they make me wait—wasting my precious minutes! I'll make them pay for every single one."

"Perhaps Misery is still with Despair," the Grinning Cat said. "I heard it was quite the ordeal to get that one back to sleep after it was all riled up the other day."

"I heard about the centipede's little rampage," Greed said with a dismissive slosh of his cup. "I don't know how that mindless bug ever became a Sorrow. If it's back to sleep, good riddance. Get rid of it once and for all, I say."

Terror chuckled, a screechy sound like nails on a chalkboard. "Are you sure? If one Sorrow can be ousted, then any Sorrow could. Even you, Greed."

The Grinning Cat hissed out a laugh, while Greed just har-rumphed.

A sudden cry rose from the other side of the hill. Nightmare creatures scrambled to get out of the way of a figure stalking up the slope. Ix inched forward on her elbows to get a better look. It was a woman in a bright red dress. Her face was completely obscured by a blood-red veil pinned into her dark hair with a wickedly sharp hat pin. Her crimson gown bloomed with a bustle and long train that dragged through the grass. The cloth left a red stain dark as blood behind it.

"Wrath," Terror greeted with a crooked smile.

"Late—you're late!" Greed snapped at the same time.

"I'm not even the last one!" the Bloody Ripper snarled. She yanked a heavy mug from the pocket of her dress and dipped it into the Midnight Pool, taking a large swig and then belching loudly.

"So undignified," the Masked Charlatan sniffed.

"What did you say?" Wrath demanded, her head whipping around. But before they could get into it, a sudden rush of noise preceded the entrance of another Sorrow. Ix tensed where she lay on her stomach.

The figure ascending the hill was a woman in a gray tailcoat, with long hair spilling over her gray features. She held a gray umbrella, which was where the noise was coming from—and the water.

The umbrella was raining from the inside, soaking Misery, the Shadow Lady, and splashing into the grass. She passed so close to Ix that little speckles of water hit her face. The rain was warm, and it smelled salty, like tears.

"Oh, do put that away," Smiles hissed, the fur on his back rising as he arched away from the water.

"Always so dramatic, Misery," the Masked Charlatan taunted.

"And the last to arrive, as usual—unless we're expecting Despair?"

All the Sorrows seemed to hold their breaths as Misery pulled her umbrella closed. The rain stopped, though she still looked wet and bedraggled, dripping her way to the Midnight Pool with a chipped teacup.

"Despair should sleep for some time," the Shadow Lady said, wrapping her hands around the teacup and taking the barest sip. "Not that any of you really cares."

Ix gulped around a lump so big it felt like a rock stuck in her throat. These were the Sorrows—five of the most powerful beings in the Labyrinth. And here was Ix, a frail human hidden under nothing but a thin Shroud, crouched just a few feet away from them.

34

THE WHIMS OF CHAOS

"Now that we're all here, I propose a toast," Greed said. "Unless anyone thinks this is the year Death will finally deign to grace us with their presence?" The Masked Charlatan laughed as though it were some great joke.

Wrath snorted into her mug. "The Soul Reaper always did whatever they wanted."

"Still, it has been an *awfully long* time," Smiles pointed out, tipping his giant head. "Ten human years now. Surely even Death couldn't be *so* bored of us."

"Ha! Good riddance to them, too," Greed mumbled into his cup. "The Soul Reaper was always lording it over the rest of us."

"Cheers to that!" Wrath slammed her cup harshly into Greed's goblet. "I never liked all those nitpicky rules, either. *Do this. Don't do that.* Gah! It irritates me just thinking about it."

"And what about Jack?" Terror asked, lips souring into a deep frown. "No Soul Reaper means no one to take care of . . . mistakes."

"Are you looking at me?" Wrath demanded. "I didn't create that awful thing. He's been nothing but an aggravation to me, eating my Horned Beasts and taking control of my Lesser Nightmares!" The Bloody Ripper slammed her cup down on the rocks along the edge of the spring. "If you're going to accuse anyone, it should be Chaos. That scarecrow has *his* nasty sense of humor."

"Now, now," the Grinning Cat warned, tail lashing. "Let's not be hasty. I've nothing to do with Jack."

"Nor I," Greed added. "I would never create something in such poor taste."

"So now you all look at me . . . You always do," Misery whined, stirring a finger in her teacup. "But I've been more wronged by Jack than all of you . . . Did you even think of that? Of course you didn't. You never do . . ." The Shadow Lady went on mumbling unhappily to herself.

The Grinning Cat waggled a gleaming claw. "Well, if all of us are to be believed—and I don't know that we are—then Jack is not a creature of the Labyrinth. Which leaves only one possibility."

"He's from the Waking World!" Wrath spat. "Meddling humans up to no good."

Ix shrank away from the fury of the Sorrow. She thought about the moment that Jack's sackcloth mask had ripped, and the face she had seen for a split-second underneath.

A soul. A human soul.

Jack wasn't working for the Sorrows. He wasn't even a Nightmare. Something else was responsible for what was happening in the Labyrinth.

Ix had just started to inch closer when the next words stopped her.

"Death couldn't be dead, right?" Misery said. "It would be too terrible, too awful to contemplate."

"Death is eternal," Terror responded, padding over on bare feet to refill their cup. "I doubt anything is powerful enough to destroy the Soul Reaper. Besides, the Midnight Pool burbles up every year, so the Soul Reaper must still exist . . . somewhere."

"Maybe," Chaos mused. "But the Apparitions say that Death's Door has been closing little by little. These days, it's barely open a crack. That's why the souls have started backing up."

No wonder the Labyrinth was acting up, Ix thought. It had finally reached its breaking point.

"Well, in the meantime," Greed broke in, "perhaps it's time one of us other Sorrows steps up to fill the void of power—just until Death returns, of course."

"You say this every year," the Grinning Cat mocked. "And it always goes the same way."

"I suppose this new leader would be you?" Wrath ground out, already outraged.

"Naturally," the Masked Charlatan said, with a wave of his gloved hand. "I don't see anyone else here suited to that kind of power."

"Oh really?" The Bloody Ripper's voice was low and dangerous. A tremor shook the ground under Ix, hard enough to make her teeth rattle. A burning red glow surrounded Wrath, like tongues of fire lashing the night.

This was about to be a fight between Sorrows. Ix got to her hands and knees and crawled backward down the hill as fast as she could.

"Simmer down, Wrath," the Grinning Cat suggested. "Greed's been staring at his own reflection so long he can't see anything else. No need to get all hot under the collar over a bad joke."

"Are you accusing me of overreacting?!" Wrath shouted. She slammed her boot down, and the ground rumbled again, sending a few rocks bouncing down the hill. Right at Ix.

Ix tried to dodge. Her foot slipped against the slick Ghost Grass. A second later, she was tumbling end over end down the slope, the world spinning wildly around her. Pebbles and brittle twigs scraped her hands as she scrabbled for something to grab on to. And then there was an awful tearing sound.

When Ix finally came to a stop at the bottom of the hill, there was no longer a cloth covering her face. The Shroud lay in ragged pieces around her. Ix staggered to her feet, dizzy. She tried to run, only to find herself on her knees, staring up the hill at the five Sorrows, who all had their eyes locked on her.

"A human!" Wrath howled. "A human child dares to set foot in this realm on All Hallows' Eve!"

Ix couldn't breathe. She didn't know if the world was spinning because she was still dizzy or because she was so scared. Ripped apart by Wrath. Tormented by Terror. Devoured by Greed. Drowned by Misery. There were only bad ways to go.

The Grinning Cat chuckled. "I'll get it. I do so love a good pounce."

The giant striped cat leapt at Ix all at once. His wicked claws gleamed as he landed on her—but when his paw pushed her to the ground, the claws had retracted, leaving her trapped under the soft pad.

"Very, very foolish, human child," Smiles whispered, his glowing amethyst eyes inches from her. "You're lucky I'm in the mood for a bit of fun tonight. Grab on to the fur of my stomach."

"What?" Ix started to ask. Then she was suddenly buried as the Grinning Cat scooted forward, covering her with his body. Ix grabbed clumps of striped fur, desperately clinging to him.

"Well?" Wrath demanded.

"It seems to have gotten away," Chaos told the other Sorrows with a shrug. "Scuttled off into the dark."

"That's what you get when you leave important things to a creature known for playing with its food," Greed said haughtily. "Phantasms! A human child has infiltrated our party. Find it and bring it to me."

"No!" Wrath yelled twice as loud. "Bring it to me, Fiends—dead or alive, I don't care which." Ix heard the bang and clatter of creatures moving, and the hollers as Wrath and Greed moved off in opposite directions.

"No need to blubber so, Misery," Terror rasped out.

"But the banquet is ruined," the Shadow Lady moaned. "Just ruined. There's no coming back from this. This pall will hang over everything. And now I've spilled my cup! How could you all do this to me?" Ix heard a sniffling, and then the snap of the umbrella opening as Misery chose to wail alone under her rain cloud.

"And what about you, Chaos?" Terror's voice was sly. "Not going to join the hunt? Or maybe you're hiding something."

"No more than usual." Ix could just imagine the giant grin stretched across the cat's face.

"You know, I saw that human once before in my own domain, when it foolishly threw itself in front of me," Terror said. "I never forget a face. Or a scent. Better hurry, Chaos—wouldn't want to be caught. Wrath has never known an ounce of mercy, and Greed does so hate being denied anything."

Ix couldn't believe it. Terror knew she was there—and was letting her go anyway.

Smiles's body rippled with laughter as he stood. "A truly *ter-*

rifying threat," the Grinning Cat purred. "I'll be sure to keep it in mind."

Then Smiles took off, bounding down the hill and through Death's domain. The giant cat was so fast, Ix could barely hold on to his slippery fur. They passed groups of Nightmares drinking and laughing and partying, and clusters of Wrath's and Greed's creatures, calling to each other as they searched for Ix. Only when the noise died down and the purple flames grew far apart did Smiles finally slow, letting her slip off.

They had stopped at the mouth of a narrow passage. Ix's legs were still rubbery, and she wasn't sure her heart would ever stop pounding. But at least she could breathe again.

"Thank you," she said, looking up into the unblinking amethyst eyes of the cat. "You saved me."

"A debt I fully intend to collect on one day," Smiles promised with a crooked grin. "But you're not out of danger yet. They won't stop hunting you." He nodded at the passageway ahead, shrouded in darkness and lit by a single wavering purple flame. "When trying to escape, I always suggest the path less traveled."

Even as he said it, Ix heard the hooves of a pack of Fiends drawing closer. She wouldn't be safe until she was out of the Labyrinth.

"Won't they suspect you?" she asked, worried. "Or Terror could give you up."

The cat snickered through his teeth. "Terror's no tattletale. And the others aren't going to suspect me, either, because I have a plan. A devious one, of course."

"What is it?" Ix asked.

"This." The Grinning Cat inched away and then threw his head back, shouting, "I've spotted it—the human is over here! Come quickly, it's *running away!*" He looked meaningfully at Ix as he said the last.

She took the hint, turning and racing as fast as she could down the passage. She heard clopping hooves and a great shout, but when she reached the end of the corridor, she realized that the darkness was actually a fissure in the wall, leading back to the Labyrinth. Chaos had at least brought her to the exit before playing his little games.

Ix's boots slapped against the stones as she threw herself into the crack. The mist was so thick on the other side, Ix couldn't tell what part of the Labyrinth she had come out into. Even stranger, there seemed to already be a tear into the Waking World right in front of her.

It was too late to stop. Ix plunged into the gap. The cold mist tingled against her skin, and then she was tumbling out through an archway of hawthorn branches into a patch of silver plants that swayed beneath the moonlight.

"Ix!" said a surprised voice. It was Healer Mella. The woman hastily dropped a handful of dark plants, rushing toward her. "How did you wind up here?"

Ix looked around, gasping to catch her breath. She was in the silverweed patch right outside Covenant Keep. She was home.

Relief and exhaustion crashed over Ix. Mella barely caught her before she fell. The healer knelt carefully, lowering Ix into the silverweed and pressing a hand to her forehead. "Are you all right? You're terribly clammy."

"Tell them," Ix said, grabbing Mella's coat. The Silverweave patch under her fingers felt unbearably cold. Or maybe that was just Ix, who'd been running through Death's domain without even the Shroud to protect her. "Tell them Death is missing from the Labyrinth. And that Jack is from our side. He's human."

The last thing Ix saw before she lost consciousness was Healer Mella's wide, horrified eyes.

35

THE SEVENTH SLEEPER

The next time Ix woke, she was tucked into one of the beds in the infirmary. Healer Mella pressed a warm compress to her forehead, tutting about how the council had no idea what effects Death's realm might have on a child and how irresponsible they'd been to send her in the first place. Ix felt fine, but Mella insisted on keeping her for a few days, just in case.

As soon as Mella allowed visitors, the infirmary was flooded with council members and captains wanting to hear her account of the Sorrows. Ix told her story again and again, though she left out the part about being saved by Chaos. She didn't think being friends with a Sorrow would win her any points.

"Is it enough?" Ix had asked fearfully as she faced the councillors from her bed. "You won't purge the Nightmares? And Morrigan and I . . . we get to stay?"

Fallon Winters looked highly displeased. But Alexis Moongrave laid a hand on Ix's head. "More than enough. You've given the council a great deal to reflect upon—including our own conduct." She shot a pointed look at Penelope Wystorm and Argus Winters as she ushered them out.

The only person who didn't come to see her was Captain Kel. Ix had expected him to be the first one through the infirmary doors when she woke up. When she asked Morrigan about him, the girl got suddenly quiet, hunching in her chair next to Ix's bed.

"I thought you knew. Captain Kel disappeared—on All Hallows' Eve. He never came back after taking you into the Labyrinth."

"What?" Ix lurched up in bed.

Morrigan's face crumpled. "Captain Winters says he disappears like this all the time and that he must've taken advantage of All Hallows' Eve to get into the center of the Labyrinth. But he's wrong. Captain Kel never would have abandoned you in there! Something happened—I know it. Professor Swann looks like he hasn't slept in days."

Morrigan was right. When Professor Swann dropped by the infirmary later, Ix could see the dark circles under his eyes, and his smile was thin and drawn. He told Ix not to worry, that Captain Kel would be fine, but he was clearly distracted, absently peeling a grape from the fruit basket he'd brought.

Ollie tried to cheer her up with stories of everything she'd missed on All Hallows' Eve. He also smuggled Hanky in to visit, hiding the Inkling in his pocket whenever Healer Mella checked on them.

"It was epic!" Ollie gushed. "Vice-Captain Torrent was in charge of the Big Scare this year, and she roped Tempest into helping. At fifteen minutes to midnight, all the lights went out, and then bats suddenly swooped in from everywhere and sticky spiders rained down from the ceiling."

"They weren't real," Morrigan interjected. "Tempest rigged a bunch of paper bats and jelly spiders so they'd fall during the blackout."

"But they felt real," Ollie said, shuddering. "Everyone was

screaming and running. Then Torrent appeared in a black robe, with a real scythe and everything. People got so scared they started bailing out the windows. Valerie's cousin Emory even ran smack into Captain Rozthorn—you know, the captain who screams like a Banshee. Well, she let out such a bloodcurdling shriek, Captain Calloway thought a *real* Banshee had gotten in, and he burst into the hall with his Shadow Render blazing!"

"You forgot the best part," Morrigan said. "Cole was one of the students who jumped out the window, and he pushed Darien right into the pie and pumpkin punch. You should have seen him sopping wet and covered in whipped cream!"

Ix couldn't help laughing, picturing Darien Winters's haughty face smeared with gobs of dessert.

"Next year, we'll go together," Morrigan promised.

Ix smiled, feeling warm. "Definitely."

"Speaking of next year," Ollie piped in, "I brought your homework so you won't get behind."

Ix groaned. But she didn't really mind. Not when they stayed with her, laughing and talking, until Healer Mella shooed them out, saying it was getting late.

Ix shifted against her pillows, antsy. "Can't I go back to my room yet? I feel fine."

Mella shook her head, folding her patched coat over her arm. "Maybe tomorrow. You know I'm just trying to look out for you, don't you?"

"I guess," Ix said, resigned. Then she swallowed.

Healer Mella was also the one taking care of the crystallized bodies in the catacombs. Ever since Ix had heard what Death's absence was doing to souls in the Labyrinth, she'd wondered about her father—and whether he really was trapped somewhere.

"The people in the Crystal Sleep . . . have you made any progress figuring out how to wake them up?"

Mella sighed. "I wish I had better news. But the only way to wake someone in the Crystal Sleep is to return their soul. Without that . . ."

Ix fisted her hands into the blanket. "So if I can't find my father's soul, it's hopeless."

"It's never hopeless," Mella said softly. "There's always a chance those we love will come back to us. Don't give up, Ix. I never have."

Her expression was very kind and very sad. Ix wondered if she was thinking of her brother, the one who'd gone missing. She wanted to say something, but she hadn't figured out what before Healer Mella bade her good night and blew out the lamp.

Ix tossed and turned in the narrow bed. She hated these nights alone in the infirmary. During the day, she could keep her dark thoughts at bay, but as soon as she lay down at night, the worries crept back in.

Especially about Captain Kel. Ix didn't think he would have abandoned her while she was doing something so dangerous. But she couldn't quite forget what Aunt Tara had told her, either.

It's very easy for those obsessed with the Labyrinth to lose themselves to it.

Lying alone in the row of beds, Ix couldn't help but imagine her father down in the silent catacombs. She wished she could see him, just for a minute.

A tiny sound broke Ix from her thoughts—the soft squeak of the door opening. Ix pushed up on her elbows to see Morrigan sneaking into the infirmary.

"What are you doing here?" she hissed.

"I could hear your lonely sighs from all the way upstairs." Morrigan had that telltale blush that meant she was doing something nice but was embarrassed about it.

Ix smiled. "Thanks. It gets way too quiet here."

Morrigan plopped onto the end of the bed and poked Ix in the toes. "Says the person who's always complaining about me banging drawers and throwing things too early in the morning."

"I take it back. I miss the sound of you throwing things most of all."

Morrigan snorted. "I don't think Healer Mella would really appreciate me making a mess in here."

Ix laughed. But it was a strange laugh that caught in her throat.

Morrigan seemed to notice. "What's wrong?"

Ix hesitated. "It's silly," she admitted. "But I really wish I could go see my father. I mean, I know he won't wake up or anything. But I miss him."

"So let's go," Morrigan said, sliding off the end of the bed. "He's in the keep, right?"

"Yes . . ." Ix tugged at her sleeves. "But I've never gone without Captain Kel before. I'm not sure it's allowed."

"Well, you know what Tempest says about things that aren't allowed," Morrigan said. "It only matters if you get caught. And who's going to see us in the middle of the night? Come on."

Morrigan tugged on Ix's pajama sleeve until she slid out of bed.

"Just let me put my boots on," Ix said, balancing on one foot and then the other while she yanked on her striped socks. She'd had enough of running around the keep barefoot.

Together, they crept out of the infirmary. Morrigan swiped a tall candle from an alcove and then followed Ix toward the inner keep. They had to check several velvet curtains before they found the stairs spiraling down into the dark.

"This is it," Ix whispered when they finally reached the heavy stone door beyond the catacombs.

It took both of them to pry it open, the hinges squeaking and protesting. They shut it firmly behind them. Morrigan set aside the candle, looking around.

Ix leaned close to her father and pressed her hand over his. "I know you're not really here," she whispered. "But somehow, I get the feeling you would know what's happening—with  the Labyrinth, and Jack, and all of it. Just this once, I wish you could answer me." But of course, there was only silence.

Morrigan cleared her throat uncomfortably. "I'm sorry, you know. For being so mean to you when we first became roommates."

Ix didn't think she'd ever heard Morrigan apologize for anything. "It's okay," she said, smiling. "I was pretty nosy at the beginning, too. Besides, now I know that's just how you talk. Harsh, and a little too honest."

"Hey," Morrigan grumbled. But there wasn't any bite to it.

Ix rose and wandered through the slabs, studying the other crystal figures. "You've lived at the keep a long time, right? Do you know who the rest of these people are?"

"Not all of them. But that's Vice-Captain Crenesta," Morrigan said, pointing to a woman in a Candle Corps uniform. "She was found crystallized right here at Covenant Keep. Everybody was really scared after that."

Morrigan bent down to look at the vice-captain. "Do you think what Ollie said could be true? That someone forced the souls out of these bodies? Maybe these people's souls aren't lost but tethered to something that's keeping them trapped."

"I've been wondering about that, too." Ix hesitated. "There's something I overheard from the Sorrows that keeps bothering me. They said Jack was not a creature of the Labyrinth, which means he was created by a human."

"Creepy." Morrigan shuddered.

"I always thought whatever happened to my father, surely a Nightmare had done it, but what if it wasn't? If a person could make Jack, maybe they could do this, too." Ix swept her hand out toward all the sleeping bodies. "They'd have to have immense power and knowledge, though. Which means . . ."

"It could be someone here at Candle Corps," Morrigan finished, looking stricken.

They fell silent.

Morrigan wrapped her arms around herself. "I *really* wish we could talk to Captain Kel."

"Me too," Ix agreed.

They were interrupted by a sound outside—footsteps creaking down the rickety stairs. Ix and Morrigan shared a panicked look.

The only people who knew about this place were the councillors and the captains. If they were found here, they were going to be in big trouble. Again.

"What do we do?" Morrigan hissed. The footsteps were right on the other side of the door.

"Hide," Ix said desperately. "In the back."

At the last second, Ix remembered to grab Morrigan's candle. They scurried to the corner, slipping into the narrow gap between the farthest slab and the back wall of the chamber.

The hinges creaked as the heavy stone hissed open. Ix and Morrigan scooted back until they hit the wall. And then suddenly they were both falling backward for real, as a small trapdoor swung inward behind them, dumping them into a pitch-black room.

Ix swallowed down her yelp and righted herself before she set Morrigan's hair on fire with the candle. Morrigan scrambled to push the trapdoor closed before whoever had entered the tomb noticed it.

"Could you see who it was?" Ix whispered as they sat side by side in the dark, listening to the person on the other side of the wall. Ix could hear the click of their footsteps as they walked among the crystal bodies.

"No. But why would a captain or councillor come down here in the middle of the night?"

Ix's guts clenched. She'd been so panicked about being in trouble, she hadn't even stopped to think about why someone would be in the room with the Crystal Sleepers right now.

"And what is this place, anyway?"

Silently, Ix stood up and peered around the hidden chamber, lifting the candle and almost bumping into the low ceiling. There were no windows and no other doors that she could see. It was just big enough for a body . . .

Ix regretted that thought the moment she had it. Especially

because she'd spotted another slab, like the one her father was laid out on. On top of it was a body. A *seventh* body, hidden away back here.

"Come on. Let's get a closer look," Morrigan whispered bravely.

Ix forced herself to nod. But she was glad Morrigan grabbed her hand as they crept toward the figure.

It was a young man encased in crystal. But unlike the figures in the other room, this crystal had started cracking and breaking. A huge dark fissure cut into the stone right over the man's heart, and fat chunks of crystal lay all around him on the floor. Ix accidentally kicked one with her boot, and then felt a little sick.

Morrigan's face was horrified. "It looks like someone's been trying to hold him together."

She was right. Here and there, the cracks were filled with a sticky resin that looked like dried glue. Glittering strings were tied around the biggest chunks, binding them together with ugly knots.

Ix didn't think a soul could return to a body like this anymore.

"I wonder who it is," Morrigan said.

Ix held the candle close over the face and then gasped. The candle fell out of her hand. The metal candlestick clanged against the floor, and the flame went out as it rolled in the dust.

"Ix, what is it?" Morrigan asked, fearful.

Before Ix could answer her, the footsteps thumped closer— headed right for the secret chamber. Whoever was out there couldn't catch them, especially not with what Ix had just seen.

"We have to get out of here," she told Morrigan.

"Why? What's going on?" Morrigan gave up trying to find the candle and grabbed Ix's arms.

"It's Jack," Ix said, holding on to Morrigan tightly. "The body that's encased in the crystal, falling apart. It's Jack." This was the face she'd seen under the scarecrow's mask. She'd never forget it.

"What's Jack's body doing here?" Morrigan hissed.

Ix didn't know. But she had no time to guess. A thin line of light had appeared in the wall. Someone was sliding the trapdoor open. Ix had to get them out of here—the only way she knew how.

"Hold on tight, Morrigan," she whispered. Then she closed her eyes and slipped into the Labyrinth.

36

THE THING IN THE BASEMENT

Ix had never tried to bring anybody with her into the Labyrinth before. She could tell immediately that something was wrong. The prickle of mist on her skin was sharp and biting, and instead of the darkness embracing Ix, it felt almost like it was fighting her.

No, not her. Morrigan.

Something was tugging at Morrigan, trying to separate them. Ix held on tighter. One blink, she was surrounded by mist. With the next, she could see the hazy high walls of Terror's domain wavering around her, and then she and Morrigan were falling back into the Waking World. For one awful second, Ix thought they would be yanked back into the secret chamber and caught by whoever had been sneaking around.

But there was an even stronger pull. The red door, and the whisper behind it.

Ix stumbled on the stone floor that suddenly appeared under her feet. She let go of Morrigan, who bent over, grabbing her stomach like she was going to be sick.

"What did you do?" Morrigan asked her, coughing.

"I don't know," Ix said. "I was trying to slip into the Labyrinth, but something went wrong, and we ended up . . . here."

"Where is here?" Morrigan asked, looking around.

The room they'd appeared in was cold, and its stone walls were rough, as if the chamber had been carved right into the earth. Thin, sickly Dreamlight flames burned on the wall, all of them guttering like they might go out. Ix backed up, and something shivered against the back of her neck. It was a great silver web, stretching all the way from the ceiling to the floor.

"Does that mean there's a giant spider down here?" Ix breathed.

"That's not a spiderweb," Morrigan hissed, her jaw tight. "It's arach-needlework—Silverweave. Candle Corps only puts up nets like this to hold back the most powerful and dangerous Nightmares."

Ix swallowed. "We must be under the keep. Behind the red door."

The place Captain Kel had told her never to go. *Ever.*

"And we're locked in," Morrigan confirmed, rattling the knob on the only door. "We might be able to break it with our Shadow Renders, but not without setting off all the alarms."

Suddenly there was a voice, as cold and quivering as a curl of mist. "At last. You're here. I've been waiting so long . . . so long alone in the dark."

Ix whirled around. That was the same voice she'd heard in the hallway.

"You heard that, right, Morrigan?"

Morrigan nodded tightly as something dragged itself out of the shadows behind the web. It looked like a slab of pure nightmare, ghoulishly white in some places and dark and leathery in others. Its round, featureless head sat on a misshapen body like a great lumpy sack, with two long arms dangling to the floor. Its entire body was covered in strange stitch marks, as though it had been taken apart and sewn haphazardly back together.

The creature galumphed to the very edge of the spiderweb and lifted a hand over its face. "Come closer," it whispered. "Let me get a look at you."

On the back of the hand was a ragged tear, crisscrossed with stitches that reminded Ix of Jack's jagged smile. There was a mouth pressed against those stitches—that's what the creature was speaking through. Ix could see its lips quivering against the thread. The creature lifted its other hand, pressing it over the side of its face. An eye blinked out of the tear, fixing on Ix.

Ix shuddered. It was like the whole body was some awful outfit the creature was sewn into. It peered out at them through the rips in its hands.

"What is that?" Ix whispered, backing into Morrigan.

Morrigan shook her head. "I think it's a Memory Eater. But I've never seen one . . . like that."

The bulbous body reminded Ix a little of the larvae they'd handled in class. But something about it looked wrong.

"We should get out of here," Morrigan whispered.

"Don't go," the Memory Eater hissed, its tongue licking the edge of the stitches. "Don't you want to know the truth?"

The truth. That's what Smiles had said was behind this door. Ix couldn't leave, not yet. She shook off Morrigan's hand, standing before the creature.

"What truth? Why have you been whispering to me?"

"Because you're the only one who can hear. And of course you can. Closer. Closer," the Memory Eater begged, and Ix obeyed, until she was right in front of the web. The creature's wide eye rolled, looking her up and down. "You're the one. You must be."

Ix fisted her hands in frustration. "You keep saying you've been waiting for me, that I'm the one, but what does that mean? What do you want from me?"

The Nightmare tipped its head, as though confused by the question. "We're kindred, you and I . . ." it hissed. "Can't you feel it in your bones? You're not like them. You're like me."

Ix shuddered. Because she *could* feel something when she looked at the creature. Like there was a connection, a bond between them. Despite how horrifying it seemed, there was something *familiar* about the monster in front of her—a pull that reminded her of how it felt to step into the Labyrinth. A feeling like coming home.

Ix's guts twisted. She felt suddenly sick, every thought she'd had about being a Nightmare or something worse staring her in the face.

She only realized how close she'd gotten to the web when Morrigan hauled her back. Just in time.

"It's a Nightmare—don't believe anything it says!" Morrigan warned.

The creature had lifted its arm. Now the part of it stretching against the rip looked almost like a hand—a human hand trapped behind the crisscross of dark threads. A single finger waved in the air, reaching for Ix. The finger withdrew as the creature pressed the rips back over its face.

"I just wanted a little touch. A little skinship," it mourned.

"Back off," Morrigan snapped, though Ix could feel her hand shaking where it was fisted into Ix's nightshirt. Morrigan tugged at her. "You're clearly not thinking straight. I'm getting you out of here."

"No!" Ix and the Nightmare said at the same time.

"There's something I have to know," Ix said. She turned back to the creature. The fingers straining from behind the threads had made her sure of one thing. This wasn't a Memory Eater. "What are you really? I mean, inside there?"

"Inside here," the Nightmare said slowly. "Yes . . . I was something else before I was in this cage."

"You don't remember?" Ix turned to Morrigan. "Do Memory Eaters ever devour their own memories?"

"I don't know," Morrigan admitted. "I've never heard of anything like that. But that thing has been down here a long time. This is the Memory Eater that Captain Kel captured in Mistmorrow ten years ago. Who even knows what's left of it?"

The Memory Eater's eye bulged against the threads. It let out a long, low wail that shook Ix's bones. "Kel . . . Kel . . . yes, he did it. He was the one who did this."

Ix stared in horror. The eye disappeared as the creature threw both hands over its mouth to keen again.

"We're getting out of here!" Morrigan yelled, dragging Ix toward the door. But then the creature said something that froze both of them in their tracks.

"*I remember now.* Someone broke the eighth rule. That's where Jack came from."

Ix gaped. "You know Jack?"

"Jack was mine," the creature hissed. It was just a mouth now, its other hand curled into a fist. "I was about to get him. Someone broke the eighth rule. Someone put me in this . . ."

"What is it? What's the eighth rule?" Morrigan demanded.

But the creature wasn't listening anymore. "I don't belong in here," it wailed, the sound echoing as it grabbed on to the web with both hands. "It was Kel. He locked me in here. Buried the truth. Let me out!"

It couldn't be. It couldn't be saying what Ix thought it was saying. Her mouth went dry as bone. "Are you saying Captain Kel locked you in here . . . or that he's the one who made Jack?"

"Ix!" Morrigan said, horrified.

But the Nightmare just kept screeching. "Let me out! Let me out!" It tore at the web, human fingernails scrabbling from inside the jagged tears.

"I'm not listening to any more of this." Morrigan grabbed Ix by the collar. "You got us in here. Now get us out!"

Morrigan's demand finally shook Ix from her daze. She nodded.

It was impossible to concentrate on finding the darkness behind her eyelids with the Nightmare raging in the prison. So Ix tried something else. She looked into Morrigan's scared eyes and thought about how much she wanted to get out of here, together. She wrapped her arms around Morrigan and buried her face into her shoulder.

"Please," Ix whispered to the darkness. "Anywhere but here."

And then suddenly she and Morrigan were falling, tumbling as though dropped over the side of a cliff. It was even worse than the last time. The bottom dropped out of Ix's stomach as they slid through mist with the angry red tinge of Wrath's domain, and then all at once they were spat out. Rejected.

They splattered into cold mud. Even Ix felt like she was going to throw up this time, coughing and choking. They'd fallen from high enough that her tailbone was definitely bruised. And she had a feeling it could have been much worse.

When she finally got her breath, she looked up at a circle of trees with blood-red leaves. A few midnight mushrooms poked their heads up from the grass, and over the treetops she could see Covenant Keep. They were in the hawthorn forest.

For a moment, they just sat, looking at each other like they couldn't quite believe it.

"I never want to travel that way again," Morrigan wheezed.

"Me neither," Ix agreed, rubbing at her goose bumps. However Ix slipped in and out of the Labyrinth, she clearly wasn't meant to take other people with her.

Morrigan brushed wet, mucky leaves off her sweater. "Come on. If we sneak back in, maybe nobody will catch us."

"What are you talking about?" Ix asked, getting to her feet. "We can't sneak in. We have to tell everybody what that . . . *thing* said."

"No, we don't!" Morrigan hissed. "We don't even know what we heard. It's a Nightmare, Ix—they lie and deceive. That's what they do."

"But if it's right. If someone broke the eighth rule and created Jack . . ."

"They'll blame Captain Kel!" Morrigan said, grabbing Ix's shoulders. "You know about the bad blood between him and Captain Winters. And he isn't even here to defend himself. This is the excuse the Winters have been waiting for. They'll have him stripped of his captaincy. They might even throw him out of Candle Corps. You can't tell anyone what that thing said."

"Morrigan—" Ix started.

"No!" Morrigan swiped a hand over her eyes. "If you cost Captain Kel everything, after all he's done for you—and all he's done for *me*—then we're not friends anymore."

Ix swallowed hard. She wanted to protect Captain Kel. To forget everything she'd heard. But . . .

"Well, well, well. What do we have here?"

A flurry of leaves spiraled down as a figure stepped out from behind a twisted oak tree. Vice-Captain Wystorm stalked toward them, her mouth curved in a vicious smile. "Here I was looking for dangerous Nightmares trying to get into the keep, and instead, I find a pair that got out."

Morrigan growled.

"I can explain," Ix said.

"I can't wait," Vice-Captain Wystorm told her. "Captain Winters will want to hear this, too—and the whole council. You two are coming with me."

THE MISSING CAPTAIN

For the second time, Ix found herself facing the hastily woken council in her pajamas. But this time, she didn't have Captain Kel with her, or Professor Swann to give her a comforting smile. Just Vice-Captain Wystorm, who kept one menacing hand on her shoulder and the other on Morrigan's as she presented them to the Elder Flames.

Ix felt that nervous grin stretching across her face as she told them about the hidden Crystal Sleeper and the Memory Eater in the basement. Fallon Winters looked especially interested.

"And you say it mentioned Captain Kel's name specifically?" he asked, eyes glinting.

Morrigan glared at Ix as though to say: *I told you so!*

"It wasn't like that!" Ix tried to backpedal, to explain it better, but Captain Winters twisted everything she said to make it seem like Captain Kel was guilty.

Vice-Captain Wystorm, who had disappeared halfway through their story, slipped back into the chamber. She bowed sharply to the council and then whispered into Fallon Winters's ear.

"My vice-captain has informed me that they located the secret chamber you spoke of. However, there is no crystallized body inside."

"What?" Ix blurted out. "That's impossible! Someone must have moved it. There really was a body there, and it was definitely Jack."

"And we have only your word for that. Still, it hardly matters." Fallon Winters waved a hand. "Take a squad into the Labyrinth and find Captain Kel. He must be dragged back here and questioned at once."

Vice-Captain Wystorm nodded, her steps crisp and satisfied as she marched out.

"Smelling blood in the water, Fallon?" Tyrese Valerian asked, unimpressed.

Fallon scoffed. "Just doing what's necessary. What none of you have been willing to do all this time. Captain Kel defies the will of the council. He enters the Labyrinth for his own ends. And now, he may even be implicated in breaking the eighth rule." Ix flinched. "His obsession with the Labyrinth has finally gotten the better of him. Surely you can all see that."

There was a discouraging murmur among the councillors.

"But could it really be true? That the eighth rule was broken?" Elder Ito's face was drawn, her eyes very serious.

"The council will get to the bottom of this," Alexis Moongrave said, before turning to Ix and Morrigan. "But you have been breaking rules again, young Novices. And there must be consequences."

Ix braced herself for the worst.

In the end, they weren't expelled. But Ix had been told this was her last warning. One more infraction, and she was out—for good. No more chances. And not one single toe out of line.

When they left the council chamber, Instructor Cadence was waiting for them. And she was livid.

"It's mop duty for the both of you," she fumed, marching Ix and Morrigan back to their room. "I will see you back in the front hall at five o'clock tomorrow."

"That's only three hours from now," Ix protested.

"Keep complaining, and I'll have you clean the entire keep," Cadence warned. "I've never had a pair of Novices so determined to get themselves killed!"

Ix's mouth snapped shut.

Morrigan trudged ahead, her muddy boots swinging in her hand. She glared at Ix over her shoulder. "Traitor," she whispered under her breath.

It stung, a lot. Worse than *Ick*, and *Snot*, and *Fluke*, and everything else Arthur and Darien had ever called her.

When they reached their room, Morrigan flopped into bed, wrapping her arms around her stomach and turning pointedly away. It reminded Ix of their very first night together, when Morrigan hadn't liked her at all. She wanted to apologize, to make it all go away, but she didn't know how.

Instructor Cadence looked tired and irritated the next morning, and a little like she regretted assigning them a punishment that required being up before the sun. She handed them each a bucket and a mop and gestured to the giant front hall.

"I'll be back in one hour. I want to see this floor sparkling."

They started from opposite ends. Morrigan mopped furiously, and she kept splashing Ix with the dirty wash water, which Ix didn't think was an accident. Ix scowled. Smiles was right—nobody liked mopping.

A snicker of laughter floated down to them. Ix looked up to see Darien Winters at the top of the stairs, with Cole and a clump of other students gawking at them.

"Finally a job that suits you monsters," he called. "Oops, you missed a spot." He spat, the gob of saliva landing just behind Ix.

"Gross," Valerie said. She glared at Ix and Morrigan. "I don't know what you did this time, but can you try not to bring our *whole* Novice year down with you? Some of us still have futures at Candle Corps."

Ix hunched over her mop. She'd thought she was beyond caring what other people thought about her. But it was different with Morrigan angry and silent at her back. Ix hadn't felt this horrible in a long time. Darien threw unhelpful suggestions and wads of paper at them until Cadence reappeared to shoo him away.

The day did not improve from there. Everyone had heard that Morrigan and Ix were in trouble again. Andre inched his desk away from hers, and even Beatrix wouldn't meet her eyes.

Professor Swann looked utterly wrung out. He fumbled a textbook when an Inkling popped out at him. The wrinkled old book hit the floor with a splat.

"I heard he was up all night being questioned by the council," Darien hissed gleefully.

Nora gasped. "Does that mean it's true? What people are saying about Captain Kel?"

Ix sank into her desk, wishing a great big Wallow Worm would rise out of the floor and swallow her.

Professor Swann kept glancing over at her, like he was trying to signal her to stay after class. She made a beeline for the door the moment the bells rang.

"Ix—Ix, a moment, please—"

Ix ducked out, pretending she couldn't hear him.

"Can't face him after you stabbed his husband in the back?" Morrigan asked, shoulder-checking Ix in the hall.

"I didn't want this to happen!" Ix hissed. But Morrigan was already stomping away.

"What was that about?" Ollie asked, running up to her. "I was picking herbs with Mella this morning, but I heard that you two were dragged before the council? And had to mop the whole keep?"

"Not the whole keep," Ix said. "But . . . Ollie, it's bad."

She tugged Ollie down a side hallway, into a crooked old stairwell where they could talk. As soon as they were alone, the entire story poured out of her. It sounded even worse the second time.

"So you see," Ix finished, "I have to find a way to prove Captain Kel is innocent, or Morrigan will never forgive me. And probably Professor Swann and everyone else, too."

"I might have an idea," Ollie said, twisting his fingers like he did when he was nervous. "You said you got out of the keep unseen once—the night you saw that suspicious figure in the silverweed, right? Do you think you could do it again?"

"Probably," Ix said. The Devious Doorway still liked to play pranks on her, like sending her into the occasional musty wardrobe. But they were kind of friends now.

"Okay." Ollie breathed deep, like he was gathering his courage. "Meet me after lights-out in the Gargoyle Courtyard."

Ix blinked. "Why all the way out there?"

Ollie smiled mysteriously. "We're going to need a secret weapon."

Ix had worried how she would avoid Morrigan all evening. But Morrigan never came back. All Ix found in their shared room was an angry line redrawn down the middle of the floor, and Hanky, wrapping its silky little body around the broken piece of chalk.

Ix cradled the distressed Inkling in her palms. "She'll come back," she promised. "At least, I hope she will."

Ollie wasn't at dinner, either. For the first time in a long time, Ix ate by herself in the corner. It was lonelier than she remembered.

The bells were tolling midnight when Ix finally crept out of the arched doorway into the Gargoyle Courtyard. Hanky had tagged along, hanging from the bib of her overalls—the Inkling's very favorite spot.

"Ollie," Ix whispered as she walked through the snarling statues, whose eyes seemed to follow her in the dark. "Ollie, are you there?"

"Over here." Ollie poked his curly head out from behind a beaky statue, waving Ix over. "But be careful, I've got . . ."

"Bella!" Ix yelped in surprise as the bulldog jumped up, licking at Hanky. The Inkling scurried up Ix's pigtail to escape. "Why do you have Captain Rossi's dog?"

"She's our secret weapon: a Dreamchaser. As for how . . ." Ollie blushed. "Captain Rossi's away from the keep this weekend. Since Bella likes me, he's been letting me take her for walks."

"So you stole Bella," Ix said, excited.

"Borrowed!" Ollie insisted, tugging on the dog's leash. "And we should really get out of here."

Ix knocked on the nearest door. A second later, an identical door wavered onto the wall beside it. The Devious Doorway clacked its grinning teeth together in a greeting.

Bella stared at the Nightmare. Her tail started thumping against the ground, and she tipped her head back.

"Is she about to . . ."

"Howl—yes!" Ollie confirmed. "Go!"

They hustled through the doorway just as Bella let out a gruff, rowdy howl. Ix could only hope if anyone heard it and came running, they'd suspect one of the stone gargoyles of getting up to some mischief.

They tumbled into the cold night air in a heap. Ix thanked the Devious Doorway, which vanished with a cheerful wiggle of its handle as they stood and brushed themselves off.

They were right on the edge of the silverweed field. Ix froze, listening for the *swish* of a sickle, but there was only the breeze whispering through the bushes . . . and Bella, snorting like a Warty Hornswoggle as she snuffled the ground.

"So, what are we doing out here?" Ix asked as the bulldog stuck her nose in a hole—and then sneezed, sending snot and Dust-Puff Beetles flying everywhere. Ix grimaced. "And where does Bella fit in?"

"She's here to help us find the real culprit," Ollie said, giving the Dreamchaser a pet. "I've been thinking about that figure you saw. If they were harvesting silverweed in the middle of the night, maybe that's the person who actually made the Crystal Sleepers—and Jack."

Ix liked the sound of that. If they found the real culprit, the council would have to believe Captain Kel was innocent. There was just one problem.

"I never saw the figure's face," Ix said. "And it's been ages since that night."

Ollie shook his head. "To make really powerful things like soul tethers, you need a lot of silverweed. So whoever it is, they've probably had to come back over and over. Which means Bella might be able to track them." Ollie raised his voice higher as he bent down, ruffing Bella's cheeks. "Do you want to track down a bad guy, Bella? Do you?"

Bella got more excited with every word. A second later, they were headed into the silverweed with the bulldog in the lead. The swaying plants were even higher than before. Ix felt like they were wandering through a corn maze.

"I think I was over here last time." Ix pushed toward the edge, close to the hawthorn forest.

A metal gleam caught her eye. There, sticking out of the dirt where a graveyard of plants had been ripped up by the roots, was the sickle.

"That's it!" Ix whispered.

"Okay, Bella," Ollie said. He lifted the sickle carefully by the blade, offering the handle to the Dreamchaser. "Can you get this scent? The feeling of this person's power?"

Bella's jowly mouth panted as she took a good long sniff. Then she sat back and barked.

"I think she's got it," Ollie said. Then he was almost yanked off his feet as Bella took off running toward the forest. "She's definitely got the scent!" he hollered over his shoulder.

Branches whipped past them as they raced into the dark woods. Hanky bounced around in Ix's pocket as she leapt over brambles and trickles of streams, following the Dreamchaser zigzagging through the trees.

She was panting and wheezing almost as hard as Bella when the dog finally skidded to a halt at the base of a tall, crooked oak. The branches were gnarled, and the whole tree was bent nearly in half, as though it were reaching for them.

Ix glanced around, sharing a look with Ollie.

"There's nothing here—" Ix started to say. Then she shrieked as something surged up from the ground and grabbed her ankle.

38

THE TANGLE VAULT

It was a hand. A skeletal hand had reached up through the dirt and seized her.

Ix shrieked again, kicking at it. But the hand held on, pulling her off her feet and dragging her toward the base of the tree. Ix's fingers raked through the grass as she desperately tried to grab on to something.

"Ix!" Ollie shouted, running for her. Bella was barking and growling, circling Ollie protectively.

"Behind you!" Ix warned.

A pair of hands had popped out of the dirt behind Ollie. They slid toward him like eels in the water, their bony fingers rattling.

Suddenly Ix knew exactly what had grabbed her. These were Skelligrabs—disembodied bony hands that crawled around on their own. The weakest ones liked to tap on children's windows at night and then pretend to be branches when the lights came on. But the stronger ones were known to grab people in dark grave-yards and drag them underground.

Ix's heart pounded out of her chest. It felt impossible to think when she was this scared, but that's what she had to do. Skel-ligrabs were creatures of Terror, so the more frightened you were, the more powerful they became. The key to defeating terror was seeing what was really there and not letting your imagination run off with you.

Ix closed her eyes, ignoring the squelch of grass and mud under her as she fought to calm down. This was just a Nightmare. She could figure this out. She didn't have to be afraid—

Thunk!

The hand stopped dragging Ix as her boots thumped into the base of the tree. Bella had stopped barking, and everything had gotten quiet.

"Ix, is that skeleton hand . . . pointing?"

Ix's eyes sprang open. The Skelligrab that had seized her ankle was still holding on, but another one had sprouted up beside her. And it was definitely pointing, wiggling up and down as it gestured at a spot on the ground.

Ix pushed up on her elbows. "Maybe it's trying to tell us something," she said as Ollie and Bella bounded over.

Ollie knelt down in the dirt. "I think there's something here," he whispered, pulling up a few clumps of grass.

Hanky dropped from Ix's pocket, skittering through the grass and curling around something metal.

"What is that?" Ix asked. She and Ollie brushed the dirt away.

It was a handle. Ix sucked in a startled breath. A trapdoor! There was some kind of hidden chamber under this tree. The Skelligrab let go of Ix's ankle to give the other disembodied hand a victorious high five.

"I don't think those Nightmares were attacking us at all," Ix said. "I think they wanted us to find this."

"Bella, too," Ollie said as the bulldog waddled around the trapdoor and then sat on it with a howl. "She's saying this is where the trail ends."

It took some pushing and a lot of praise to get Bella off the secret hatch. Ix and Ollie grabbed the rusted metal handles together and heaved the trapdoor open. The space beyond was pitch-black, and there didn't seem to be any kind of rope or ladder.

"How do we get down there?" Ix wondered.

The Skelligrab snapped its fingers to get her attention. The skeletal hands had all gathered together, lining up expectantly by the hole and waving them over.

"You're saying you'll . . . give us a hand?" Ix guessed, making Ollie groan at the pun.

The Skelligrab gave her a thumbs-up.

254 LESLIE VEDDER

Ollie went first so he could make a Dreamlight. The Skelligrabs arranged themselves like handholds and footholds, helping them down into the hidden chamber. It felt strange to grab on to bony fingers that grabbed back.

"I can't believe Nightmares are helping us," Ollie whispered.

Ix could believe it. She'd spent her whole life with Nightmares of one kind or another. They'd made her an outcast in Brittlewick and even caused trouble in Covenant Keep. But she'd also come to understand them. Sure, there were some dangerous Nightmares people needed to be protected from. But a lot more Nightmares were misunderstood. And if it weren't against the rules to even talk about them, maybe people could learn to live alongside them just fine.

Ix dropped the last few feet with a soft "Oof!" and Ollie lifted his Dreamlight to the opening above them.

"Bella, you stay there—" he started. But it was too late.

Bella whined and then leapt into the hole like she was doing a belly flop. Skelligrabs shot out of the wall, catching the pudgy bulldog and slowly lowering her to the floor.

". . . Or you can come with us, I guess," Ollie finished, as Bella slobbered all over his pants.

The Skelligrabs skittered by their feet as they looked around. Even Hanky climbed out of Ix's pocket, curious.

They were in a small, cramped hollow, not much bigger than the storerooms at Covenant Keep. Stones paved the floor and climbed halfway up the wall, but the rest was dirt, giving off a thick, musty smell. Giant twisted roots plunged through the ceiling, coiling around the room like they were strangling the whole chamber.

"I think this is a Tangle Vault," Ollie said, tracing one of the roots with awe. "When Candle Corps was just starting out, before they had Dreamlight seals, they kept dangerous things in vaults buried underground, where any dangerous Nightmare energy would be absorbed into the roots of a tree."

Ix shivered, thinking about the ghastly, gnarled tree above them. "Sounds like a perfect villain hideout to me. Let's see what we can find."

Ollie nodded, holding his Dreamlight high as they spread out. On one side of the room stood a set of bookshelves filled with pewter cauldrons and burnished copper teakettles and all manner of gleaming vials. On the other side sat a towering apothecary cabinet, with drawers that got smaller and smaller as they went up.

"There are probably herbs and potions in there," Ollie said. "I'll see if I can recognize anything." A couple of Skelligrabs followed him, offering him a boost to reach the highest drawers.

Bella seemed to have made up with the Nightmares. She had flopped on her back, her back leg kicking in delight as a few rattly hands tickled her belly and tossed Hanky playfully between them.

Ix bent down to look at the books on the sagging bottom shelf. A couple looked like old medical texts, with creepy drawings of people's insides. Others were wrapped in chains, like the forbidden tomes she'd seen on the shelf behind the librarian's desk. One was called *The Ancient Origins of Soul Tethering*, and another, *The Undead of the Labyrinth*.

Ix showed Ollie what she'd found.

"Someone could definitely figure out how to tether souls with these," Ollie agreed, running his finger down a red book bristling with bookmarks. "And I found a lot of silverweed and other powerful Labyrinth plants in the apothecary drawers. But . . ."

Ix nodded, miserable. "There's no sign of who's been doing all this. If we show this to the council, Fallon Winters will just say it's more evidence against Captain Kel."

"I'm sorry, Ix." Ollie gave her a hopeful smile. "Maybe Bella can pick up another scent trail in the forest."

The Skelligrabs helped Ix and Ollie climb back out of the Tangle Vault and then hoisted Bella up after them, heave-ho-ing the heavy dog between them.

"Thanks," Ix whispered, pinkie-shaking with one of the Skelligrabs before they left.

Bella took them on a rambling path through the midnight forest. In the end, the Dreamchaser only led them back to the keep, to a door on the other side of the very same silverweed field. A couple of knocks later, the Devious Doorway dropped them back in the Gargoyle Courtyard.

"We're right back where we started," Ix groaned, frustrated. "The real culprit *has* to be someone at Candle Corps, but we have no idea who. And we have nothing to help Captain Kel."

Ollie was quiet. Ix wasn't even sure he was listening. In fact, he'd been distracted all the way back to the keep, fiddling with something in his pocket.

"Do you think someone could ever have a good reason to capture a soul?" he asked softly. "Like, if they thought they were helping someone?"

Ix's stomach swooped. "Ollie, what are you talking about?"

"I'm not sure yet." When Ollie finally looked up, his expression was the most serious Ix had ever seen it. "There's something I have to check. Someone I need to talk to."

"I'll go with you," she said.

Ollie shook his head. "No. I need to do this alone. Please— trust me."

"Okay," Ix said, though she had a bad feeling about it.

"I'll tell you everything tomorrow," Ollie said. "Meet me at breakfast—and bring Morrigan."

Worry squirmed around in Ix's guts. "Tomorrow, you promise?"

"I promise. And in the meantime, hold on to this for me." Ollie pushed something into Ix's hand. It was just a black square of cloth, but it had a strange shimmer.

"Is it Silverweave?" Ix asked, holding it up to the moonlight.

"It's not Silverweave," Ollie said. "Or at least, not entirely. Look, I've got to get Bella back. Just—be careful, Ix."

"You too," Ix whispered, but the bulldog had already pulled Ollie away.

Ix stared at the strange piece of cloth in her hand. There was something familiar about it, as though she'd seen it somewhere before, but she couldn't place it. Still, it was important to Ollie, and Ix knew she was prone to losing things. So the second she snuck back into her room, she tucked it into the pocket of her Candle Corps coat for safekeeping.

Ix couldn't shake her worry as she fell asleep that night, and the bad feeling only increased the next morning. Ollie had said breakfast—but no matter how long she waited, he never came to the cafeteria. His room was empty, and his roommate, Andre, had no idea where he'd gone.

Guts churning, Ix walked the whole length of the dining hall again. Morrigan glared as Ix approached her table.

"There's no seat for you here," she growled, kicking her boots up on the second chair.

"I'm looking for Ollie," Ix insisted.

"Why, do you want to stab him in the back, too?" Morrigan asked, driving her fork viciously into a slice of zucchini cake.

"No," Ix snapped, losing her temper. She was suddenly very tired of Morrigan putting all the blame on her when this hadn't been her fault. "Ollie was supposed to meet me here—both of us actually! And he might be missing, but you don't care about that, because you're the high-and-mighty Morrigan Bea who doesn't care about anyone but herself!"

Morrigan sprang to her feet, her hair crackling with red sparks. She'd just lunged for Ix when Tempest appeared, seizing each of them under an arm.

"Very lively Novices this year," he called cheerfully in a loud voice. More quietly, he added, "I'm pretty sure I know what this is about. And believe me, you don't want to do this in the dining hall in front of everybody."

Belatedly, Ix realized every table was staring at them. Whispers flew through the cafeteria.

Tempest dragged them out into the hall before he let them go. Morrigan tugged at her wrinkled shirt, glaring at Ix.

"You know what she did—"

"I know what the council did," Tempest cut her off. "And more importantly, I know Captain Kel wouldn't want you fighting like this. You're friends, remember?"

"*Friends*," Morrigan huffed.

"None of that matters right now!" Ix broke in. "Ollie is missing!"

She dropped her voice. "We were out last night looking for some-thing to prove Captain Kel innocent." She paused to give Morrigan a significant glare. "But Ollie said there was something he needed to look into. He was supposed to meet me this morning, and now I can't find him."

"Have you checked everywhere?" Tempest asked, worried. "His room, common areas . . . how about the infirmary?"

Ix shook her head. "I'll ask if Healer Mella's seen him."

Morrigan glared. "I'm going, too, because unlike you, Ollie *is* still my friend."

Tempest sighed. "And I'm going, too, because I'm afraid of what you'll do to each other if you're left alone."

As soon as they reached the infirmary, Ix could tell something was wrong. There was a crowd of people gathered at the door, and the woman holding them back was Captain Rozthorn.

Ix and Morrigan pushed their way to the front. Captain Roz-thorn caught them before they could enter. Then a soft, sniffling voice spoke up.

"Let them in, Roz." It was Healer Mella. Her eyes were red and puffy from crying. "I'm so sorry. I couldn't stop him," she said into her handkerchief.

There were more people in the room, Captain Ito and Instruc-tor Cadence, all looking grave. Even Fallon Winters had lost his sinister smile. When they moved aside, Ix saw why.

On the infirmary bed lay a small crystallized figure.

"Ollie!" Morrigan gasped.

Ix's stomach wrenched.

Unlike her father and the others, Ollie didn't look peacefully asleep. His hand was thrown out in front of him, as if in surprise. One look at him, and Ix was sure. Ollie's soul hadn't just slipped away. It had been stolen.

This was all her fault. She should have gone with him. He never should have been alone.

"What happened?" Tempest asked.

"It was Captain Kel," Mella said, her voice quivering. "He took Oliver's soul—I don't know how—and then disappeared through a Door to Nowhere. I should have followed him, but I was so worried about Oliver . . ."

Ix felt like she'd been plunged into one of Terror's icy wells. *Captain Kel took Ollie's soul?* She tried to imagine that, but she just couldn't.

"There, there, Allison," Captain Winters said, patting her hand. "This isn't your fault. Captain Kel should have been dismissed years ago. He's never been the same since the unfortunate incident with Vice-Captain Bea."

"Fallon," Captain Ito snapped, glancing at Morrigan.

But Morrigan didn't seem to have heard. She had fallen to her knees, devastated. "This isn't possible! It isn't!"

"I saw him myself," Healer Mella told her.

Morrigan shook her head as though she could make the whole scene disappear. "He wouldn't do that. Never," she whispered, eyes brimming with tears. Then she sprang to her feet and ran, pushing her way through the gawkers in the hall.

"I'd better go after her," Tempest said. He squeezed Ix's arm. "Can you get back to your room okay?"

"Sure," Ix said. She wanted to be alone anyway. She'd been wrong—about everything. And now Ollie was paying for it.

39

THE MEMORY EATER

H̶ours later, Ix pressed her ear to her bedroom door, listening to Instructor Cadence's sharp footsteps echoing up and down the hall as she patrolled the South Wing.

All the students had been confined to the dorms for their own safety. Only Morrigan hadn't come back. Ix wondered if she was still up in the bell tower. Ix had tiptoed up the belfry stairs to talk to her. But listening to Morrigan sob, she hadn't been able to go up. Instead she hunched into her coat, clutching Hanky close while the Inkling vibrated in her hands like a comforting purr. In the end, she left without saying a word.

After all, what could she possibly say? Ix wanted to cry herself every time she thought about Ollie frozen in crystal.

She'd spent all afternoon pacing and thinking in her room, but the more she thought, the less sense it all made. Maybe she could imagine Captain Kel hiding that crystallized body in the secret chamber—maybe even breaking the eighth rule, if he had a really good reason. But no matter how hard she tried, she couldn't imagine him ever doing anything to hurt Ollie.

Instructor Cadence's footsteps disappeared as she finished her rounds. Ix scrambled into the closet, pushing sweaters aside and slumping down on the shoes. It was always best to enter the

Labyrinth from a seated position, so you didn't fall on your face.

Only one creature knew the truth about Jack. Ix had to go back to the Memory Eater.

She hesitated for one second, imagining Alexis Moongrave's stern face. This was definitely more than one toe out of line. But Ix had to get the truth this time. For Morrigan, who hadn't stopped crying. For Professor Swann, who looked stricken and scared sitting outside the infirmary. And especially for Ollie, whose soul was trapped somewhere, just like her father's. Because if it wasn't Captain Kel, then the real culprit was somewhere in this castle. And only they knew how to bring Ollie back.

"This one's too dangerous for you," Ix whispered to Hanky, tucking the Inkling into one of her boots. Then she closed her eyes and slipped into the Labyrinth.

The mist and darkness swirled around her, welcoming her like an old friend. She stepped out onto the familiar paving stones of Chaos's domain.

Standing before a thick wall of mist, Ix chewed on the end of her thumb. She had never tried to slip through to somewhere specific before. She closed her eyes, remembering the red door and the feeling she'd had when she ended up in the Memory Eater's prison the first time.

Ix poked her head into the mist, only to see the same bedroom she'd just left. She pulled back, disappointed.

Ix concentrated harder on the red door, remembering all the times she had stood before it in her dreams. The next time she parted the veil, she was looking into Covenant Keep's tearoom, which had a pink door and always smelled like strawberries.

"Come on," Ix hissed.

She knew it didn't work to rush. But she couldn't help it. She plunged her hand into the mist again, thinking *red* as hard as she could. Her fingers met something wet and sticky. She'd opened a doorway into Wrath's domain, right into a patch of Bloody Cat-tails. Something growled menacingly, and Ix stumbled back so hard she fell on her butt.

She was met with snickering. "Playing with mist portals is best left to the experts," Smiles said, stretching languidly out on the stones. "Or at least those with sharper claws." He unsheathed his, as though to demonstrate.

"I have to get somewhere," Ix told the Grinning Cat.

"Somewhere?" The giant cat sniffed. "Every portal you open has *somewhere* on the other side."

"I have to get somewhere specific," Ix said, frustrated. "I have to find the red door again. The one that was in my dreams. I have questions . . ."

Smiles chuckled. "You have questions for a door?"

"I have questions for the creature behind the door. The *thing* down in the basement. You said it was the truth, remember?" Ix paused, a thought striking her. "Do you know what it really is?"

"The truth? I wouldn't know it if it was coming from my own mouth." Smiles rested his head on his crossed paws. "But it sounds to me as though your portal problem is one of imagination. You're imagining a door you have no connection with, when you ought to be imagining the creature with whom you do."

Ix's breath caught. "The Memory Eater."

It scared her, to imagine how she was connected to a thing like that. But Smiles was right.

She stood before the mist again. This time when she closed her eyes, it wasn't the red door she pictured, but the creature behind the Silverweave web. Her fingers tingled with the cold of the basement when she slid them through the veil.

"Do say hi to her for me," Smiles said, just as Ix stepped into the mist.

Her? she thought. Then she had to catch herself on the wall as she stumbled into the forbidden chamber on the other side.

The spiderweb prison glistened in the low light. The creature behind it perked up, pressing the jagged holes in its hands over the places where its eyes should be.

It seemed calmer this time. Like it was more itself—or *herself*, if Smiles was to be believed. There were more rips along its sewn-together body, as though it had been tearing at the seams from the inside. Between the stretched threads, Ix caught glimpses of dark hair and tan skin and swishing dark cloth. There was a new rip over its mouth, the threads snarled and knotted at each end.

"I knew you'd come back," the creature whispered. "My memory has been returning to me in bits and pieces. Ever since you reminded me that I'm something else inside here."

Ix licked her lips and tried to ignore the cold fingers walking down her spine.

"I've come for the truth. About Jack."

"*Jack, Jack, Jack*," the creature hissed. "Jack is something that never should have existed. A human soul that's been devouring little bits of Nightmares, feeding on the Labyrinth to stay alive."

Ix thought of all the strange things Jack seemed to be cobbled together from. As if he'd been building himself a body out of odds and ends. "But how? Where did he come from?" she asked.

The Nightmare bent forward. "What happened to Jack and

what happened to me . . . they happened on the same night. Ten years ago, someone entered Death's domain—someone who never should have been there."

It all came back to ten years ago. The creation of Jack. The Nightmares attacking Covenant Keep. Death disappearing from the Labyrinth. And Ix's father losing his soul.

"Was it Captain Kel in the Labyrinth that night?" Ix asked, her throat so tight she thought she'd choke.

Slowly, the creature shook its head. "No. Kel found me later . . . in Mistmorrow."

Ix sagged in relief. Morrigan was right. Kel was innocent. Healer Mella must have been mistaken about what she'd seen. But Ix would have to untangle that later. The creature was still talking.

"He shouldn't have taken me away. I was looking for something. Something very precious to me." The Nightmare let one hand drift into the air, the human fingers stretching through the thread as though trying to grasp some distant memory.

Ix inched closer. "Then who was it? Who made Jack?"

"It's all so fractured." The creature clutched at its head. "My memories . . . this shell is eating at them—eating at them all the time. But I might remember . . . if you let me out."

Its voice turned soft and inviting.

"With your Nightmare power, you could do it. You could break these seals holding me. Then I'll take care of Jack and set everything in the Labyrinth right."

For a moment, Ix was mesmerized by that whisper. She pinched herself before she said something she'd regret. "No. I don't bargain with Nightmares."

The lips behind the stitches curved into a smile. "Someone has taught you the rules. But sometimes they're worth breaking. Your father knew that."

Ix's mouth fell open. "You knew him?"

"Oh yes. He walked the Labyrinth many times." The creature's voice was like silk. It moved forward until they were only inches apart, the silver web shivering between them. "You have his eyes," it whispered. "And his curiosity. He was there that night, too. Looking for something he should have left alone."

Ix had thought she'd come here for the truth about Captain Kel. But maybe this was the real truth she had been searching for all along.

"What happened to him?" Ix asked desperately, gripping the strands of the web. "Please, you have to tell me."

"I could tell you many things." The creature inched forward, its human fingers sliding over hers. "About him. And about what you are. If only you give me your name, *little wishling*."

It was that nickname, *little wishling*, that got her. That was what Aunt Tara had called her when she was young. And what her father had called her, too. Without thinking, she answered.

"Ix Tatterfall."

Ix realized a second too late what she'd done. She'd given a Nightmare her full name. She yanked her hands free, lurching back, but it was too late.

"Tatterfall. Tatterfall. I knew it," the creature crooned, sounding positively gleeful. "Of course it would be you who released me."

"Release you?!" Ix said, feeling sick. "There's no way I'm going to—"

"Ix Tatterfall," the Nightmare said. Its voice echoed like thunder in her head. "Call your Shadow Render. Slice through this seal and *set me free*."

Ix tried to make her mind blank. To tell herself she hadn't heard. To pretend this creature wasn't strong enough to make her obey. But she could feel her will crumbling. *Stay down, stay down*, she begged her hands, fisting them in her overalls to hold them still.

And then something jerked. It was like a hook had caught right into the core of her being and yanked her out of the dark place she'd hidden.

Ix's arms didn't move. Instead, a pair of ghostly hands rose from her side.

Her soul, Ix realized in terror. Her soul was following the Nightmare's orders, pulling itself from Ix's body.

Ix watched, helpless, as the ghost hands called her sickle-shaped Shadow Render. One shimmery foot lunged forward out of Ix's body. She felt like she'd been yanked apart.

"No!" she cried, as her ghost arms slashed the Shadow Render full of Nightmare power into the web. It cut easily, the long strings of Silverweave snapping.

The creature roiled gleefully in its stitched-together sack. "And now these threads. Free me from the awful prison of this Memory Eater."

Ix's brain went fuzzy as she watched a ghostly version of herself—a darkly glimmering Ix soul—step forward, tethered to the real Ix by only the barest connection. It raised the hand sickle, bringing it down over a giant crisscross of threads right in the creature's center. The Shadow Render caught on the thread. And stopped.

"Free me, free me," the Memory Eater chanted, impatient. But no matter how her soul hacked, it couldn't cut through the stitches.

Ix's horror turned to relief. But it only lasted a moment before her soul was thrown back into her body, hitting her like a snapped rubber band.

"Not powerful enough," the creature lamented. "No matter. I'll find something that is. I've been away from the Labyrinth for far too long."

Ix stumbled back against the wall as the Nightmare loomed over her.

"I couldn't have done it without you. You have my eternal gratitude." The creature reached for her, stroking both its Nightmare fingers and its human ones against Ix's cheek.

All Ix's energy seemed to drain out of her as she slumped down the wall. The last thing she felt was cool human fingers against her forehead.

"Sleep, little wishling. The fireflies will come for you. You will be safe here—safe from everything that's about to happen."

Ix struggled to keep her eyes open. She saw the guttering Dreamlight flames and the Memory Eater shuffling away. And then she found herself lost in a memory she didn't recognize.

She was looking up—up at a mobile of little moons and Starlight Spiders. From her crib? A figure was leaning over her. It was her father, Nathan Tatterfall. His face was warm and alive in a way Ix had never seen it, his lips curved in a radiant smile. And soft fingers were brushing her cheek . . . but whose hand was that? And whose voice was crooning in her ears, a soft and lonely lullaby?

She woke to someone shaking her.

"Ix. Ix! Answer me. Are you okay?"

Ix forced her eyes open. Tempest leaned over her, his face grim with worry. Over his shoulder, Captain Ito looked deathly serious.

"What happened?" Ix croaked out.

Tempest's face fell. "The Memory Eater escaped. You set it free. I'm sorry, Ix—it's gone."

40

DEATH BELLS IN THE GARDEN

Ix had ruined everything.

She stood at her bedroom window, clutching her empty bag to her chest. Thunder rumbled in the dark clouds outside. She was supposed to be packing. But every time she reached for her things, misery overwhelmed her like she was covered in Loathing Leeches.

But this was no Nightmare malady. There was no quick fix. Ix had done this to herself—and to everyone else. She'd broken the rules and accidentally released one of the most dangerous Nightmares ever captured. She hadn't even managed to help Ollie. Now she was going to be expelled, banished, or locked up. And she deserved it.

After she woke up in the Central Tower, Ix had tried to tell everyone what the Memory Eater said about Captain Kel. But no one would listen. No one would even look at her. Even Tempest only gave her a pained half smile before Fallon Winters swept in, his eyes hard and angry.

"I knew you were working with the Nightmares. Was this your plan all along?"

"No! It was an accident. I didn't—" Ix protested.

Fallon waved his hand, signaling Vice-Captain Wystorm to

take her away. "Enough of your lies. Once I've dealt with you, we'll see to the issue of Morrigan Bea as well. Covenant Keep is no place for Nightmares."

"I told you I'd see you get what you deserve," Vice-Captain Wystorm hissed as she escorted Ix to her room. "And soon, the rest of your little friends will follow."

Ix felt sick. She hadn't just ruined things for herself. She'd ruined them for Morrigan, too, and all the Nightmares in the keep. She should disappear, before she hurt anyone else.

She tore herself away from the window, shoving things carelessly into her bag. One pair of striped socks rolled under the bed. Ix dropped onto her stomach, reaching for them, only to find that Hanky had grabbed the socks and wouldn't let go.

Ix's eyes prickled. "Come on, Hanky. I don't want to leave, either, but I don't have a choice." Still Hanky clung stubbornly to her socks. All its little Inkling friends piled on, too, fighting her tight grip.

Anger flashed through Ix. She shoved the socks away, sending all the Inklings tumbling end over end.

"Fine! You stay here, then—no one's kicking you out, after all."

"So that's it? You're just going to run away?"

Ix jerked up so fast she banged her head. Morrigan stood in the doorway, arms crossed.

"Morrigan . . ." Ix swallowed around a lump. "What else am I supposed to do? This is all my fault."

Morrigan's black skirt swished as she sat down next to Ix. "I told Captain Kel something like that once. That he should just get rid of me because I screw up everything. You know what he said?" Morrigan pulled her face into a stern frown and lowered her voice.

"Everybody makes mistakes. You can't change what you've done. All that matters is what you do next. And you can't do anything if you run away."

"You do a terrible Captain Kel impression," Ix told her, sitting up. She pulled Hanky and the socks into her lap, picking off little dust clumps. "But you're right. About this—about everything. I'm sorry I didn't listen before."

Morrigan shook her head. "I'm sorry, too. I got so angry I couldn't think straight. Maybe if we'd worked together, things would have turned out differently." She shot Ix a guilty look. "I know you went back to the Memory Eater to clear Captain Kel's name."

"Captain Kel isn't the one who made Jack. Not that it matters," Ix said. "I ruined everything. Ollie's still crystallized, and the council won't believe anything I say. And Fallon Winters wants to throw you out, too."

Morrigan scoffed. "No one's getting rid of us that easily." She gave Ix a considering look. "Have you actually been officially expelled?"

"Well, no. But only because everyone's too busy going after the Memory Eater."

"Then you're still a member of Candle Corps." Morrigan lurched up from the bed, sending balled-up socks and notebooks flying. "Which means we have one more chance to make this right. To save Ollie. And Captain Kel."

"How?" Ix asked, desperate.

Morrigan tugged Ix to her feet. "I don't think Captain Kel disappeared by choice. If he could get back, he would . . . for you, for me. Definitely for Professor Swann—they're madly in love!

There's no way he'd be gone this long unless something happened to him."

"But if that's true, there's one thing that doesn't make sense," Ix said. It was the same thing that had been bothering her in the basement.

"Healer Mella," they said at the same time.

"Why did she say it was Captain Kel who crystallized Ollie?" Ix asked, hopping a little as she pulled her boots on.

Morrigan shook her head. "Either she was tricked, or . . ."

"Or she's the one who did it," Ix whispered. "But that can't be. Right?"

"That's what we have to investigate. Come on."

Morrigan ducked into the closet and grabbed their Candle Corps coats.

"Why do we need those?" Ix asked, though she was already pulling hers on.

Morrigan yanked her hair out of the collar and snapped her heavy Soul Lock shut. "Captain Winters is dead set on expelling me, right? So if this is my last act as a member of Candle Corps, I'm going down in this coat." She popped the little silver lock closed around the buckle of Ix's coat, too. Ix didn't have the heart to tell her it was fake, not when the gesture made her feel so warm.

Hanky was turning happy exclamation points on the floor. Ix swept her socks back under the bed and tucked the little Inkling into them. "Stay safe," she whispered. Then, pulse pounding, she darted after Morrigan into the hall.

It was easier to go unnoticed than Ix expected. The whole castle was in a commotion. Doors to Nowhere slammed shut as captains slipped into the Labyrinth to hunt for the Memory Eater and

Embers relayed orders down the halls. They had to flatten themselves behind a tapestry as Vice-Captain Weisgard and Tempest passed barely a foot from them, carrying a Silverweave net. Ix almost thought Tempest caught a glimpse of them as they slipped down the stairs—but then someone called his name, and he moved off.

The infirmary was deserted. Ollie's body had been moved, and there was no sign of Mella.

"What are we looking for?" Ix asked.

"I'm not sure exactly. Something that proves Healer Mella's betraying Candle Corps."

Ix rifled through the desk, inspecting the sheaves of paper and potions in red glass vials.

"You think she keeps proof of her secret evil plans out in the open?" Morrigan asked.

"Where, then?"

"Places nobody's supposed to look, of course." Morrigan moved to the cabinet beside the desk. She eyed the locks on the bottom two drawers, then lifted her boot and smashed one with her heel.

"You're going to break it?" Ix asked, horrified.

Morrigan smashed her foot down again. "What? You think we can be in any more trouble than we already are?"

"Good point." Ix knelt and removed the mangled lock while Morrigan kicked open the other one.

Ix peered inside. There were all kinds of dried plants tied together in little bundles. Squat jars of colorful liquid sat in a neat row alongside scraggly pouches, one stained a rusty-red color that looked suspiciously like blood. But Ix had no idea what any of them were.

Morrigan pulled open the other drawer. She gasped. "Ix, look."

Ix peered over Morrigan's shoulder. The things inside looked like shiny stones—until Morrigan lifted one out, and Ix realized it was a mouse frozen in crystal. There were at least two other mice in the drawer and one gecko, its eyes bulging in fear.

"I don't get it," Morrigan said. "Are these animals in the Crystal Sleep? I didn't think animals' souls got lost in the Labyrinth."

"They don't," Ix said. She'd asked Smiles about it once. The Grinning Cat didn't know what happened to animal souls after they died, but they never passed through the Labyrinth.

We Sorrows are entirely for you humans, Chaos had said with a razor smile. *The souls of other creatures are of no interest to us.*

"That can only mean one thing," Ix said, studying the frozen mouse. "These creatures had their souls forced out and trapped somehow. Mella must have done it—and I'll bet she did the same thing to the people in the Crystal Sleep."

"But why?" Morrigan hissed. "She's a healer. She's supposed to help people. What does she possibly have to gain from stealing people's souls and making a creature like Jack?"

Ix chewed on the end of her thumb. Then suddenly the strange question Ollie had asked before he went missing came back to her: *Do you think someone could ever have a good reason to capture a soul? Like, if they thought they were helping someone?*

Ix's eyes widened. "Jack. That's it, Morrigan! *That's* what this was all about."

She raced back to the desk. Under the papers lay a hand-painted portrait in a cracked frame of two little children with golden hair. Mella and her twin, even younger than they'd looked in the old Candle Corps logbook.

But that wasn't the last time she'd seen that face.

Ix held it up. "Jacora Mella. *Jack*. His face is older, but he's her brother, I'm sure of it! I don't know what happened to him or exactly what he is now, but Mella must have done it. That's why she hid his body after we found it—because someone at Candle Corps would have recognized him. We can go to the council with this!"

"No, we can't," Morrigan insisted. "Because the body disappeared, remember? They'd have only your word. Maybe if your last name was Winters or Wystorm and you weren't about to be expelled, that would be enough. But not for us."

Us Nightmares, Ix filled in.

"We need proof. *Real* proof," Morrigan finished.

Ix shoved her hands into her pockets, thinking. Her fingertips brushed something soft. It was the square of cloth Ollie had given her for safekeeping. Suddenly it all came together.

Healer Mella wouldn't need to secretly harvest silverweed from her own crop in the middle of the night. So if it really was her that Ix had seen that night, she must have been harvesting something else.

"There is proof," Ix said. "And I know where to get it—because this is *not* Silverweave." She waggled the cloth at Morrigan, who just looked baffled.

"What?"

Ix didn't have time to explain. She took off at a run, trusting Morrigan to follow.

They busted through a locked door beneath Duskwatch Tower, stepping out into the silverweed she'd run through with Ollie the night before. She could still make out Bella's paw prints in the dust. This time Ix stuck to the edge, searching until she found an arch where two hawthorn trees had grown together. The archway she'd come through on All Hallows' Eve. The doorway that just happened to be open into Mella's private silverweed patch, the very night Captain Kel went missing.

Ix's mind raced back to that moment. The moment Mella turned around, startled, dropping the plants she'd been holding. Not shimmering silver plants but black leaves and dark purple blossoms. Death Delphinium, found only in Death's domain in the very heart of the Labyrinth.

"What are we looking for?" Morrigan demanded as Ix stepped into the silverweed, pushing the spiny stalks aside.

"This," Ix breathed. Right there, hidden in the silverweed, was a patch of dark flowers. "These are Death Bells. You can use them to trap souls—and they are definitely not supposed to be grown outside the Labyrinth."

Morrigan's eyes were wide. "We can take this to the council. We can clear Captain Kel's name and save Ollie!"

"And stop her," Ix said. She traded a triumphant smile with Morrigan.

"I do wish you hadn't found that," said a cold voice behind them.

41

THE FLAMES OF WRATH

Ix and Morrigan whirled around.

Healer Mella stood framed against the darkening sky. Storm clouds roiled over the high towers of the keep, and her stitched and patched coat whipped around her in the wind. All pretense of her kind smile was gone.

"It's too bad," she said. "If you two were just a little less clever—if you'd just left well enough alone—you could have kept your souls. Now you'll have to join dear Oliver. He also poked his nose where it didn't belong."

Morrigan gripped Ix's hand tight.

"You were the person Ollie wanted to talk to," Ix whispered. "He figured out what you were up to."

"Yes. I've been using these flowers to create Deathweave—a material that traps souls. I found the recipe in an old forbidden tome and arranged to have it spun by the spider weavers. Not that they knew what they were spinning, of course."

Suddenly, Ix remembered the inky fabric she'd seen Mella shoving into her pocket in Spindlecrook. "That's what you're using these for."

Mella smiled. "Among other things. Death Bell poison can force a soul out of a body. But it's my Shadow Render needle that allows me to tether them to whatever I want."

Mella laid her hand over one of the patches on her coat, stroking it fondly. They looked exactly like the square of cloth Ollie had given Ix. The cloth that *wasn't* Silverweave.

Ix felt sick. "Those patches—that's where you're keeping the souls you've stolen." They were trapped right there in her coat, under the crisscrosses of threads. Ix should have realized that, because when she'd first counted the patches, there were six. But there were seven now—a brand-new one for Ollie, just below her heart. "You trapped all those people in the Crystal Sleep. Even my father."

Mella shrugged. "Some of them got in the way, and some I needed for research. As for your father, he was just in the wrong place at the wrong time." She stalked toward them. "Ten years ago, a man dreamed himself into the Labyrinth and was wandering Death's domain when he saw something he shouldn't. He became the very first patch on my coat."

Mella took another step, backing them toward the forest, out of sight from the keep windows. Fear rolled down Ix's spine. No one knew where they were. No one even knew they suspected Mella. If she got rid of them, she could get away with all of it.

"Give Ollie back!" Morrigan shouted. "How could you do that to him?"

"What have I really done? Just tucked him out of the way for a little while." Mella's face softened. "I'm not a cruel person. I haven't hurt anyone. Their souls are all safe. And I'll stitch them back together, as soon as I have what I want."

All at once Ix understood. "You're trying to save Jack. Your brother."

A flicker of pain crossed Mella's face. Then she scowled. "You really do know far too much. And nothing at all. Jacora was always sickly. He was never suited to being in Candle Corps, but he stayed for me. And then, almost eleven years ago, he died in my arms. He told me it was his time—but I couldn't let it end like that."

Ix shuddered, thinking about Jacora's crumbling crystallized body held together with resin and bits of string.

"You can't save him from death," Ix said. "There's barely even a body left anymore. He's too far gone. What you're doing—it isn't right!"

"You think I don't know that?" Mella spat. "You think I haven't agonized over this? I've come much too far to turn around now."

Ix had to do something. She had to get them out of here. But how? Healer Mella stood between them and Covenant Keep. The only thing behind Ix was the hawthorn forest.

"And what about Captain Kel? Did you take his soul, too?" Morrigan demanded.

"What happened to him is his own fault. He saw me crossing through the Labyrinth on All Hallows' Eve and caught me picking a few of these." Mella crumpled one of the Death Delphiniums between her fingers. "I left him chained up in Death's domain, right by the Soul Reaper's door. I couldn't have him getting in the way."

"Of what? What are you going to do?"

Mella's eyes glittered. She pulled her gleaming Shadow Render needle from the air. The trailing thread swirled in the stormy wind. "You were right about one thing. Jack's body is too far gone. But at last, I've figured out how to bring him back. I need to stitch Jack's soul into a body that hasn't crystallized. And I happen to have left one in the Labyrinth."

"You're going to steal Captain Kel's body," Ix whispered in horror.

"You can't!" Morrigan yelled.

"Given more time, I might have picked someone else. But I've had to move my plans up, thanks to you." Thunder rumbled through the dark sky as Mella stalked toward them. "I sewed something inside that Memory Eater husk that absolutely cannot be allowed to escape. That creature needed to stay locked up in the keep. But I'll get it back. I'll fix everything. As soon as I've dealt with you."

Ix's back hit the trunk of a tree. She craned her head around, desperate. Then she saw it—a curl of mist seeping through an archway of branches.

Suddenly, she knew exactly what to do.

Mella reached into her pocket and pulled out a Deathweave patch. "There's nowhere to run," she told them.

But she was wrong. Because this was the place Mella had been opening her door into the Labyrinth. The veil separating the Waking World and the Between World was always thinnest in places where tears had been opened again and again.

Mella lunged for them.

Ix called her Shadow Render. Just a bit of it. The tiny curved tip of the sickle appeared between her fingers, and she darted forward, slicing at Mella's coat.

Her Shadow Render had been powerful enough to free the Memory Eater. Surely she could dislodge a single patch of cloth.

The blade caught on the threads. Then there was a *rrrip!* and the Deathweave tore loose, swirling in the winds. Ix managed to snatch it just before Morrigan hauled her back out of Mella's reach.

"Run!" Ix yelled, shoving the patch in her pocket. Then she grabbed Morrigan's hand and threw them both into the misty archway.

The world shifted around them, the cold mist burning away

into hot steam as she and Morrigan burst into the Labyrinth. Walls of rough-cut stone loomed above them. Rusted chains hung from heavy bolts, crisscrossing the corridor and snarling in the branches of twisted trees. Smoky red light filtered through the haze, and everything hissed and seethed.

Wrath's domain.

They ran until they were gasping for breath. When they were sure Mella wasn't following them, they slumped against the wall. Ix braced her hands on her knees.

"What do we do now?" she asked. "Should we try to get back and tell one of the captains?"

"They've all been sent out, remember?" Morrigan snapped. "By the time we find someone and convince them to believe us, Mella will already have stolen Captain Kel's body."

"But you heard what she said," Ix protested. "Captain Kel's chained up in front of Death's Door, in the very center of the Labyrinth. Even if we wanted to stop her, how would we get there?"

"You were in Death's domain before."

"Sure. On All Hallows' Eve, when the Apparitions of Death opened the way," Ix shot back, swiping at a bead of sweat on her forehead. "No one knows how to get to the center of the Labyrinth."

"So you're saying we should just give up?" Morrigan yelled, fuming.

Ix found herself snapping back. "No! And why are you yelling at me?"

"Why are you?!" Morrigan returned, just as heated.

Stop fighting!

That sounded like Ollie's voice. Ix dug frantically into her pocket, pulling out the Deathweave patch she'd managed to rip off Mella's coat.

"Ollie?" she asked, holding it up.

For a moment there was no sound. Then Ix heard a strange buzzing. That definitely wasn't Ollie, though. It sounded more like . . .

"Oh no!" She wrenched her head around. "Quarrelswarm Wasps." No wonder she and Morrigan had been at each other's throats. They'd fallen prey to one of the Nightmare creatures of Wrath's domain.

The buzzing grew louder and louder. At last Ix spotted the pulsing swarm. Hundreds of wasps moved together like a dark cloud, zooming toward them.

Ollie's soul would have to wait, Ix thought, tucking the cloth back into her pocket.

"Come on!" Morrigan shouted, taking off.

Ix didn't need to be told twice. Even just the buzzing of Quarrelswarm Wasps could make a person unreasonably snappish and angry. Like she and Morrigan had been.

"This way," Ix said, pointing toward a narrow side passage. She almost tripped over a Stubbed Toad that hopped into her path, but Morrigan yanked her into the narrow passage just in time.

"Thanks," Ix gasped as they watched the swarm pass. As soon as it was gone, they set off again. It wasn't safe to stop and rest in Wrath's domain. Unlike the slow crawl of Misery or sudden shock of Terror, Wrath was relentless.

Wrath's quadrant was the most dangerous in the Labyrinth. The Horned Beasts of all kinds loved to fight, and Giant Werewolves and Jimber-Jawed Hounds snapped and growled at each other in the Brickle Bushes. Half the domain was wild overgrowth, deadly sharp-needled pine forests and rocky hills where giant juts of flame burst from the ground like geysers. Everything seemed to be covered in barbs and prickles and spikes. Wrath's domain was all sharp edges.

The narrow passage banked in front of them. Abruptly, Ix and Morrigan stepped out into dark pines. Ix counted to ten and took a deep breath before she spoke. That was the trick to surviving Wrath's domain. Always keep your cool. Stop and ask yourself why you were upset and whether getting angry would really solve any of your problems. And definitely never act without thinking.

"There might be a way to get to the center of the Labyrinth and save Captain Kel," Ix told Morrigan, who perked up. "We could ask one of the Sorrows to take us."

Morrigan wrinkled her nose. "You really think Wrath would help us?"

"Probably not Wrath, but maybe . . ."

Ix never got the chance to finish.

A low growl filled the air. A huge Jimber-Jawed Hound had come up behind them, stalking them through the trees. Yellow eyes narrowed in its gargoyle face, its hackles rippling.

"Not again—" Ix croaked.

"Run!" Morrigan shouted.

42

TEMPESTUOUS TAR

Ix and Morrigan raced into the spiny trees. But the hound was right behind them, barreling through the undergrowth.

Ix threw a glance at Morrigan. The girl's face was grim and angry, and little bits of her red Dreamlight power sizzled around her. It had been a pack of Jimber-Jawed Hounds that pushed Morrigan's mother to the limit, forcing her to transform into a wolf to save her squad.

They burst through a row of trees and skidded to a stop. A great black pool spread out before them—a tar pit, seething and boiling with fat bubbles. Ix could see an archway in the wall on the other side, maybe an opening into another part of the Labyrinth.

"If we could get across the tar pit, I think we could get away," Ix said, pointing.

"That's way too far to jump!"

There was a growl at their backs. The hound crouched in the brambles, its long toothy jaw quivering with ropes of spit.

Morrigan pushed Ix behind her. "You find a way across. I'll hold off the beast."

Morrigan's hands blazed as she conjured her Shadow Render, the claws leaping from her knuckles. Red power glowed around her, making ears and a lashing tail, stronger than Ix had ever seen it.

Anger made you powerful in Wrath's domain, but it also made it easier to lose yourself. If Morrigan transformed, became a full Bea Wolf, she would be lost to the Labyrinth.

"Morrigan . . ." Ix started, scared.

"If you're worried about me, then find a way across—fast," Morrigan snapped. Then she shoved Ix out of the way, just as the Jimber-Jawed Hound leapt at them.

Morrigan ducked the snapping jaws, raking her claws down the Nightmare's leathery hide. They barely left a scratch.

"Go!" Morrigan shouted.

Ix darted down the bank, looking for something, *anything*, that could get them out of this mess. She could hear the snarls and the sounds of the fight at her back. Even Morrigan couldn't hold off something like that for long—

Then she spotted it. A calcified tree was sunk halfway into the tar pit, gleaming white as bone. They might be able to jump to it if they had a running start.

Ix didn't stop to think. She took a deep breath and threw herself from the bank. She stumbled when she landed, her boots sliding on the smooth bark. But she'd made it.

Ix turned around. "Morrigan!" she cried. "This way—hurry!"

Morrigan's red tail snapped up and whipped the Nightmare across the face. Its giant head lurched away. Morrigan took off running and launched herself over the tar pit, arms wheeling. Ix caught her around the waist. Jets of steam burst up from the tar, leaving them both coughing.

"You did it!" Ix gasped out.

The Jimber-Jawed Hound paced along the tar, growling. Then it leaned back and howled. More shapes skulked out of the forest—

not just one, but a whole pack of Jimber-Jawed Hounds eyeing them from the bank.

Ix shuddered. "Come on. Let's get out of here. It's a shorter jump to the other side."

But Morrigan didn't move. Her angry tail swished, her eyes fixed on the hounds. "That's what my mom was facing when she transformed. It could even be the same pack."

"Morrigan, don't. We're in Wrath. You can't get mad," Ix begged, grabbing her arm.

Morrigan threw her off. "Stop telling me what to do! You don't understand. I lost my mom because of creatures like that—"

"Morrigan, look out!"

The tar was boiling, splashing around their feet. And getting higher. Ix dragged Morrigan back from the edge before her boots stuck in it.

"What's happening?" Morrigan cried.

"It's Tempestuous Tar! The angrier you get, the more turbulent it becomes." Ix shook her. "At this rate, it'll rise up and swallow us. You have to calm down."

"I'm trying!" Morrigan said, not at all calmly. "But it's like it's consuming me . . . my anger and my Nightmare power . . ." The red flames writhed around her.

The log under them shook as the smoldering tar crept up another inch. In a second, it'd be over their toes. Ix racked her brain. What had Instructor Cadence said about Wrath?

Kindness has a way of tempering anger and reminding us what we cherish.

Ix gasped. "Morrigan! Tell me what you like about me!"

"What?" Morrigan demanded.

"It's a trick—in Wrath, if anger's getting the better of you. Remember all the things you like about someone."

"Well, right now, I don't like anything about you," Morrigan groused.

"Fine, I'll go first!" Ix grabbed her shoulders. "I like how you always save me a piece of pumpkin cake, even when you say you won't."

Morrigan wrinkled her nose. But she tried. "I . . . I like the way you pick up Inklings and put them in your pockets. Except when they end up living in my shoes."

The log stopped shaking. The bubbles simmered down around their feet. It was working! Ix grinned, her heart soaring.

"I like your Shadow Render. I wish mine had a tail."

Morrigan rolled her eyes. "I like your stripy socks, even though you leave them all over the floor." Her red flames died down to a few sparks in her wild hair.

"I like how brave you are," Ix said seriously. "How you're never afraid to say exactly what you're feeling."

Morrigan's ears were a little pink. "A lot of people *don't* like that about me." She hesitated, then said all in a rush: "You're the first person who ever wanted to be friends with me even though I'm a Bea Wolf. You make me feel like maybe I'm not a monster . . . or if I am, maybe it's not such a bad thing. That's what I like about you."

"That's what I like about you, too," Ix admitted.

The tar was a low burble now. Ix heaved a sigh of relief as they leapt across it and slumped down against the Labyrinth wall. The hounds slunk off into the trees.

"That was a close one," Morrigan said.

"Too close," Ix sighed.

"Way too close," a third voice added.

This time, Ix was certain she hadn't imagined it. "Ollie?" she cried, whirling around.

"Hold on, I think I've just about got this figured out." A second later, a figure was wavering to life in front of them. Ollie pushed his glasses up his nose, looking at his glowing hands with fascination.

"Ollie!" Ix surged up and tried to throw her arms around him, only to stumble right through his insubstantial form. That was when she noticed he didn't have any feet. Instead, he was floating, like one of the sleepwalking souls in the Labyrinth.

"I think I'm soulwalking right now," Ollie whispered. "This is how the founders of Candle Corps entered the Labyrinth centuries ago."

"What does it feel like?" Morrigan asked.

"Kind of like I'm lucid dreaming." Ollie spun in a quick circle, trailing his ghostly fingers through a pair of bristling thistles. "It's weird not to be in a body. But at least you can't end up on the wrong end of a Brickle Bush."

Ix really wanted to throw her arms around him, but she knew she'd go through him again. "I'm so glad you're okay, Ollie—well, not okay, obviously, you're a soul, but . . ." Ix gave up, her shoulders slumping. "I'm so sorry. I should never have left you alone last night."

"It's not your fault," Ollie said. "When I figured out it was Healer Mella, I thought I could talk to her, maybe change her mind. But I got crystallized instead."

"We'll get you back to your body," Morrigan promised. "But we have to stop Mella first. She's got Captain Kel."

"Right," Ollie agreed. "But how do we—" Then he stopped, frowning as something caught his eye. "What is that?" he asked, pointing a glowing finger at something under Ix's feet.

That's when Ix noticed a crack had opened up under her boot. It stretched down the stone passage, growing wider and more jagged until it became a fissure. Floating halfway through the dark gap was one of the Apparitions of Death. The Nightmare reached out a shadowy hand, beckoning them.

"It's a portal to Death's domain," Ix said. "The Apparition must have made it."

"Why is it helping us?" Morrigan asked.

Ix shook her head. "Maybe it wants us to stop Mella. Or maybe it heard us calling out. Either way, the path to Death is open."

Ollie floated closer, curious. "This isn't like a mist portal, is it?"

"It's not." Ix bit her lip. "I have a feeling there's no turning back once we go through. So if you want to turn around . . ."

"Well, you just told me you like how brave I am. So I can't back down now," Morrigan said, throwing her hair back and grinning.

Ollie's eyes were bright. "I could never give up without knowing how it ends," he said.

"Well, then." Ix stepped up next to her friends. "Nightmare girls and bookworm boys forever?"

"Still too corny," Morrigan teased. "But there's no one I'd rather face Death with than you two."

Ix couldn't agree more. Hearts hammering, they stepped into the portal together.

43

DEATH'S DOOR

When the three of them came through the cracked fissure, they were in the very heart of Death's domain.

Ix had passed through the edges on All Hallows' Eve, with the ring of Death Bells and the winding River of Shades. But this time, they had come out in a wide-open field. Ghost Grass swayed under their feet. The walls made a circle around them, cut with dozens of passages that all led here. The very center of the Labyrinth. Purple ghost flames danced in the air, and black spider lilies grew all the way to the giant door at the center.

"Death's Door," Ollie whispered.

Ix shivered, looking up. The door to death rose like a black tower above them. Strangely, it seemed to be covered in chains. Rusty metal links wound around it, leaving it open the barest crack—just enough for a single soul to slip through at a time. Farther away, along the walls, she could see hazy, translucent forms—souls that had made it all the way here, to the center of the Labyrinth, but couldn't get through.

"Captain Kel!" Morrigan yelled.

Ix tore her eyes away from the door. There, chained to an obsidian rock that rose like a gravestone, was Captain Kel. He was on his knees with chains wrapped around his torso, holding his arms behind him. His Candle Corps jacket was torn, and blood ran down one side of his face as though he'd been struck by a rock. He didn't seem to be moving.

"Captain Kel, wake up!" Morrigan shouted as they ran for him, Ollie floating along.

"Stop them, Jack!" Healer Mella's voice rang out.

A second later, the scarecrow leapt in front of them. It landed in a squat, its gangly limbs akimbo. A few sticks came loose, and an old coin rolled out of his sleeve.

"Pesky little pesklings," Jack said, straightening. "You've picked an ever-so-fitting place to die." He spun a circle with one hand in the air, as though he were dancing. "Isn't it lovely? It positively screeches *the end*." He stopped abruptly, staring at them with his empty eyeholes. "The end is a beautiful thing, you know."

Ix gulped, horrified all over again now that she knew what Jack really was. A dead human soul tethered and trapped in the Labyrinth. Unable to cross Death's Door.

"Don't kill them, Jack," Mella warned. "As I said, I don't want to hurt anyone."

She stood near a crumbling wall covered in ivy and bindweed. A deep black fissure cut into the stone. Mella must have her own portal right into the heart of Death's realm—that was how she'd gotten here ahead of them.

Her eyes flitted over Ollie's shimmering soul. "Be very careful, Oliver, dear. You don't want to get too close to that door—you might slip right through. You were much safer in my coat."

Ollie looked scared, but he stood his ground. "I'd rather take my chances with my friends than be trapped in there, knowing I couldn't stop you." To Ix and Morrigan, he whispered, "We have to get that coat."

"But how?" Morrigan hissed back.

"I'm working on that—"

They were distracted by a groan. Captain Kel raised his head weakly. "All of you, run. Get out of here."

"Not without you!" Morrigan said, conjuring her Shadow Render. She glared at Jack, her fiery wolf tail lashing.

Healer Mella clapped. "Touching, truly. Except for the part where you keep getting in my way. I'll be sure to take care of you this time. Just like this thing."

Mella laid a hand on the wall. With horror, Ix realized there was a creature trapped in the seething vines.

"The Memory Eater!" she gasped.

It wailed in agony. Mella laughed. "Overestimated your- self, didn't you?" she taunted the creature. "You really thought after ten years, weakened by the seals of Covenant Keep, you could undo all those stitches I put into you? Mine may not be the most powerful Shadow Render, but I know precisely how to use it."

Ix's mind whirled. "What did you sew inside there?" she de- manded.

"The thing that foolishly tried to take my brother from me. Just as you have been."

Ollie nudged Ix's shoulder. Or, he tried, anyway. All she felt was a pins-and-needles tingle where his arm went through hers. Then she saw what he'd seen—a cluster of Pepper Puffs, right at Mella's feet. The seeds must have drifted in from Misery on All Hallows' Eve.

Ix's heart swelled. "We're not afraid of you. And we're not going to let you get away with this." Then she raced forward and kicked the Pepper Puffs with all her might—right up into Mella's face.

"Agh—CHOO!" Mella sneezed, as the pollen went up her nose.

"Morrigan! Get the coat!" Ix shouted.

Morrigan didn't have to be told twice. With a ferocious leap, she launched herself at Mella's back, wrenching the coat and all its trapped souls away from her. Mella shrieked.

"Ix, catch!" Morrigan shouted. Ix snatched the coat out of the air.

"How dare you—ACHOO!" Mella could barely speak through her sneezing. She rounded on them with furious, bloodshot eyes. "Jack, seize them!"

Jack crowed with laughter. Perched on a rock, he tipped his head back and reached into his gaping mouth, flinging three coal-like lumps into the Ghost Grass.

The stones hissed into smoke, releasing two silvery, long-armed Wraiths and one Moaning Ghoul. The ghoul's face looked like it was made of thick green putty forever running down. It moaned low and ghastly. All the creatures' eyes glowed green. They belonged to Jack.

Ix conjured her hand sickle, clutching Mella's coat close.

"It isn't a party without friends," the scarecrow said. "And they'll need arms to be *seizing* you with, so the rest of my lovelies will just have to wait." Jack petted his stomach.

"Let them go, Allison, they're just children!" Ix heard Captain Kel yelling.

The two Wraiths flew at Morrigan. She swiped at them with both hands, snarling. Ix ducked under the arm of the Moaning Ghoul, its chains clanking as it chased her into the obsidian stones.

"Run, Ix!" Morrigan growled.

Ix took off. Ollie whizzed around her, not sure what he could do.

"Help Morrigan!" Ix told him. "She's got two of them. But be careful, Ollie—those things are *made* for chomping on souls."

"We can handle it," Ollie promised. Even here, in Death's realm, he didn't look shy or scared anymore. He looked like a member of Candle Corps—a light of Spinar, shining against the darkness.

Ollie zoomed away. Through the stones, Ix caught a glimpse of him circling Morrigan, taunting one of the Wraiths.

She was so busy watching her friends that she forgot to look where she was going. One moment she was running, and the next Ix had tripped over something like a long slab of rock. She landed on her knees and found herself staring into the peaceful, sleeping face of Jacora.

It wasn't a rock. It was the body from the hidden chamber— Jacora's body, encased in crumbling crystal. Mella had brought him here.

The Moaning Ghoul seized Ix's moment of distraction, grabbing her by the arm and yanking her up. Ix shrieked. She sliced out desperately with the sickle. The Shadow Render caught the creature's gooey arm, severing it and sending it flying. It flopped around for a moment in the Ghost Grass, and then began crawling back toward the ghoul, dragging itself by its fingertips.

She had to get to Captain Kel. Without him, they didn't stand a chance.

Ix pressed her back to an icy obsidian slab, looking around.

Morrigan and Ollie were holding off the Wraiths, and the Moaning Ghoul was busy reattaching its arm backward. And Jack—

"Peekaboo. Found you."

The scratchy voice was right behind her. Ix screamed as the scarecrow's face popped over the slab, his eyeholes dark and empty.

"I do love a game of hide-and-seek," Jack said gleefully. "But you lost. So you have to give me something. The coat? Or should we become friends?"

His long, crooked arms stretched toward her.

"She's already got plenty of friends," said a familiar voice. Then suddenly Tempest was right next to her, swinging his Shadow Render.

The glowing pole crunched against Jack's shoulder. Ix heard a sound like wood splintering. One of Jack's arms sagged, and he leapt back, hissing.

"Tempest!" Ix shouted in relief. "How are you here?"

"Well, I couldn't let my favorite Novices get in trouble without me," he joked, pulling her up. His Candle Corps coat glowed around him, and a Dreamlight flame blazed high above his head. "I saw you sneaking around and found all the evidence you left in the infirmary." He raised his voice so Mella could hear him. "You should have been more careful opening your portal to Death's domain. I was able to follow you here, and so will the rest of the captains when they've returned. We've got you beat."

Mella gave him a nasty smile. "I guess that depends what you're willing to lose right now," she said, holding a curved hand sickle to Captain Kel's throat.

44

THE LOST SORROW

"No!" Morrigan screamed.

"Give yourselves up, or he dies," Mella warned. She yanked back on Kel's hair, exposing more of his neck.

"Tempest, don't," Kel shouted. "Your duty is to Candle Corps. My life is a small price to pay to stop her."

A hundred emotions warred across Tempest's face. The boy squeezed his eyes shut. Then his arms sagged.

"Sorry, Captain. I can't." He held his hands up, letting his Shadow Render disappear.

"I'll be taking that coat back," Mella warned, snatching it from Ix. She held out a hand. "Oliver's patch, too. Now, on your knees, all of you."

This can't be happening. That was what Ix thought as the Wraiths seized Morrigan and Tempest. The Nightmares forced them down, all in a line next to Captain Kel, with Morrigan on one side and Ix on the other. Ix tried to struggle, but the ghoul held her arms tight.

"For you, Oliver, this will have to do." Mella drew the thread from her Shadow Render and looped it around Ollie's shining wrists—a glowing strand of light, just like the one she'd used on Aunt Tara. With two quick stitches, Mella bound Ollie's soul to the Deathweave and then tossed her coat aside. Ollie tugged at the end of his tether, his eyes wide.

"Please, Healer Mella. This isn't you!" he said. "I know you thought you were doing the right thing. You didn't want to lose someone you love."

Ix's heart guttered. Her eyes fell on Mella's coat, lying in a heap on the Ghost Grass. Her father's soul was in there, too, closer than it had ever been, and Ix still couldn't save him.

Tempest glared up at Mella. "You won't get away with this. You can never go back to Candle Corps, and they'll never stop hunting you. This won't get you what you want."

"But it will," Mella said. "Once I have Jacora back, nothing else will matter."

She dug something out of her pocket—a long glittering thread. Silverweave, Ix realized. That's what she would use to bind Jack's soul to Captain Kel's body.

Mella beckoned the scarecrow. "Jack, come here, it's time. Aren't you tired of being lonely?" she crooned. "Don't you want to be human again?"

Jack nodded, tottering toward her.

"Jack, don't listen to her. This isn't what you want!" Ix cried.

"Silence," Mella hissed.

But Ix couldn't be silent. Only one person could stop this now: the blond boy in the portraits, the one who had told Mella it was his time.

"I don't know what happened to you, but this isn't right," Ix went on. "This isn't who you are. The real you died. That's your body over there, encased in crystal."

Jack's head swung around to look over his shoulder.

"Please, Jack. You're lonely and sad, right?" Ix said breathlessly. "I've been lonely like that, too. But this won't make it better. It will only make it worse."

"Jacora, don't listen to her. *Jack!*" Mella snapped.

But the scarecrow wasn't paying attention. He staggered over to his glittering body. Jack gazed down at it as though mesmerized.

"Such a beautiful, terrible nightmare I've been trapped in for so long." He knelt down, laying his sackcloth cheek against the stone. "Such a perfect place for an ending. An ending that never comes."

"What have you done to him?" Mella cried.

"It's what *you* did to him," Morrigan said, glaring. "You chose all of this, and not for him—for yourself!"

"Enough!" Mella's eyes blazed with anger and grief. "Clearly, I'll have to take care of you pests first."

She stalked down the line, staring at each of them in turn.

"Do you know what happens when you break someone's Soul Lock in here?" she asked viciously. "The soul becomes untethered, flung to the far reaches of the Labyrinth. And the body . . . well, this is a dangerous place. Most of them get eaten by something before they can even begin to crystallize."

Mella stopped at the end of the line, fingering the heavy lock on Morrigan's coat. Morrigan stared up at her defiantly as Mella conjured her tiny Shadow Render. The point glinted wickedly as she held it over the lock.

"Wait!" Ix cried out. "Break my lock first," she begged. "I'm the one who set the Memory Eater free. It should be me."

"Well, if you insist . . ." Mella moved to Ix, cradling the lock in one hand and raising the needle with the other. Ix held her breath.

"Think very carefully about what you're about to do," Captain

Kel said. He said it while looking at Mella. But Ix knew he was talking to her.

"I've made my decision. Say goodbye," Mella said. Then she stabbed the needle down. The lock cracked, splitting apart and crumbling.

"Ix!" Morrigan and Ollie screamed.

The ghoul let go of Ix's arms as she collapsed boneless onto the ground, forcing herself to stay still as a corpse.

"You monster!" Morrigan accused.

"Sounds to me like you're ready to join her." Mella stalked toward Morrigan.

Ix didn't waste a single precious moment. The second Mella's back was turned, she leapt to her feet, conjuring her Shadow Render. But she didn't attack Mella. Or the Wraiths. Or even try to free Captain Kel.

She ran for the Memory Eater. Because she had finally realized what was inside that husk. What Mella was afraid of. What could set the whole Labyrinth to rights.

Nightmare power burned in Ix's hands—more and more and more. Her small hand sickle hadn't been powerful enough to break Mella's threads and free the thing inside the Memory Eater. But Ix was part Nightmare, and her power was strongest in the Labyrinth.

The Shadow Render that blazed to life in her hands was no small sickle. It was a gleaming scythe, with a long handle and a great curved blade like a half-moon. Ix was a Nightmare of Death's domain, and this was her weapon's true form.

"No!" she heard Mella screaming. But nothing could stop her now.

Ix brought the scythe down with all her might. The glittering blade slashed right through the bindweed. It caught on the crisscross of Mella's threads—and then sliced through.

A sound like a thunderclap rang out as the husk of the Memory Eater fell away, releasing the Sorrow that had been missing for ten years. The Soul Reaper.

Death had finally returned to the Labyrinth.

Ix stared, not quite believing her eyes. She'd thought she was right—she'd *hoped*—but she couldn't be sure until a tall figure rose from the bits of thread and decay. A long black robe swept all the way to the ground. A hooded cowl hid the figure's face in shadow, only wisps of black hair slipping out.

Human hands rose from the billowing sleeves. All at once the chains were unwinding from the great door, and it flew open with a bang.

It was like being caught inside a wind tunnel. Death's Door raged like a storm, sucking everything toward it. The two Wraiths whirled through the air, disappearing into the darkness. The Moaning Ghoul held on to one of the black stones. Then its arm came off again, and both pieces were flung into the doorway. Captain Kel's chains snapped, and he dove forward, grabbing Morrigan and Tempest before they were swept away. With his other hand, he snatched Healer Mella's coat. Ollie's shimmering soul clung to the end of the tether.

Death stood serenely in the middle of the maelstrom, both hands raised as though drinking in the power.

Ix felt her feet start to slide against the Ghost Grass. She yelped, scrambling for something to hold on to. Her boots lifted off the ground. Then something grabbed her—a rough, scratchy hand of old wood and bone and a bent corkscrew. Ix looked up in shock. It was Jack. The scarecrow held on to Ix with one hand and the bindweed with the other, his hat flapping off his head.

"Hold on!" Jack told her.

Ix stared at him in amazement. All the pieces he'd made himself out of were being stripped away. The sticks and bones. The straw and birds' nests and bent nails. All of it was being sucked into the doorway.

Mella screamed. Ix glanced back to see her clinging desperately to the edge of the door.

"You can't take him from me!" she raged at the Soul Reaper. "I only wanted one thing. I was so close—"

Her fingers slipped. Ix looked away as Healer Mella was sucked into the darkness. Then the door swung shut again, only open a crack. But the chains were gone. Death's Door was free, and the souls would be able to pass through normally again.

Ix stumbled as Jack's hand became suddenly insubstantial in hers, his coat and the last few pieces of his scarecrow body falling away. The sackcloth mask landed on top of the pile. When Ix looked up, it was at a young man with golden curls and a Candle Corps coat. Jacora Mella's shimmering soul.

His lips curled into a soft, sad smile as the Soul Reaper turned to him.

"It's been a long time, Jack," Death said.

45

THE EIGHTH RULE

"I've been waiting for you, Death," Jack said. "For an awfully long time. But perhaps I could have a moment more." He turned to Ix.

Ix didn't know what to say. Suddenly Morrigan bowled into her.

"I thought you were dead!" Morrigan shouted. Ix couldn't tell if she was happy or angry, and she didn't think Morrigan knew, either.

"How did you survive Mella breaking your Soul Lock?" Ollie asked breathlessly.

"Seems you still have a few more secrets," Tempest joked, mussing her hair.

"My lock was fake," Ix admitted. "Captain Kel gave it to me so that I could join Candle Corps, but I've been wandering the Labyrinth for years without needing one."

"A mystery I'd still like an answer to," came a gruff voice.

Captain Kel limped over, holding Mella's coat folded over one arm. He'd protected it and all the precious souls inside from being sucked through Death's Door. Ix touched one of the patches, tears prickling in her eyes. Maybe they could finally get her father back.

Jack's translucent hand hovered over the coat. There was nothing

scary about him at all like this, Ix thought. He looked very kind—
and very sad.

"I'm sorry for all the pain my sister and I have caused."

"Is she really gone for good?" Morrigan wanted to know.

"Yes," Jack said with a melancholy smile. "There's no coming
back from that door."

"What happened to her?" Ix asked. "She wasn't dead, so why
did the door want her?"

"I believe I can best answer that."

Death swept over to them, taller even than Captain Kel. Mor-
rigan took a nervous step back and bumped right into Tempest.
Ix's skin prickled, as it always did in the presence of the Sorrows.
But she still felt that strange connection between them. There was
something about the tip of the figure's hooded head, the way the
Sorrow bent down to her . . . It was like they'd met before.

The voice that came from the shadowed robe was whispery but
no longer hoarse and frightening the way it had been from inside
the Memory Eater.

"Allison Mella's soul was forfeit from the moment she broke
the eighth rule," Death explained.

"The eighth rule?" Ollie repeated.

"I thought there were only seven," Tempest said at the same time.

"What is the eighth rule?" Ix whispered.

"Never steal a soul from the Reaper. Once a human soul has
crossed over into Death, it must never be returned."

Suddenly Ix understood why the founders of Candle Corps
had hidden the eighth rule. Even the possibility that you could get
a loved one back was too powerful a temptation.

Jack traced a cross-stitch on Mella's coat. "When I died, my sister couldn't let go. She came all the way to the Labyrinth, prepared to fight Death itself to keep me from crossing over. But to her surprise, the Soul Reaper was nowhere to be found. Allison was always clever with her Shadow Render, and as twins, our connection was already strong. She tethered my soul to hers—stitching us together and stealing my soul from the Reaper."

"When Jack's soul failed to pass through Death's Door, the eighth rule was broken, and the Labyrinth became unbalanced," the Soul Reaper told them. "I had been gone for some time, but I returned to the Labyrinth to search for Jack's missing soul and set things right."

"So what went wrong?" Morrigan asked.

"My sister," Jack said, looking mournful. "She knew she could never fight a Sorrow and win. So she came up with a way to trap Death instead. She worried Death would be able to escape any prison she built—unless it didn't remember what it was. Allison secretly fed a Memory Eater, growing it until it was powerful enough to swallow the memories of a Sorrow. Then she used me to bait a trap."

"I never thought a human could challenge me," Death said. "Here in my own domain, Mella released the Memory Eater. It scrambled my thoughts, my memories, and swallowed me whole. The next thing I knew, I was rampaging in the Waking World."

"In Mistmorrow, that was you . . ." Captain Kel shook his head, amazed. "All those years I spent searching for the Soul Reaper, trying to put the Labyrinth to rights . . . you were under the keep the whole time."

"When I realized what Mella had done, I tried to stop her," Jack said. "But I only managed to tear a few stitches before I lost my memories, too. I forgot I was Jacora Mella. I even forgot I was human. I wandered Death's domain for years, unable to leave, unable to cross over. When the Labyrinth finally reached its breaking point, I escaped Death's realm and wandered the domains of the other Sorrows. But loneliness gnawed at me like a hunger. So I started eating other Nightmares and fashioning a Nightmare body for myself, until I was a monster of my own making."

Jack looked at Ix.

"You reminded me who I was. Now that my sister has passed through the door, my soul isn't tethered here any longer. I'm free. Thank you, Ix Tatterfall. Let me do one last thing before I go."

Jack held his hand over the coat in Captain Kel's arms. Slowly the threads began to unravel. Ollie sighed in relief as his tether came free, all the patches dropping off one by one. Little balls of light, brighter than any Dreamlight Ix had ever seen, drifted into the air. The souls Mella had trapped.

They flickered around Ix, dancing like will-o'-the-wisps. One of them whizzed over Morrigan's head, and then they all began to flit away, darting and disappearing like fireflies.

"What's happening to them?" Ollie wanted to know.

"They should return to their bodies and wake up. You will, too, when you return home," Jack promised. "And now, it's time for me to go, too. Long past time."

The Soul Reaper lifted a hand, gesturing toward the door, which creaked open.

"Thank you," Jack told Death. Then he walked away, growing more and more translucent until he disappeared through the gap.

Ix's mind was reeling. But there was one thing she still didn't understand. She turned to the Soul Reaper.

"Why were you gone from the Labyrinth in the first place? If you had been there to stop Mella, none of this would have happened."

"That is true," Death said. "And you of all people deserve to know the truth. You see, even though I am a Sorrow, I fell in love with a human." Death reached up and pulled the cowl back to reveal a tan face, long pitch-black hair, and the darkest eyes Ix had ever seen. "And twelve years ago, I had a child."

Morrigan and Ollie gasped. Even Tempest made a strangled noise.

"Me?" Ix asked in disbelief.

The Soul Reaper placed a hand on Ix's head, smiling. "When I told you that you have your father's eyes, I wasn't lying. But there's a little of me in you, too. Especially in that scythe you wield."

Ix couldn't believe it. Suddenly, so many things in her life made sense. The reason Nathan Tatterfall had been so afraid of Candle Corps. Ix's mysterious mother. And after the Soul Reaper returned to the Labyrinth, her father's obsession with finding Death's domain, because he was looking for his lost love.

As long as you are with me, little wishling, Death will surely come for us.

That's what Smiles had heard him say. Not because Ix was a Nightmare, but because she was the daughter of Death.

Ix could feel her friends' eyes on her.

"Ix . . ." Morrigan said softly.

But Captain Kel caught her shoulder. "Let's give them a minute. Tempest, why don't you show me that portal you came through?"

Ollie flitted after them, throwing worried looks over his shoulder.

Distantly, Ix was aware of them moving away. But she couldn't tear her eyes from the Soul Reaper. No, not the Soul Reaper. *Her mother.* It felt so strange to look into a real face, after all the years she'd spent wishing and wondering. Ix thought she had Death's nose.

Her mother was a Sorrow—the most powerful Sorrow. And the one whose disappearance had caused so much heartache.

Ix bowed her head. "You left the Labyrinth for me. So everything that happened . . . with Mella, and with Jack . . . it really is my fault," she whispered.

The Soul Reaper bent down from her great height and rested a hand on Ix's shoulder. "No, Ix. You were my little wish-come-true. My mistakes, and Mella's mistakes, they were ours alone." She tugged on one of Ix's raggedy braids. "I have guarded this door for countless lifetimes. But you taught me something I could never learn here in the Labyrinth: joy. And in that joy, I at last understood how precious the souls that slip through this door are. And how irreplaceable.

"That's why I ended up in Mistmorrow. Even with my memories eaten away, I was trying to hold on to you and Nathan—to get back to something so precious."

All the souls had disappeared except for one. It hovered over Death's outstretched palm. Ix thought she knew whose it was.

"That's my father, isn't it?"

"Yes," the Soul Reaper said.

A crack slid open in the ground beside them, and four Apparitions of Death appeared, carrying a crystallized body. They set it before the Soul Reaper.

Ix watched with her heart in her mouth as Death leaned down, gently pouring the soul back into her father's body.

The crystal began to crack along the surface. Just as the last drop of light fell through Nathan Tatterfall's lips, the crystal burst into dust that swirled around them like glowing dandelion seeds. Her father groaned and slowly got to his feet, covered in crystal glitter that gave him an otherworldly shine.

"Dad?" Ix said, unsure. It was almost like meeting a stranger, but a stranger she'd grown up beside her whole life.

"Ix! Is that you? You're so big . . ." He threw his arms around her, crushing her into a hug. "I thought I would never see you again. Either of you." He reached up, grabbing the very dignified Reaper and pulling her into a very undignified hug.

"Nathan, honestly. In front of everyone?" the Reaper grumbled. But she wasn't looking at Captain Kel and the others. She was looking at the clump of Death Apparitions, as if embarrassed for them to see this.

Ix was laughing so hard she could barely breathe. She hoped her smile wasn't creepy this time. She grabbed them both—her *parents*—and held on as tight as she could. And Ix found she did remember this, in some deep-down tiny corner of her heart: how it felt to be loved, and safe, with their arms around her. Maybe she'd never really forgotten. Maybe a little bit of that love had been inside her all along.

She pulled back, looking up at them excitedly.

"I have to introduce you to all my friends. And Aunt Tara. She'll be so glad to see you—and she'll never believe who my mother is!"

Nathan smiled. But it was a sad smile, his eyes shining.

"Ix," the Soul Reaper said gently. "Your father can no longer leave the Labyrinth. And neither can I. I have many things to put right. And ten years is simply too long. Nathan Tatterfall's soul is part of this place now."

Ix's heart crumpled. "No. It can't be. That can't happen." She swiped a hand across her wet cheeks. "I can't lose you—I just met you!" It was too unfair.

Captain Kel had returned to her side. He put a comforting hand on Ix's shoulder.

"I'm so sorry," Death said.

"So that's it?" Ix demanded. "He'll go through the door? He'll die?"

"No," the Soul Reaper said. She swept a hand out, and Ix suddenly had the feeling the entire Labyrinth could hear her. "Today, for the first time, a lesser Sorrow is born. The Melancholy of Regret." In a whisper so low Ix barely heard it, she added, "You are Nathan Tatterfall no longer."

Ix's father closed his eyes. A tear rolled down his face. "I'm so sorry, Ix," he said. "I was so obsessed with the Labyrinth and everything I'd lost. I forgot to treasure what I still had."

His was a particular sadness—a sadness tinged with the wistful longing for what could have been. The Melancholy of Regret.

Ix was crying harder now. The tears blurred her father's face. She tried to do what she'd been taught—to count her blessings, so that the sadness couldn't make a home inside her. But she just ached and ached.

Her mother carded soft fingers through her hair. "It's all right to be sad. Sometimes you will be sad, and angry, and scared, and so many other things." The smile on Death's lips was bittersweet. "It is no easy thing to live in a world with so many sorrows, but remember, Ix—the Sorrows are not here to torment us. They're here to teach us things. To remind us how precious what we have is.

To cherish the time and the people we are given. Only those who refuse to live with and alongside their sorrows are ruled by them."

The Soul Reaper straightened to her full height.

"I'm afraid our time is growing short. Only the creatures of Death may stay in this domain. But we will see each other again."

"Come here, Ix," her father said.

Ix hugged them both one last time, trying to soak up the feeling before she backed away. She scrubbed the last tears off her face.

"I'll come see you every All Hallows' Eve," she promised.

Her father smiled. "And I'll tell you our story—how I fell in love with Death."

"I'd like that." Ix's throat was tight. "I'll have so much to tell Aunt Tara when I go back."

"You mean to visit, right?" Captain Kel said, raising an eyebrow. "Because it would be a shame for Candle Corps to lose you."

"What?" Ix gaped at him. "I thought I was getting expelled."

"After helping save both Candle Corps and the Labyrinth?" Tempest scoffed. "I'll tell the council about every brave thing you did. I'll even embellish a little if I have to. By the time I'm done, they'll be begging you to stay."

"What Tempest means," Captain Kel said with a significant look, "is that you're welcome back, if that's what you want."

Ollie gave her a glowing smile. "You *have* to come back. I haven't even been able to hug you properly yet!"

"Don't make me beg," Morrigan said, tossing her hair. "I'm no good at it."

Ix felt tears prickling her eyes again, but this time they were happy tears.

She thought about her life back at Candle Corps—the rattling paintings and Hanky under the bed and the army of cats, her friends and her classes and her teachers, and especially Professor Swann, with his kind smiles and his rumpled sweaters. She thought about all the people and places and Nightmares she had come to love so much—all the things she would miss if she left them behind.

She wanted to stay at Candle Corps and make it better—a place where everyone's first answer wasn't to eradicate Nightmares, but to try to understand them. A place where humans and Nightmares could live together.

Most of all, Ix didn't want to have any regrets.

"I want to go back to Candle Corps," she told them.

Then, with one last glance at her mother and father, Ix Tatterfall followed her friends toward the passage out of the Labyrinth. Morrigan grabbed her hand and Tempest pulled them all into an awkward hug, even Captain Kel, who groaned at his injuries, while Ollie laughed and buzzed around them, shimmering.

And Ix knew the feeling that rose up in her chest. A warm feeling, soft and powerful.

Belonging.

EPILOGUE

On the eve of the Solstice Festival, Covenant Keep sparkled with snow.

It had been six weeks since Ix and the others returned from the Labyrinth. Though the council had agreed to let Ix stay at the academy, they had decided it was best not to tell everyone she was the daughter of a Sorrow. So Ix Tatterfall had a secret again.

"Sorry, sorry!" Ix panted as she skidded into the ballroom, with Hanky clinging to one of her pigtails. "I got stuck behind a door on the second floor."

"Really?" Morrigan asked, stringing tinsel around the banisters. "That's how you got all that orange cat hair on your sweater?"

Ix grinned sheepishly. "Okay. I was under the stairs *before* I got stuck behind the door. But Peanut Butter's kittens are just so cute! They're like tiny fuzzy potatoes."

Morrigan smirked. "I knew it. Get over here already—Professor Swann saved us a spot by the tree."

Ix looked around as Morrigan led her through the bustling ballroom. Everything sparkled and gleamed—the decorations, the chandeliers, and even the people. The keep cats were in their element, swiping at tinsel, crawling up the trees, and lounging around like fuzzy speed bumps under everyone's feet.

It was Candle Corps tradition to wear something that shone on

Solstice Eve. Ix had braided silver ribbons into her hair, and Morrigan's dark blouse looked like it was dusted with stars. It seemed everyone was dressed in sequins and silver—everyone except Captain Kel, who was stubbornly wearing his captain's coat as usual. Professor Swann leaned up to wrap a shimmering scarf around his husband's neck. Tempest slung an arm around Ollie, who beamed and waved them over.

In the very center of the room stood a great gleaming tree. The dark boughs blazed with hundreds of Dreamlight flames in little glass baubles. Instructor Cadence had told them that every member of Candle Corps made their own glowing ornament each year. Even the Balefires, the Flames who traveled to the far-flung corners of the kingdom, sent globes back to the castle, so that the light of all of Candle Corps shone as one. A symbol of their pledge to Spinar on the darkest night of the year.

Families of all those at Candle Corps had been invited to the celebration, and guests had been pouring into the keep all week in anticipation of the great banquet the next day. Even Aunt Tara had promised to come.

"Ix, there you are!" Professor Swann said when she and Morrigan fought their way through the crowd. He held out a cup decorated with holly leaves. "Here, try some of this—peppermint pickle tea. It's fascinating."

Behind him, Ollie desperately waved his hands, making a gagging motion.

Ix was saved by a commotion on the other side of the room. Beatrix had opened a box infested with Whirlygiggles, little gossamer-winged butterflies that made you laugh uncontrollably. She and the other Novices were all in stitches. Valerie was trying to hold her breath, which was the best way to get rid of the giggles, but every time the others looked at her puffed-out cheeks, they burst out laughing again.

Captain Rossi chuckled at the pinched look on Instructor Cadence's face. "Ah, let them be, Julia. It's all in good fun," he said, slapping her hard on the back.

Ix looked around at all the people in the hall. Vice-Captain Weisgard chased after Bella with a string of lights in her mouth. Some of the captains clinked glasses with Tyrese Valerian, who stood with his arm around Torrent's shoulders. Ix didn't see any sign of Fallon Winters, but everyone else was celebrating.

Standing there in the shining ballroom, a feeling bubbled up in Ix, as warm and sweet as fizzy cider.

Morrigan was staring at her.

"What?" Ix asked. "Am I smiling all creepy again?"

"Not creepy," Morrigan said, tickling Hanky on her shoulder.

"I've got our ornaments." Ollie held up the box with their Dreamlight globes nestled inside.

Ix let her grin stretch wider. "We should all hang each other's. Since we're friends."

Morrigan scoffed. "We're not friends." At Ix's and Ollie's wide-eyed looks, she went on, "Because *friends* doesn't even begin to cover it. After all we've been through, we're *best* friends."

"Right," Ix said, as the three of them traded ornaments.

The red flame inside Morrigan's blazed strong as a bonfire, and Ollie's glowed a beautiful gold. Ix's Dreamlight was still more like a guttery, wheezy candle. But sitting between Morrigan's and Ollie's, and surrounded by all the other lights on the tree, it was perfect.

When Ix drifted off that night, she found herself in a dream.

She knew it was a dream because she was looking up at the giant solstice tree glimmering with lights, but somehow it was rising from the mist of Chaos's domain. A few Mistcats reached up to bat at the Dreamlight baubles, while more wiggled up the inner branches to cause trouble.

"I wholeheartedly approve."

Ix turned around to find the Grinning Cat sauntering into her dream.

"Smiles!" Ix said. She hadn't seen the Sorrow since everything that happened in the Labyrinth. She'd begun to wonder if she ever would again. "I didn't know if you'd come visit me anymore."

"Death has kept us all busy putting the Labyrinth back to rights. Working through a backlog of souls that built up while the door was jammed. Weeding out the wild patches getting out of hand. It's all very smooth, measured . . . one might even say *orderly*." Smiles shuddered at the word. "There's such an inevitability about Death and all her boring choices."

Ix imagined all the Sorrows with kerchiefs tied over their heads as the Soul Reaper ordered them around, making them clean and weed and ferry souls through the Labyrinth. She tried to stifle a giggle.

"You laugh, but Wrath explodes at the slightest setback, Terror is forever running away. Greed has the bad habit of pushing his work off on everyone else. And Misery . . . well, she'll do her part, but you will *never* hear the end of it."

"And what about you, Smiles?"

"Me?" Smiles blinked his eyes innocently. "My conduct is exemplary. I even encourage the others with helpful little quips and suggestions."

Ix thought that probably meant he poked at them and egged them into fighting with each other.

"But Death has the final say—as always. On everything. So when your mother brings down the hammer—or should I say, the scythe—everyone falls in line."

Ix laughed a little, feeling warm at the thought of her mother—and her father. There was still an ache inside her from losing them, and maybe there always would be. But it helped to know they were together again.

There was one more thing she had to know. She turned to look Smiles right in his glowing amethyst eyes. "Did you always know who I was?"

Smiles hummed thoughtfully. "Did I know . . . ? I had certain suspicions, of course. Conjectures aplenty. Even a hunch or two by the end. But *knowing, for sure*, that's a different thing entirely."

"But is that the reason you befriended me?" Ix pressed. "Because you thought I might be the daughter of Death?"

The Grinning Cat sniffed. "Now that would be an utterly boring and predictable reason to start a friendship—and you know I am neither of those things." He laid his head on his paws, tickling Ix with his striped tail. "I simply met an interesting little human who foolishly wandered the Labyrinth by herself. What do I care whose daughter she is? Ix . . . what did you say your last name was?"

"Never going to happen, Smiles," Ix told the cat, grinning right back at him.

"Give it time," Smiles promised, chuckling. "Besides, I haven't forgotten you owe me a favor. And I fully intend to collect—when the time is right."

A GLOSSARY OF NIGHTMARES

BLACKOUT BAT: A thumb-sized bat with velvety charcoal-black fur that loves to eat Dreamlight, causing sudden blackouts. Totally harmless unless you're afraid of the dark.

BUPKIS BIRDS: Fluffy purple-and-blue birds with easily ruffled feathers, which call out nonsense to each other to baffle, befuddle, and bemuse. Don't talk to a Bupkis Bird, or you may find yourself speaking nonsense.

CREAK-O-DILE: A crocodile-like Nightmare with a metallic body and teeth covered in rust that squeaks whenever the creature snaps its jaw or swings its tail. Listen close—you'll hear the Creak-o-dile's screeching steps long before you see it.

DIRE FROG: A long-legged frog with bulging red eyes that shine like lamps in the dark. An omen of bad luck and dread. Don't get into a staring contest with a Dire Frog—but if you do, definitely don't blink first.

DREARY LONGLEGS: A slow-moving Nightmare spider that likes to climb on people who are droopy and in the doldrums. Dreary Longlegs are attracted to gloomy moods, so getting rid of this Nightmare is as easy as turning your frown upside down.

DUST-PUFF BEETLES: Plump brown beetles with buzzy wings that fly in swarms and stir up giant clouds of dust whenever they take off. Bother a Dust-Puff Beetle, and you'll definitely have something to sneeze about.

FRIGHT BAT: A midnight-black bat whose scratchy-scratchy wingbeats cause sudden bursts of terror. A swarm of Fright Bats is called a screech—which is definitely what you'll do if they come upon you in the dark.

INKLING: A small darkness-dwelling Nightmare that looks like a splotch of ink, with long thin arms and legs. Gooey and harmless, Inklings like to hide in cracks and crevices, in the pages of old books, and in your sock drawer.

JIMBER-JAWED HOUND: A gargoyle-like hound with a thick gray body and huge fangs protruding from its jaw like tusks. One of the most dangerous Nightmares in the Labyrinth. Don't get close enough to count the fangs.

MISTCAT: A mischievous blue-and-white cat with cold curls of mist-like fur. Sneaky and fickle, the Mistcats love to play hide-and-seek, but be careful, lest you wind up following one into the Labyrinth.

MONEY-GRUBBER MOUSE: A whiskery green mouse that covets money and will chew holes in pockets to steal whatever's inside. Watch out, or these little sneaks will make off with your last precious coin.

NARCISSUSNAKES: Jewel-bright snakes with a poisonous bite that makes you obsessed with your looks. If facing one, hope you have a hand mirror—these vain serpents are transfixed by their own reflection.

ORNERY OWLS: Little horned, spotted owls that get puffed up and annoyed and then stubbornly refuse to do anything. Especially drawn to sit on the shoulders of people who are sulking.

SEETHING SERPENT: A giant fanged serpent with four burning red eyes. It grows bigger and bigger the more furious it becomes. Though enormous when angry, a calm Seething Serpent can fit inside a jam jar.

SKELLIGRABS: Disembodied skeletal hands that skitter around on their fingers and grab people to give them a fright. Mostly pranksters, but if you're in a pinch, they might lend a hand.

SLEEPLESS MICE: Tiny gray mice no bigger than a thimble, which cause insomnia by scratch-scratch-scratching away under beds and keeping you up all night. Especially active when you have a trip, a test, or an important game to wake up for.

STUBBED TOADS: Lumpy rocklike toads that like to lie in wait and then roll right into your path, especially when you're hurrying. Watch your feet, or these rocky rollers will send you sprawling.

TEASEL WEASEL: A snaggletoothed weasel Nightmare that likes to tease out threads and bits of yarn from clothes and rugs. Watch out for loose threads, or a Teasel Weasel might make your plans unravel!

UNSCORPITY: A gleaming scorpion with a long double stinger and pearly green-black scales, which can make you suspicious of even your closest friends. Unscorpity are weak on their tails being pinched—and on being tickled.

WARTY HORNSWOGGLES: Grumpy Nightmares with hairy, warthog-like snouts and bodies, lizard legs, and long, hairless rat tails. These moody monsters never back down from a challenge, but their snort is worse than their bite.

WEIGHTY SLOTH: A Nightmare sloth that climbs onto your back, causing the feeling of an ominous, crushing weight on your shoulders. The Weighty Sloth may look small and cute, but don't underestimate the heavy toll it takes at full size.

WOEBEGONE WOOLIE: A raggedy sheeplike Nightmare that likes to charge and knock people down over and over until they give up. Woolies might seem like pushovers, but if you anger one, you'll be the one getting pushed over!

ACKNOWLEDGMENTS

Some books come all in a rush. Some books simmer for a long time under the surface before a spark of inspiration finally brings them to life. That was *The Labyrinth of Souls*. Thank you, reader, for picking up this weird little book and getting swept away into the Labyrinth with Ix Tatterfall.

This journey would not have been possible without so many people! Thank you to my amazing agents, Carrie Hannigan and Ellen Goff. From the first moment *The Nightmare Before Christmas* came up, it felt like this project was meant to be. Also to Rhea Lyons, Soumeya B. Roberts, and all of HG Literary!

Thank you to my incredible editor, Rūta Rimas. You brought so much love and so much joy and made this book come to life. Ollie, a very slobbery bulldog, and especially Hanky would not be the same without you!

To Abigail Larson, who made me gasp from the very first cover sketch and brought all the weird and wonderful things about this story to life! Your illustrations throughout the book are beyond what I ever could have imagined. The second I saw the Inkling, I was in love.

And to Alex Campbell, whose design brought it all together and made it look amazing!

I am so grateful to Karter Powell for being a champion of this book and making so many of my author dreams come true. The entire team at Penguin went above and beyond—it truly takes a village to bring out a book, and I could not ask for a more fantastic team.

A special thanks to my wonderful early readers: Kyle, Christie, Suzanne, Claire, and so many more. You have no idea how much your enthusiasm means to me! I store up those words like a chipmunk hoarding nuts for the long, cold winter. And to the fantastic Colorado authors group, who make every event rock!

To my family, especially my grandmother, and also my wife's wonderful family, who has made me one of their own. ❤

A grudging thanks to my two very spoiled house cats. You are the inspiration for all the cat shenanigans in this book. And also the reason for many, many Band-Aids.

And finally, to my partner, Michelle, who somehow knows how to make everything better—from cookies, to bad days, to scenes that aren't working in my books. You are my heart, and every book I write is for you.